When she ~~~~~~~~~~~~~~~~~~~~~~~~~~~~~~~~~
strawberries out of the shopping bag. They were beauties, plump and rosy, and so ripe that the box that held them was blotted here and there with deep red strawberry stains.

Pamela knew that the knitting club wasn't responsible for Randall Jefferson's death. Whoever murdered him, probably with the yam-shaped rock from the rock garden, had simply tucked the body under the nearest booth, and that booth happened to be the knitting club booth. Then, later (during the parade?), the murderer—or someone—had quickly reached under the table's canvas skirt and placed an aardvark on the dead man's chest.

That was where things got odd . . .

But still, what could the knitting club have to do with it?

Books by Peggy Ehrhart

MURDER, SHE KNIT

DIED IN THE WOOL

Published by Kensington Publishing Corporation

DIED
IN THE WOOL

PEGGY
EHRHART

KENSINGTON BOOKS
KENSINGTON PUBLISHING CORP.
http://www.kensingtonbooks.com

KENSINGTON BOOKS are published by

Kensington Publishing Corp.
119 West 40th Street
New York, NY 10018

First Printing: September 2018
ISBN-13: 978-1-4967-1329-2
ISBN-10: 1-4967-1329-X

eISBN-13: 978-1-4967-1330-8
eISBN-10: 1-4967-1330-3

10 9 8 7 6 5 4 3 2 1

Printed in the United States of America

For Matt, my son,
and
Angela, my craft-loving daughter-in-law

ACKNOWLEDGMENTS

Abundant thanks, again, to my agent Evan Marshall; John Scognamiglio at Kensington Books; and Eileen Watkins, my New Jersey writing friend.

Chapter One

"Do you think anyone will actually buy these?" Roland DeCamp, trim in a navy polo shirt and crisply pressed khakis, studied the aardvark he'd plucked from the group arrayed before him. He examined its stubby legs, rabbit-like ears, and long snout, running his fingers over its knitted surface. "Not a bad job, if I say so myself," he concluded. "I think I'm getting the hang of this knitting business."

"Actually"—Bettina Fraser reached across the table to lift it out of his hands and set it back among its fuzzy turquoise companions—"I believe that's one I made."

"I beg to differ—" Roland picked it up again and pointed to the shiny black buttons that marked its eyes. "I particularly remember using these buttons. Your buttons were different—see, look here." He seized another aardvark by the scruff of its neck and turned its head toward Bettina. "Not as shiny."

Pamela Paterson slipped around the table to join Bettina. "They all turned out beautifully," she said. "The one with the shiny eyes is definitely yours, Roland." Pamela was the founder and mainstay of the Arborville knitting club. Bettina was her best friend, but Roland was the only male member of the club. Sometimes he needed someone on his side. "And I'm sure we'll sell them. Sports mascots in the school colors—well, one of the school colors at least. Who could resist? And it's for such a good cause."

Arborville High School's colors were turquoise and gold, and the occasion was Arborfest, Arborville's annual town celebration, held the Sunday after Mother's Day. The knitting club, known to its members as Knit and Nibble, had been at work for weeks producing the aardvarks now arrayed on the table. Money from the sale of the creatures was to go to the high school's athletic program. On a corner of the table not occupied by aardvarks was a pile of flyers describing the knitting club.

Arborfest had begun at eleven a.m. with a parade down Arborville Avenue, featuring Boy Scouts and Girl Scouts, Cub Scouts and Brownies, the mayor and town council in vintage cars, and the high school's marching band. Now the festival was in full swing. Two rows of booths faced each other across the asphalt expanse of the library parking lot. The Arborville chapter of the Community Chest was represented, serving slices of a huge sheet cake celebrating the group's one hundredth anniversary in the town. And the Lions Club and Chamber of Commerce had booths, as well as the library, the recreation center, and the historical society. The Arborville pizza parlor, When in Rome, offered samples of three kinds of pizza, and the Chinese takeout restaurant offered dumplings, fried on the spot, creating a tantalizing aroma. The Co-Op Grocery's booth highlighted its bakery, with trays of gingerbread cookies shaped like the letter *A*, for Arborville. Inside the library, a display of old photos and newspaper clippings focused on the high points of the high school's athletic program.

On a stage at the end of the parking lot, the high school's jazz-rock band was playing a lively tune. It featured enthusiastic horn parts, and the horns glinted golden in the midday sun. Beyond the parking lot, in the grassy expanse of Arborville's park, a petting zoo had been set up, with lambs, baby goats, and rabbits. Pony rides were available for the children, and a clown capered about on the lawn, pausing now and then to juggle a bright collection of balls.

"Yes," Pamela repeated, to Bettina this time. Roland had wandered off to join his wife, and they were sampling pizza at the When in Rome booth. "It's a very good cause."

"I'm sure he'd agree." Bettina nodded toward a sturdy young man in a turquoise "Arborville Aardvarks" T-shirt. He caught Bettina's eye and strolled over.

"How are you doing?" he asked.

"Brad Striker," Bettina explained. "The new football coach. I interviewed him for the *Advocate* last fall." Pamela reached out her hand and supplied her name. The coach had the square jaw and strong brows of a comic-book hero, and he grasped her hand without smiling.

"I'm glad to see the knitters approve of high-school sports," he said, letting go of her hand after a firm squeeze and reaching for an aardvark. "Not like that"—he paused, as if censoring the word he'd planned to use—"that . . . that *idiot* history teacher."

"Did you see last week's *Advocate*?" Bettina asked Pamela. The *Arborville Advocate* was the town's weekly newspaper, and as the paper's chief reporter, Bettina covered most of the town news.

Pamela hesitated. "I know I brought it in." No one

actually subscribed to the *Advocate*—it just arrived, generally midweek, at the end of one's driveway. "I'm not sure I read the whole thing."

"Randall Jefferson can be a very nasty man," Bettina said. "But, freedom of the press and all. He must be busy, with the school year winding down, but he took the time to sit down and unburden himself on the subject of high-school sports."

"Not in favor?" Pamela asked.

"Most definitely not in favor." Bettina laughed. "You got that right. The high-school sports program should be abolished, especially football. He noted that the students are stupid enough already without rattling their brains on the football field, and if they spent more time studying history they'd be better citizens. People who don't remember the past are condemned to repeat it and so on."

Brad Striker didn't laugh. "Like I said, an idiot." He shoved his hands in his pockets and swung his head from side to side as if he was scouting the crowd for the object of his irritation. "They say he's got so much money he wouldn't even have to work if he didn't want to. Why doesn't he just stay home and mind his own business then?"

"Can't the students do both?" Pamela inquired. "Sports and history?" Pamela herself had never enjoyed team sports, preferring to get her exercise by doing errands on foot, a luxury that the tiny town of Arborville allowed.

Brad Striker frowned, as if even a compromise was an insult. "Idiot," he muttered again and wandered off toward a rowdy group of young men wearing T-shirts just like his.

Bettina touched Pamela's arm. "I don't think he meant you were an idiot," she said soothingly.

Pamela, meanwhile, was handing over two aardvarks to a tall, smiling man who immediately gave one to each of the excited little boys bouncing at his side. "Our first sale," she said, smoothing out two twenty-dollar bills and placing them in the metal cash box.

Young couples in shorts and T-shirts strolled with their children, balloons on long strings bobbing along behind them. Teenagers stood in tight knots, segregated by gender, the girls giggling and watching the boys, and the boys trying not to be obvious about watching the girls. Older couples ambled along, pausing to greet old friends.

"Such a perfect day for this," Bettina said, beaming. "The booths look so nice, and the volunteers worked overtime to finish the rock garden. That handsome Joe Taylor really got them organized." She turned toward the library to survey the little plot, bordered by carefully arranged rocks, then turned back toward the crowd. "Oh, look!" she said suddenly. "Richard Larkin is here with his daughters." Bettina nodded toward a tall man in torn and faded jeans standing with two young, twentyish women. "Why don't you go over and say hello? This is his first Arborfest. I can certainly manage the booth myself for a while."

Pamela had been the object of her friend's matchmaking efforts since the previous fall, when Richard Larkin—recently divorced—moved into the house next to Pamela's own.

"I said hello to him this morning," Pamela said. "He was bringing in his newspaper while I was loading the aardvarks into my car."

"Well, go say hello again." Bettina gave her a friendly nudge. "Ask him if he's having a good time. You said you'd think about dating again when Penny started college, and now she's already finished her freshman year and you're still all alone in that big house."

"Penny is home for the summer," Pamela said. "And he's really not my type."

Richard Larkin wasn't unattractive. Pamela would grant that, though the jeans seemed an affectation—too artistically torn and faded, like something a city hipster would buy at a SoHo boutique, and his hair was too shaggy. He was smiling now, in a way that softened his strong features. She looked away when his gaze turned in her direction.

"Why don't you take a walk anyway?" Bettina said. "You did all the booth setup before the parade. I can handle things for a while—" She paused to accept a twenty-dollar bill from a grandmotherly woman and hand over an aardvark.

"Lovely idea," the woman commented. "So clever."

Pamela eased herself around the side of the table. "I *am* a little hungry," she said, "and those dumplings smell heavenly."

"Will you bring me one?" Bettina asked.

"Just one? I think they're kind of small."

Bettina patted her ample waistline. "I know you could eat ten of them and not gain an ounce, but I'm not so lucky. And I'll never understand why you wear the same jeans every day when you could show off that tall skinny figure of yours." Pamela indeed was dressed in her summer uniform of jeans and a casual cotton blouse. Bettina, who loved clothes, was wearing a floaty sundress in shades of scarlet, purple, and green. The scarlet was nearly the same shade as her hair.

"I'd like an aardvark," said a little voice at Pamela's side. She looked down to see a pigtailed girl not much taller than the table handing over a twenty-dollar bill.

Bettina completed the transaction, and Pamela

went on her way to fetch dumplings. "No hurry," Bettina called after her. "Take your time."

Pamela detoured around a knot of giggling girls, found herself bouncing along with extra spring in her step, and realized she was moving in time with the syncopated drums and tootling horns of the jazz-rock band. She smiled and glanced toward the stage.

"Hello, Pamela!"

At the sound of her name, Pamela stopped suddenly. She'd been so distracted by the music that she'd almost stepped on Nell Bascomb's toes.

"It's fun to hear the kids play this old music, isn't it?" Nell said. "I think that's 'Take Five.' Harold and I used to love to go down to the Village to hear jazz." Nell was a fellow member of Knit and Nibble and a long-time Arborville resident, much livelier and more outspoken than her white hair and wrinkled skin would suggest. "We just got here, and Harold is already off talking to his pals from the historical society. Bettina's Wilfred is there too. How are we doing with the aardvark sales?"

"Four sold so far, twenty-one to go."

"Oh, look—" Nell pointed toward the knitting club booth, where Bettina was dealing with a small crowd, handing over one aardvark after another.

A tiny boy with a balloon came hurtling by and was quickly scooped up by his mother. "Shall we go pet a goat?" she asked, smoothing his hair back from his forehead.

"I'll give Bettina a hand," Nell said. She took a few steps and paused. The jazz-rock band had wrapped up "Take Five" with a flourish and conversations going on around them were suddenly audible. "Brad Striker," Nell said. "Over there."

Standing near the rock garden, Brad Striker was

holding forth to a man dressed like he was, in a turquoise T-shirt with the Arborville Aardvark logo. The subject seemed to be Randall Jefferson's op-ed piece in the *Advocate*, and the language Brad was using wasn't confined to the fairly mild word "idiot."

"I have to say that Randall had a point," Nell confessed, "though he could have been much more diplomatic. I was happy to do my part with the aardvarks, but football does rattle the brain."

Pamela sighed. "Well, everyone will have the summer to cool off. And Randall Jefferson definitely has his supporters at the high school." She continued on her way toward the dumplings.

But Bettina had said to take her time, so she detoured around the row of booths that flanked the park. The lawn was the rich green of late spring, and the May sun made the colors of everything seem brighter. Children scampered here and there, watched by parents chatting in groups. A clown shaped a long balloon into a yellow dachshund.

A terrified shriek, out of keeping with the atmosphere, drew her attention to the petting zoo. Within a low wire fence held up by stakes, a young woman was trying to introduce a hesitant little girl to a baby goat. The goat stared with huge eyes at the girl as the girl backed into the embrace of her mother. Other children weren't so hesitant. The goat stood patiently as many tiny hands explored its furry coat.

"Hey, Mom," said a voice behind her. "Waiting for your turn to pet a goat?"

Pamela turned to see her daughter Penny, accompanied by Richard Larkin and his two daughters. Like their father, they were tall and blond.

"Interesting event," Richard said, letting his eyes

rove over the crowd. "I guess these kinds of things are a big deal in little towns."

"Dad!" His oldest daughter, the one named Laine, laughingly jabbed his arm. "You sound like a complete snob."

He blinked a few times. "I meant—"

"We know what you meant, Dad." This came from Sybil. She grabbed Penny's arm. "Come on, let's go pet a goat." The three of them bounced off together, little Penny with her short dark curls between the two lanky blondes.

Suddenly Pamela and Richard Larkin were alone—at least as alone as it was possible to be in the midst of Arborfest.

"I . . . uh . . ." Richard rubbed his forehead and let his eyes rove over the crowd again. "How is your group doing with the armadillos?" he asked suddenly.

"Aardvarks," Pamela said. "They're aardvarks."

"Of course," he said. "I meant aardvarks."

"Pretty well," Pamela said. "It's for a worthy cause, you know. The high-school sports program." When he didn't respond, she went on. "Kind of controversial."

"Um."

If he's not interested in the topic, why doesn't he just excuse himself and go away, Pamela wondered. But his eyes looked so desperate. "Did you see the op-ed piece in the *Advocate*?" she asked. Maybe he just needed a conversational topic.

"Is that the thing that turns up at the end of the driveway every week?" he said with a laugh. "I usually run over it with my car."

"It's the Arborville weekly," Pamela said. "Bettina writes for it—most of the articles, in fact. Lots of people in town enjoy it."

"Oh"—he blinked, clapped his hands briskly, and

looked around. "I think it's time to go buy an aardvark," he said. And he was gone. From the stage came the sound of horns as the band started up again.

At the dumpling booth, Pamela waited her turn, watching as Jamie Chin tended a batch of plump dumplings and enjoying the tantalizing aroma of the smoke drifting up from the wok. She came away with two sets of chopsticks and a small paper plate containing four dumplings. Waving at Wilfred as she passed the historical society booth, she was soon back at Bettina's side.

"Richard Larkin bought an aardvark," Bettina said before she even reached for the plate of dumplings. Then she captured a dumpling with a pair of chopsticks and conveyed it to her mouth. "Ummm . . . heavenly." She smiled and reached for another.

"How are we doing?" Pamela surveyed the table, where only a few clusters of aardvarks remained.

"Eat your dumplings," Bettina said, "then we'll take stock."

"Bean sprouts and shrimp," Pamela said, after biting into the warm, spicy tidbit. "Yum." She finished off the first dumpling in two bites and started on the second. Meanwhile, Bettina opened the metal box that had been serving as the till. She counted the bills, mostly twenties, and announced that they had taken in $280.

Pamela reached down to pull the remaining aardvarks from the cardboard box they'd arrived in and lined them up with the ones on the table. "Nine left." She paused. "But wait—there should be more than two hundred and eighty dollars then. There should be three hundred and twenty dollars, for sixteen aardvarks sold."

"Two missing!" Bettina looked stricken, her hazel

eyes wide. "I was here the whole time—except for the parade."

"But they were all still in the boxes then," Pamela said, "tucked away inside the booth. We hadn't set up yet."

"Someone has stolen two aardvarks." Bettina's lips twisted as if she was about to cry.

"Dear wife, what has happened?" It was Wilfred, Bettina's husband, his usually cheerful face mirroring his wife's unhappiness.

"Someone has stolen two aardvarks," she repeated. "There are nine left but we only have money for fourteen."

"Misfortunes never come single," Wilfred murmured and leaned across the table to pat Bettina on the shoulder. "But perhaps they went to children whose families couldn't afford twenty dollars." He slid his hand down her arm and grasped her fingers. "It's not the end of the world. Come away with me, dearest, and say hello to the people at the historical society booth."

Pamela watched them make their way through the milling crowd, Wilfred's white-thatched head bending toward Bettina's. Husbands could be a great comfort, she reflected. But she was glad when a woman offering a twenty-dollar bill and claiming an aardvark distracted her from pursuing that thought to its logical conclusion.

To distract herself further, she re-counted the money they had taken in so far. The recent sale had brought the total to three hundred dollars, but there were now only eight aardvarks waiting to be sold. Very puzzling. It was possible someone had gotten into the boxes while she and Bettina were at the parade. They'd made no secret of the fact that the boxes contained the aardvarks as people bustled here and there that morning preparing their booths. She'd chatted with someone from the Arborville Chamber of Commerce in the booth next door, and a few volunteers had been making sure the rock garden behind the library hadn't sprouted any weeds since its completion. Joe Taylor had exclaimed, "Nice varks!" and complimented her on the clever idea of enlisting the knitting group's support of the sports program.

The next few hours passed quickly. Penny stopped by with Richard Larkin's daughters to say that they were all going to walk to Richard's house and hang out for a while. Nell and Harold came by to check on sales and report that the historical society had recruited three new members. Pamela sold four more aardvarks. Bettina returned and insisted that Pamela take another stroll around the parking lot.

Pamela made a slow circuit, pausing to watch the ponies climb up a ramp into their truck. The petting zoo was closing down as well, and one of the lambs scampered away as it was being led through the gate in the zoo's temporary wire fence. It dashed across the grass and was captured at last near the tennis courts. Families trooped out of the park and along the edge of the parking lot, heading toward the street.

Back at the booth, Pamela discovered that only one aardvark was left. "I think that's it," Bettina said. The asphalt area between the two rows of booths was emptying out as well, and booths were being dismantled. The chimes from St. Willibrod's, the grand stone church on Arborville Avenue, sounded the hour. It was five o'clock, time to pack up.

Bettina tucked the lone aardvark into one of the cardboard boxes they'd arrived in while Pamela climbed on a chair to detach the Arborville Knitting Club banner they'd strung across the front of the booth. She gently rolled it up, and then began to detach the canvas they'd tacked around the table the previous evening. But as she pulled the front panel loose, she stopped and stared. She felt her body twitch as if a tiny, local earthquake had affected the spot of parking lot where she stood.

A person was under the table, a man. He was lying on his back, and on his chest was perched a knitted turquoise aardvark. She looked up. Bettina was cheerfully counting the money again, fingers busy as she slipped bills from one hand to the other.

Bettina paused.

"Pamela?" She raised her brows. "You look like you've seen a ghost."

Chapter Two

From behind her, Pamela heard another voice, the voice of an excited child. "Mommy!" the voice said. "There's a dead person under there. The aardvark killed him."

"What?" Bettina raised her brows even farther. She hastily dropped the stack of bills back into the metal box, slammed the cover shut, and eased herself around the side of the table.

Pamela had pulled off half the canvas panel. That section drooped in loose folds, creating an opening that revealed the top half of a middle-aged man, his legs and feet still hidden. The man was wearing a linen sports jacket in an elegant shade of gray, and a white dress shirt with a starched collar. A carefully knotted bow tie finished off the outfit, its blue and gray paisley complementing the gray of the jacket. The turquoise aardvark was balanced squarely on his chest.

"How could this happen?" Bettina wailed. Pamela put her hands to her breast, as if to check that her heart was still beating. She closed her eyes and took two deep breaths. The earthquake sensation hadn't lasted long, but she felt shaky and reached a hand toward the table to steady herself. She closed her eyes again. But the scene was so mysterious she had to look closer.

She lowered one knee to the asphalt and ducked her head to clear the edge of the table. She knew enough not to disturb a crime scene by touching anything, but she stared at the aardvark, trying to determine whether it was hiding a wound. The smooth cotton shirtfront seemed undisturbed, however, and there was no sign of blood. She let her eyes wander to the man's head. There were no injuries to his face that she could see, and the neat gray hair lay smoothly against his scalp. Her eyes were drawn to the tie. Who would wear a bow tie to a town festival, she wondered, and a dress shirt that had been starched and pressed to perfection by a professional launderer? The collar was especially crisp—but what was that near the back, above the collar of the perfectly tailored linen jacket? Something dark. She bent closer. It was a stain, a stain the dark red color of dried blood, like blood that could have trickled down from a spot on the back of the head.

"That's Randall Jefferson from the high school," said a woman's voice behind her. Simultaneously, a child began to cry. Pamela stood up and turned. A blond woman in shorts and a T-shirt was stroking the hair of a little girl who was nestled against her bare legs. The woman was glaring at Pamela in an accusing way, as if Pamela was somehow responsible for the spectacle.

Only a handful of people had remained in the parking lot when Pamela began deconstructing the booth. Now a small crowd began to assemble, composed of that handful plus the tenants of the other booths. Pamela watched as a man bobbed forward, stooped to look through the opening in the canvas, and then took off at a run toward the police station at the far edge of the parking lot. She looked back at the crowd, some faces awed, others just curious. "Randall Jefferson," a few people murmured to each other. "From the high school, you know."

Wilfred had been one of the first to arrive, and now he stood off to the side, stalwart in his plaid shirt and overalls. Bettina huddled next to him with her face buried in his chest, the fabric of her sundress bright against his denim.

The heavy metal and glass door of the police station swung back, and two officers emerged, followed by the man who had dashed off to summon them. The officers trotted across the asphalt, and in a moment they were at Pamela's side. Pamela recognized one of them as the officer she had most recently seen directing traffic around a crew that was repaving a section of Orchard Street. In a pleasant voice that struck her as more suited to telling children not to skateboard on the sidewalk, he ordered the crowd to back up.

"It's Randall Jefferson," offered a middle-aged woman in yoga pants and sneakers. "From the high school."

The other officer bent down to examine the visible half of Randall Jefferson, then pulled out his phone.

Once the crowd had moved far enough from the booth to satisfy the officer, he focused on Pamela. "I'm Officer William Anders," he said. "Was it you who found the body?"

Pamela nodded. "It's my booth—our booth really." She gestured toward where Bettina stood with Wilfred, watching the proceedings now, but with Wilfred's arm tight around her bare shoulders. "We're part of the knitting club. And we were selling these"—she took a few steps toward the opening in the canvas and

pointed at the aardvark on the dead man's chest—
"aardvarks . . . to benefit the sports program." Officer
Anders had taken out a small notepad and a pen. He
was looking at Pamela encouragingly, so she went on.
"Halfway through the afternoon we noticed two were
missing. We had money for fourteen but there were
only nine left. We started out with twenty-five." She
dipped her head to look through the opening in the
canvas again. "I guess this is one of the missing ones."

"Were you at the booth all day?" he asked, pen
poised for her answer. Not only was his voice not the
voice she'd expect from a police officer, but his rosy
cheeks and light brows made her wonder if it was possible for him to ever look stern.

"At least one of us was," Pamela said. "Sometimes
both. After the parade, that is. But we didn't put any
aardvarks out until we came back from the parade.
They were in two cardboard boxes behind the table."

"And this canvas?" He pointed at the flap of canvas.
"Did it go all the way around?"

Pamela struggled to suppress a tiny laugh. "Of course.
I think we would have noticed him under there otherwise."

"And when did the canvas go on?"

"Yesterday," Pamela said. "People came out after
dinner to get a head start on setting up the booths.
It stays light so late this time of year. Bettina and I
worked on it, and her husband Wilfred helped." Pamela
looked toward them, and Wilfred gave her an encour-
aging smile. "We all went home at about eight-thirty.
A few people were still working on the booths then,
and the library was still open."

Officer Anders nodded. "Wait over there," he said,
pointing toward the space between Pamela's booth
and the remains of the Chamber of Commerce booth.

The men who had been deconstructing that booth had joined the curious crowd at the far edge of the parking lot.

Pamela didn't move. "I noticed something," she said, feeling a quiver of nervousness and wondering if it was quite her place to speak up. But before Officer Anders could answer, she went on. "There's blood on his collar." As the officer's boyish face turned stern, sterner than she would have thought such a face could look, she raised her hands in self-defense. "I didn't touch him," she said. "You can see the blood if you bend down and stick your head under the table." Now the officer almost looked amused.

"You did that?" he said.

"I was kind of in shock. I'm not sure I knew what I was doing." She shrugged. "But anyway, someone could have hit him on the back of the head with something hard and heavy, and the blood started dripping while he was still more or less upright, and it dripped down onto his collar. Then when he collapsed they put him under the table."

"And added an aardvark?"

"Maybe that came later."

Instead of making another note on the little notepad, Officer Anders stepped around to where the other officer was unrolling a ribbon of crime-scene tape. He leaned toward the other officer's ear and said something, then they both returned to the front of the booth and bent down to look through the opening in the canvas. Officer Anders stuck his head under the table.

From the street came the rising and falling whine of a siren. It grew so loud that Pamela flinched. Then suddenly it was silent, and a huge silver van with the logo of the county sheriff's department careened around the corner. The crowd of onlookers scattered onto the lawn, and the van stopped just short of where they had been standing.

Officer Anders moved off to talk to Bettina and Wilfred. The other officer watched as two people in loose-fitting white outfits climbed out of the van, and then he led them to the front of the knitting club booth. Pamela backed away until she was standing among the plantings behind the library. A man who she recognized as Detective Clayborn had joined the two officers and the people in the white outfits.

Pamela wondered how soon she'd be able to leave. She was longing to be at home, in her safe, comforting house, maybe with Bettina and Wilfred there too—though Bettina might be longing to be in her own safe, comforting house. She watched the people in the white outfits make several trips between the van and what was now the crime scene, complete with yellow crime-scene tape strung from the supports of the booths on either side of the knitting club booth.

As she watched the methodical way the police and the people from the sheriff's department went about their work, Pamela gradually relaxed. The adrenalin jolt she'd felt when she discovered the dead man under the table had carried her through her impulsive inspection of the body and her interview with Officer Anders. But now the adrenalin had subsided, and she just felt tired. She'd been on her feet all day, either standing in the booth or exploring the other festival offerings.

A pretty wooden bench was part of the library garden, donated in memory of a beloved librarian, as a notation engraved on its back testified. Pamela stepped around an azalea and settled herself on the bench, sighing and feeling her shoulders sag. From this new position she couldn't see much of what was going on at the crime scene, so she entertained herself by studying the rock garden.

When the enterprise was first proposed, a call went out on the town listserv for donations of rocks. Pamela herself had responded. Every time she did any digging in her yard she encountered huge chunks of the sandstone that had provided the building material for so many of the Revolutionary-Era houses in Northern New Jersey. She set them aside as trophies and over the years had collected quite a pile. Now she studied the rock garden, wondering if she would recognize any of her own rocks.

One at the near edge looked familiar, like the one that had emerged when she spent an afternoon the previous fall planting a crepe myrtle. She had nicknamed the rock "the yam," for its tapering shape. She stood up, took a few steps, and bent to examine it more closely. Yes, it was definitely her rock, a yam formed from dark pink sandstone—except something at the larger end looked darker than the natural sandstone color. It looked almost black.

She studied the area around the rock. The soil had recently been disturbed, as if the rock had been snatched from its original position in the artful border of the garden and then hastily tucked back into place.

Pamela made her way through the shrubbery back to the edge of the parking lot, where she was greeted by Detective Clayborn.

"I was just coming to talk to you," he said.

He had a lived-in face, a face that couldn't have ever been handsome, even when he was young, and now it showed its years. But the slight tightness around his eyes suggested that he didn't miss much.

"Are you feeling okay?" he asked. "I understand you

found the body." Pamela nodded. He nodded back. "Officer Anders asked you some questions. I'd like to go over them." He was holding a little notepad too.

Pamela repeated her description of setting up the booth the night before and leaving for the parade with the aardvarks still in boxes inside the booth, and she insisted that once she and Bettina set the aardvarks out, at least one person was always at the booth.

Detective Clayborn frowned. "But midway through the afternoon two of the aardvarks were missing."

"It was mysterious." Pamela shrugged. "There were nine left, but we only had money for fourteen. We should have had money for sixteen, three hundred and twenty dollars."

"Who made the aardvarks?" he asked suddenly. Something about the upward tilt of his chin made the question seem like more than simple curiosity.

"All of us," Pamela said, trying not to act nervous. "There are six of us, but I made more than my share. I made ten."

When he looked up from whatever that answer had provoked him to write on the notepad, Pamela said, "Did they show you the blood on his collar?"

Detective Clayborn's face relaxed. Did he practice cultivating certain expressions, Pamela wondered, expressions suitable to different aspects of his job?

"You were helpful in that murder case last fall," he said, "but let's not make a habit of doing our work for us." He even managed a little chuckle. "That's what you pay taxes for."

"Hey, Mom!" a voice called from the edge of the crowd that still lingered at the edge of the parking lot. Pamela looked over to see Penny waving and looking worried.

"Is it okay if I go home now?" Pamela asked. "My daughter has come for me."

Detective Clayborn smoothed the pages of the little notepad back into place and closed the cover. "We're finished for the present."

Pamela took a few steps toward where Penny waited. Then she turned back toward Detective Clayborn. "There's blood on one of the rocks in the rock garden," she said. "The one shaped like a yam, at the edge near the memorial bench. I didn't touch it, but somebody did. The dirt around it has been disturbed."

The skin around his eyes tightened. "We're finished for the present," he repeated.

Pamela looked around to see if Bettina and Wilfred were still there, but it seemed they'd been dismissed too.

Under the watchful eye of a third officer who had apparently been summoned to keep the crowd at bay, Penny ventured to the center of the parking lot to meet Pamela. She reached her arms out for a hug, and Pamela pulled her close, letting her chin rest on her daughter's curly hair.

"What a day," Pamela sighed.

Penny stepped back and surveyed her mother. "One of Laine's friends texted her and said the police were all over the parking lot. Somebody put a dead body under the knitting club booth."

The officer tending the crowd approached, a warning expression on his young face. Pamela and Penny headed toward the driveway that led out to the street, Penny's arm around her mother's waist. Before they turned the corner, Pamela looked back and noticed one of the people in the white outfits lifting the yam-shaped rock into an official-looking bag.

* * *

At home there was a phone message from Bettina saying they were welcome to come across the street for dinner—otherwise she'd be over first thing in the morning.

But Penny got busy in the kitchen, and soon she'd put together a salad with leftover chicken and toasted some whole-grain bread. After they ate, Pamela settled down with her knitting and found a documentary about foxes on the Nature Channel.

"Foxes, Mom?" Penny said, laughing. "Okay, I'll keep you company." Catrina the cat joined them on the sofa, sleek and contented—and a far cry from the forlorn kitten Pamela had rescued the previous winter.

Chapter Three

Pamela had already dealt with the reporters that arrived just as she ventured outside to retrieve the *Register* from the front walk. Now she was unfolding the newspaper on the kitchen table as she waited for water to boil for her coffee. A slice of whole-grain bread sat ready near the toaster. Catrina, with considerably more appetite than Pamela's, was noisily finishing off a few spoonfuls of cat food.

Penny stepped in from the entry. "There's coffee at work," she said, in answer to her mother's unspoken question.

"But you need more than that." Pamela jumped up and reached for a knife to slice off another piece of bread.

"I'm really okay, Mom," Penny said. And she looked okay, despite the startling experience of the previous evening. Her eyes were bright and her skin, set off by her dark curls, glowed.

"Have I seen that outfit before?" Pamela asked. Penny was wearing a bright yellow dress with a gathered skirt. A parade of red roosters marched around the skirt's hemline, and a necklace of large red beads set off her pretty neck.

"The dress is from Laine's favorite thrift store. We found it when I went into the city with her last weekend." Penny cocked her head toward the entry. "I think there's someone—" she began, but her words were interrupted by the doorbell.

Pamela started across the kitchen, but by the time she stepped into the entry, Penny had already opened the door and Bettina was inside. She carried a large shopping bag.

"Off to work, I see," she exclaimed, surveying Penny with a smile. "And how's the job?"

"Great," Penny said. "I'm learning a lot." Penny had a summer job at an upscale home furnishings store in Manhattan. "And I'm going to miss my bus." Penny slipped past Bettina and hurried down the front walk.

Bettina turned to Pamela. "And you," she said. "How are you, my dear?"

"Strange dreams," Pamela said. "How about you?"

"Not even dreams." Bettina indeed did not look like her usual well-put-together self. Aside from a dab of lipstick, her face was bare, and the dark circles under her eyes testified to a restless night. "I kept seeing his face, and his eyes staring straight up at nothing, and then the aardvark on his chest."

From the kitchen came a sudden insistent hoot. "It's the kettle boiling!" Pamela led the way to the kitchen. "Coffee! Come on in."

Bettina followed. "By the way," she said. "I saw Richard Larkin just now. Such a thoughtful man—he asked if you were okay, and he made a point of telling me how much he enjoys reading the *Advocate*." She set the shopping bag on the table and moved the newspapers aside. "Have you looked at the *Register* yet?" she asked.

Pamela answered from the counter, where she was pouring water from the kettle into a paper cone half-full of freshly-ground coffee. "I had just unfolded it when Penny came down, and then you arrived." The promising aroma that arose from the moistened grounds lifted her spirits, but Bettina's next words made them sink again.

"I don't know when the people from the *Register* showed up," she said. "I certainly didn't see any reporters yesterday. But here it is on the front page—the booth, the aardvark, and the headline: MURDER AT ARBORVILLE TOWN FESTIVAL. And right underneath, still in big letters: BODY OF HIGH SCHOOL HISTORY TEACHER FOUND IN KNITTING CLUB BOOTH."

"A few of them were waiting for me this morning," Pamela said.

She had always felt that daily rituals were important—all the more so when normal life had been disrupted. So she reached down two cups and two saucers of her wedding china and set them on the table next to Bettina's shopping bag. And because she knew Bettina liked cream and sugar, she moved the sugar bowl from the counter to the table and stepped to the refrigerator to pour a dollop of cream into the little cut-glass pitcher that matched the sugar bowl.

"And, yes, I *will* have some toast," Bettina said with a smile. "And jam, though I know you never eat it."

Newspapers and shopping bag out of the way, they concentrated on their breakfast for a few minutes. Toast finished, Bettina wiped her fingers and added a bit more sugar to her coffee. "At least they didn't say, 'well-loved,'" she observed.

"Who?" Pamela had barely nibbled her toast, but she'd taken several swallows of coffee, appreciating its rich bitterness.

"Randall Jefferson, of course," Bettina said, sounding a little startled. "Not to speak ill of the dead and all of that, but no one could stand him. Didn't you know?"

"Penny never said anything. But I think she had a nice woman for American History."

"Well," Bettina said, setting down her coffee cup. The resigned expression on her face suggested someone delivering necessary but unpleasant news. "He was completely full of himself, made no secret of the fact that he didn't have to work—old family money and so on—and looked down on anyone and everyone."

"I guess you're more in touch with what people talk about in town," Pamela said.

"The *Advocate*, you know. My finger is on the pulse of Arborville. Also there's Wilfred and the historical society. It was obvious Randall Jefferson thought they were nothing but amateurs. So he didn't have any fans there."

"Will you be seeing Detective Clayborn today?" Pamela asked.

"I hope so," Bettina said. "I've got to get something written up soon if there's to be anything about the murder in this week's *Advocate*." She lifted her coffee cup and inspected the contents. "Is there more coffee?" she asked, already rising.

"Help yourself," Pamela said.

"And more toast?"

"Please do."

Bettina filled her cup, slipped a piece of bread into the toaster, and returned to the table for cream and sugar. "There's really not much in the *Register*, aside from that photo and the basic gruesome details," she said. "But by the time I get in to see Clayborn he might have heard from the ME about when Jefferson was likely killed."

"It had to be Saturday night," Pamela said, "after dark and after the library closed. Everybody would have gone home from working on the booths, and the parking lot would have been deserted. And when you see Detective Clayborn, ask him about the murder weapon."

"It was something heavy, I imagine. Jefferson was clunked on the back of the head. That much got into the *Register*."

Pamela was just about to tell her about the rock when Bettina's toast popped up and the doorbell rang.

It was Wilfred. He gave Pamela a quick hug and followed her into the kitchen. Bettina looked up from the toast she was buttering. She greeted Wilfred with a smile, then a quick intake of breath. "Ooops!" she said, raising a hand to her mouth. "I forgot about the strawberries." She picked up the shopping bag. "A gift for you, from Wilfred. He stopped by the farmers market in Newfield Saturday."

Pamela looked in the bag. "So many! Thank you. I hope you kept some for yourselves."

"We did," Bettina said.

Wilfred shook his head sadly. "We might have to ration them out, dear wife. Newfield is quite a ways away, and I'm afraid the Co-Op is going to be off-limits for a while."

"What on earth happened?" Pamela and Bettina exclaimed in chorus.

"Randall Jefferson is the talk of the town, you might say." Wilfred pulled out a chair and leaned on the table to lower himself into it. "Randall Jefferson and the Arborville knitting club. No one liked him, but he *was* an Arborville-ite, they're saying, *and* a respected teacher at the high school"—Wilfred's normally deep and pleasant voice modulated into the high-pitched whine that Pamela recognized as his impression of Arborville's leading gossip—"and that knitting club has something to answer for even if they didn't do it, and who can even be sure about that?"

Bettina took a large bite of toast. Pamela jumped up. "I'll make more coffee," she said.

"Not for me." Wilfred stood up again. "I've got work to do at home. It's best to keep busy."

"I'll be along in a few minutes," Bettina said.

When she was alone once more, Pamela lifted the strawberries out of the shopping bag. They were beauties, plump and rosy, and so ripe that the box that held them was blotted here and there with deep red strawberry stain.

Pamela knew that the knitting club wasn't responsible for Randall Jefferson's death. Whoever murdered him, probably with the yam-shaped rock from the rock garden, had simply tucked the body under the nearest booth, and that booth happened to be the knitting club booth. Then, later (during the parade?), the murderer—or someone—had quickly reached under the table's canvas skirt and placed an aardvark on the dead man's chest. That was where things got odd. But still, what could the knitting club have to do with it?

Pamela loved her life in the tiny town of Arborville, New Jersey, at least most of the time. She loved the walkability of the town that let her do most errands on foot. She loved the hundred-year-old wood-frame house that she and her architect husband had rescued from decline two decades ago and decorated with antique-store and tag-sale treasures. She loved the fact that she and her daughter had been able to remain there after the tragic construction-site accident that left Pamela a widow. She loved her work-at-home job as associate editor of *Fiber Craft* magazine.

At the sink, Pamela rinsed the breakfast things. She'd make a plan for the day, and everything would feel normal again, and the police would figure out who killed Randall Jefferson. First, she decided, she would read the *Register*. It would be best to actually know what the media was reporting about the murder. Then she would take a walk, but not in the direction of the Co-Op. And she'd check in with her boss at *Fiber Craft*. Work was always a good antidote to worry. And finally, she'd browse through her recipe books for a shortcake recipe and surprise Penny with strawberry shortcake for dessert.

She was staring gloomily at the *Register*'s front-page photo of the knitting club booth festooned with crime-scene tape—thank goodness she had at least removed the Arborville Knitting Club banner before she discovered the body—when the phone rang.

An unfamiliar voice responded to her "hello." Detective Clayborn would like to speak with her, the voice said. Could she come to the police station at her earliest convenience?

That would be her walk, but not the restorative communication with nature that she had pictured.

Should she change her clothes, she wondered. No, the jeans and cotton blouse she'd put on that morning were decent, as were the Birkenstocks. But upstairs in the bathroom she pulled her loose hair back into a low ponytail and added a bit of lipstick. Maybe earrings weren't necessary for an interview with the police.

A knitted turquoise aardvark was perched in the middle of the desk, between an untidy pile of paper and an open laptop. It was the brightest thing in the room, except for the neon-orange flyer pinned to the bulletin board (and considerably out of date) announcing that alternate-side parking would be suspended for Good Friday.

"Thank you for coming." Detective Clayborn rose from behind the desk and extended his hand. His handshake was quick and efficient. The fluorescent lights were even less flattering to his homely face than the bright sunshine of the previous day had been. "Please sit down," he added. The chair was a straight-backed wooden chair, as if the Arborville police station had been furnished a century ago and not altered since, except for electric lights, modern telephones, and computers.

"The crime-scene unit has finished with this," Detective Clayborn said, nodding toward the aardvark. Pamela reached a hand toward the creature. "But I haven't," he added. Then, "Go ahead—you can touch it."

She hesitated.

"What I want to know," he said, "is who made it. Was it someone in your group?"

"Oh—" Pamela almost smiled. "You're thinking the killer could have made it, separate from the twenty-five we made, and put it on the body right after he did the murder. So it sat there all night—no need to wonder if someone was sneaking around while most people were at the parade."

Detective Clayborn frowned. "I was thinking that, yes . . ."

Pamela moved the aardvark to the edge of the desk and examined it closely, laying it on its side, bending its rabbit-like ears to-and-fro, and lifting its stubby tail. "It's one of mine," she said at last. "I dropped a few stitches on this one but it was the part that would be on the belly so I figured no one would notice. I'm usually very fussy, but we had a lot of aardvarks to knit and not much time."

Detective Clayborn reached across the desk. Pamela gave the aardvark a gentle shove until it was close enough for him to grab. He studied its belly. "I can't see it," he said. "But I'll take your word for it. And this was one of the original twenty-five?"

"Definitely," Pamela said. "It was the last one I did. I finished it Friday night."

He stood again and stepped around the desk. "Thank you," he said. "The department appreciates your help." At the door, he thanked her again and then paused. "I should have bought one," he said. "My nephew would have liked it."

Pamela smiled. "We have one left."

"Best not to complicate the case with a conflict of interest," he said, a faint smile softening the folds that bracketed his mouth.

Pamela paused. "By the way—" The door was open now, but she didn't step through. "Did that turn out to be blood on the yam-shaped rock?"

The skin around his eyes tightened and the smile vanished. "We will release information to the media as it becomes available, and if it seems appropriate."

"Two aardvarks were missing," Pamela said as she stepped into the hall. "I wonder where the other one will turn up."

Pamela's trip to the police station had been roundabout. She'd walked down the hill to County Road, the busy thoroughfare at the bottom of Orchard Street, skirted the nature preserve at the edge of town, and then climbed back up the hill when she reached the cross street where the library and the police station were located. A walk to town on her normal route would have taken her along Arborville Avenue and past the Co-Op Grocery, with the morning comings and goings of the town in full swing. If Wilfred had been accosted by people who should have been minding their own business, she would have been an even more likely prey.

But now, stepping out onto the asphalt apron at the police station's entrance and blinking in the May sunshine, she realized that she was starving, too starving to take the roundabout route back home. On a normal day, on her normal schedule, one piece of toast sufficed until she took a break from her computer at eleven or so. Today she'd barely nibbled her breakfast toast, and now it was after noon, and she was eager to make up for the breakfast she'd skipped.

The police station was nearly at the corner of Arborville Avenue. She cut across the bit of lawn that separated it from the library and dashed across the street, hurrying to put Arborville's commercial district behind her. Borough Hall, a small brick building, marked the spot where "downtown" Arborville became "residential" Arborville. She was happy to see no one at all on her side of the street except a handsome young man in jeans and a T-shirt. He was on his hands and knees in the patch of dirt between the sidewalk and the steps that led into Borough Hall, bending attentively toward a clump of salvia.

Something bright glinted on the sidewalk, and she stooped to pick up a penny. The young man looked up, and she recognized him as Joe Taylor, the same person who had admired the aardvarks at the festival.

"The knitter!" he said, rocking back into a kneeling position.

Pamela steeled herself for whatever might come next, but his smile was genuine, if a little goofy, as if compensating for his good looks. And the expression in his clear eyes was admiring.

"I really did like the aardvarks," he said. "Doing things with your hands—that's what it's all about." He smoothed the soil around the base of the rangy plant he'd been working on and picked up a garden trowel. "My grandmother knit," he said. "I wish I'd known her better." Still on his knees, he moved a few feet to the right and scooped out a trowel-full of earth. Several plastic pots of salvia waited nearby. "You'll be lucky," he observed, nodding toward the penny in her hand. "I wish I'd seen it first. I'd have played the lottery today."

"Oh—it's just a silly superstition," Pamela said. "But I always pick up pennies when I see them on the sidewalk. I never play the lottery though."

"I do," Joe said. "The same number, once a week—431985."

They talked for a few more minutes, and Pamela made it the rest of the way home with no further encounters. She was grateful that Mr. Gilly, the super of the big apartment building at her corner, was nowhere in sight—he could be very chatty. And she skipped her usual detour to peek around the length of wooden fencing that hid the apartment building's trash from the street. Other people's trash could be treasure, and Pamela had been amazed to discover castoffs as nice as things from her favorite thrift store.

At home, she made a quick sandwich with cheese the Co-Op stocked from a farm in Vermont, put two pork chops out to thaw for dinner, and climbed the steps to her office. As she'd suspected, her boss at *Fiber Craft* had had a busy morning, and an email message with ten attachments lurked in her in-box. She clicked the message open and read: "Please look at these submissions and let me know by tomorrow which you think would be suitable for the next issue, or any future issue."

Just as she was about to open the first attachment, the computer chimed to signal the arrival of a fresh email, and Bettina's name appeared in boldface at the top of the email queue. Odd, she thought. She had seen Bettina only a few hours ago, and when Bettina wanted to get in touch she usually just crossed the street. What could she have on her mind?

She clicked on the boldface "Bettina" and up came a startling message: "Check AccessArborville. The 'Killer Aardvark' is the talk of the town."

Chapter Four

AccessArborville was the town listserv. Pamela didn't subscribe to the posts, but she had an account and visited the website when she wanted to communicate with her fellow townspeople. Not long ago, after a satisfying afternoon rearranging an out-of-control flower bed, she had offered free daylily tubers to anyone who wanted them.

Now she went into her "Favorites" file, and soon she was reading the most recent comment in the thread KILLER AARDVARK: "I am not sure how the high school will replace Randall Jefferson. He may have acted at times as if he was too good for Arborville, but he was a brilliant teacher who brought credit to the town. And he was a great American. That knitting club has a lot to answer for."

Previous messages asked why Pamela Paterson hadn't yet been arrested, how anyone could suggest the aardvark wasn't placed on Jefferson's chest by a member of the knitting club (and we all know what *that* would mean!), and even hypothesized that the knitting club was a front for a group that did not support patriotic values. One person was of the opinion that Pamela Paterson was being spared because she and Detective Clayborn were involved romantically.

Pamela heard a moan and a sigh that she recognized as coming from herself. She closed her eyes in search of comforting darkness, but the glare from the computer screen gave the darkness a reddish tinge. She hurriedly clicked on the X that would banish AccessArborville from her computer and sent a quick reply to Bettina: "It's just the AccessArborville cohort, isn't it? Not the whole town." Then she retreated to the soothing world of *Fiber Craft*. The first attachment she opened contained an article about early Indonesian textiles, complete with photographs. The photographs showed weavings in vivid shades of red, blue, and gold, with parades of stylized lizards marching along their borders. She sank gratefully into her work.

In the winter, gathering darkness outside Pamela's office windows told her dinnertime was near. But sunset on these long May days came too late to signal quitting time. After she'd read half the articles her boss had sent, she checked the clock and decided the rest could wait until the next morning. Penny would be home from work soon, and Pamela wanted to get a head start on a dinner that was to include strawberry shortcake.

Catrina greeted Pamela at the bottom of the stairs and led her eagerly into the kitchen, where Pamela spooned a few scoops of cat food into a bowl and set it in front of the excited cat. That chore taken care of, she put four small red potatoes on to boil and, in a separate pot, two eggs. Then she took her oldest, most favorite cookbook down from the shelf and turned its yellowed and food-stained pages to the recipe for homemade shortcake.

Shortcakes were basically biscuits, but with added

sugar unless one liked all of one's biscuits sweet. In her caramel-colored bowl with the white stripes, she mixed flour, baking powder, salt, and sugar, then she held a stick of butter over the mixture and cut narrow slices until she judged she'd done five tablespoons' worth. She reached for a second knife and worked the two knives against each other in the flour until the butter bits had almost disappeared. The next step was to sprinkle milk over the now faintly yellowish flour mixture and work the mixture until it formed a clump.

The pastry cloth lay ready on the kitchen table, dusted with flour. She dusted flour on her hands too, and on the clump of dough, and rolled and patted and squeezed the dough until it became a smooth round.

She lifted the dough and dusted more flour under it, then returned it to its spot on the pastry cloth and patted it into a larger, thinner round. The recipe said to use a biscuit cutter to carve out the biscuit shapes, but Pamela had never owned a biscuit cutter despite her fondness for old-fashioned kitchen equipment. Instead she used a glass tumbler, placing it upside down on the dough and rotating it until the rim pushed through the dough and reached the pastry cloth. In this way she formed eight perfect rounds and set them one by one on a buttered cookie sheet. The recipe recommended splitting them while still warm and spreading them with butter before piling on the fruit. She'd time their baking so they came out of the oven right when she and Penny sat down to eat, and the biscuits would still be warm enough to melt butter by dessert time. They would eat two of them tonight and save two for the next night and the rest would go to Bettina.

A quick poke with a fork showed that the potatoes were done. Pamela drained them, and drained the eggs, and piled potatoes and eggs together in a shallow bowl to cool. She checked that the pork chops had thawed and sorted the ripest strawberries into a colander. Once they were rinsed and dripping into the sink, she picked up a small knife. She was just performing the delicate operation of stem-removal on the first strawberry when the front door opened and Penny called out, "Hi, Mom! I'm home."

Penny sailed into the kitchen as energetic as if she hadn't just put in a full day of work with a bus commute at each end. Even her yellow dress with the red roosters looked as fresh as it had looked ten hours earlier. "Oh, Mom," she said. "Manhattan is just . . . the best—so many different kinds of people, and everybody is so busy and doing such interesting things. And the people who come into the store are all furnishing their lofts, and the things they buy are so elegant—" She paused for breath.

"And so expensive, and those people are so rich," Pamela interjected, but with a smile so she didn't sound like a spoilsport.

"Why did you ever leave, Mom?"

Penny had never asked her that before. Pamela looked at the strawberry she was holding, its stem still attached. She set the strawberry down and turned away from the counter. "We wanted to have you, and we wanted a house so you could have a room of your own and a yard to play in," she said.

"Aww . . . Mom." Penny let her smooth forehead crease and puckered her mouth as if acknowledging a great sacrifice

"We loved living here," Pamela said.

"You didn't just do it for me?"

"Not *just* for you."

"You could move back to the city. After I graduate.

I'm not going to be one of those people who graduates and comes home to live with mom."

"I'll think about it," Pamela said with a smile.

Penny started toward the door. In the doorway she paused and half turned. "You're not going to try to solve this murder, are you?" she asked, her smooth forehead creasing again. "I was really worried the last time. And if Bettina tries to talk you into it, please just tell her no."

"I don't see what Bettina and I could do," Pamela said. "I'm sure we don't know anything that the police don't know."

"Okay," Penny said. "Good." And she headed around the corner and up the stairs.

"Come back down in half an hour," Pamela called.

Pamela resolved not to mention Wilfred's experience at the Co-Op or the "Killer Aardvark" theme that had overtaken the town listserv. Penny would be at work in the city every day for the rest of the week, and hopefully she and her Arborville friends had more interesting things to do than pay attention to the gossip of people with no lives of their own.

After Pamela got the oven started and picked up the strawberry she'd set down, her thoughts returned to the conversation she'd just had with Penny about leaving the city. She'd never imagined that Penny *would* move back home after college, but then she'd never thought much at all about a time that had always seemed so distant. Yet Penny's freshman year had flown by. Only three years remained. She didn't know what she'd do then. The house was huge for one person, but selling it would be like parting with a piece of herself, all the memories of being newly married and falling in love with a house in need of rescue. She and her husband had lavished their time and talents on it, and even though he was gone, the work he'd done remained. She felt welcomed by him every time she walked in the door.

Pamela went back to work on the strawberries. She carved out the stems, sliced the plump berries into quarters, and piled them in a favorite oval dish, white china with a scalloped edge and faded gold along the rim. Soon her fingers were red with strawberry juice, and the sweet but faintly spicy strawberry smell had overtaken the smell of boiled potatoes. When all the strawberries were destemmed and sliced, she sprinkled a teaspoon of sugar over them. It didn't seem that long ago—though it was years and years—that Penny would come in while she was preparing fruit and ask hopefully, "*Will sugar be added?*"

Now the oven was ready, and it was time to start the shortcakes. And since she was thinking about dessert, she filled the cut-glass cream pitcher with the heavy cream she kept on hand for Bettina's coffee. The rest of the meal went together quickly. The pork chops were set sizzling in the frying pan. The potatoes were stripped of their delicate red skins and sliced into a bowl. The hard-boiled eggs were tapped on the counter until the shells were fractured all around and the glistening white ovals slipped easily into her hand. Then they too were sliced and added to the potatoes. The salad was finished off with chopped celery and a dressing of mayonnaise, a bit of cider vinegar, powdered mustard, and salt and pepper.

A plate of sliced tomatoes would have been the perfect addition to the meal, but Pamela's own tomato crop had just gone into the ground the previous week, and she'd used up the batch she'd bought at the Co-Op when she did last week's shopping.

Penny reappeared in the doorway just as Pamela

was setting the cookie sheet with its nicely risen and slightly browned shortcakes on a trivet to cool. She was picturing how satisfyingly the butter would melt on the sliced shortcakes and how pretty the strawberries would look piled up and garnished with heavy cream.

"Can you set the table while I tend these pork chops?" Pamela asked, standing at the stove and poking at the pork chops with a long fork.

"Mom?" Penny asked, her voice rising above the jangle of silverware as she collected knives, forks, and spoons from the silverware drawer. "Did you know everyone in town is talking about the 'Killer Aardvark'"?

Pamela gave one of the chops a particularly savage poke. Maybe she *should* move back to the city. You could be anonymous there.

It was Tuesday morning. Penny was out the door, Pamela's coffee cup was empty, and all that remained of the toast were a few crumbs scattered on the vintage 1940s tablecloth with its border of purple flowers and orange fruit. Catrina had been fed and had padded off for a nap after nibbling delicately at a few table-spoons of food. The *Register* lay loosely folded, ready to join a week's worth of *Register*s in the recycling basket. Mercifully, the Arborfest murder had migrated to an inner page, much of today's front page taken up by a story about the latest (unpopular) doings of the gov-ernor. The coverage of the murder had added nothing significant to the previous day's report, except that the ME had put the murder sometime after six p.m. and before six a.m., and the murder weapon had been identified as a rock from the library rock garden—the yam-shaped rock, Pamela was sure. As far as suspects went, the police were pursuing various lines of inquiry.

Well, Pamela had said to herself as she read the article, Bettina and I had already figured out that he was killed after dark and after the library closed, but before people started showing up the next morning to put the finishing touches on their booths. And if it's the yam-shaped rock, I already knew all about it because I found it.

Five submissions to *Fiber Craft* lurked upstairs, waiting to be evaluated. Bettina would undoubtedly talk to Detective Clayborn today, or at least try, and would undoubtedly drop by to make her report. When she showed up, Pamela would take a break and make another pot of coffee, but for now duty called and she headed for the stairs.

She'd barely reached the landing when the doorbell rang. Reversing direction, she knew even before she reached the bottom of the stairs that it was Bettina—or at least a visitor who had dressed that morning in an ensemble colorful enough to do justice to a sunny May day. Through the lace that curtained the oval window in the front door, a bright but indistinct shape was visible, glowing against the green yard and the street beyond.

It was Bettina, and she began speaking even before she stepped over the threshold. "Clayborn didn't want to talk," she said breathlessly, "but I wore him down. Nothing much interesting in today's *Register*, as you probably noticed, but more goodies emerged after his interview with the *Register* reporter yesterday. *Lots* more goodies." She paused and let Pamela close the door behind her. "And speaking of goodies, how about a blueberry muffin?" She flourished a bag. "I didn't have to venture into the Co-Op—I had them at home. Do you still have butter out from your toast?"

In the kitchen, Bettina opened the bag and set blueberry muffins on the plates Pamela hastily supplied. She'd obviously slept much better than the previous night, and was her usual fastidiously groomed self, eye shadow keyed to the aqua waves that zigzagged here and there on her dress, where they intersected with splotches of bright orange and fuchsia. The fuchsia was reflected in her carefully applied lipstick.

"So—" She addressed Pamela's back. Pamela was standing at the counter pouring coffee beans into her grinder.

"Hold on," Pamela said. "I just have to do this." The grinder spun, beans clattered for a few seconds in the chamber, and then the sound smoothed out to a whir. The dark and pungent smell of coffee filled the little kitchen.

Bettina seized the kettle from the stove and measured in four cups of water. Once it was back in place with a burner alight under it, she reached two cups and saucers from the cupboard where Pamela kept her wedding china. Pamela slipped a coffee filter into the plastic cone atop her carafe and poured in the ground beans. Then she busied herself setting out cream and sugar, knives and spoons, butter, and napkins while Bettina talked.

"What do you want to hear about first?" she said. "The suspect who hasn't been arrested? The murder weapon? That's in the paper, but I know more. The blood? The fingerprints and DNA?"

"How about the murder weapon?" Pamela said, though she already knew. It was tantalizing to hear that there was a suspect, but she'd save the best for last.

"A rock from the library rock garden," Bettina said, "but the *Register* had that. What it *didn't* have was how the cops found out about the rock." Pamela paused in the act of pouring heavy cream into the cut-glass pitcher that matched her sugar bowl. "A *confidential informant*," Bettina said, whispering and looking from side to side in a parody of a television snitch.

"Oh, that silly . . . *man*!" Pamela laughed. "I'm the confidential informant. I was sitting near the rock garden waiting because I knew he'd want to talk to me, and I recognized one of the rocks I'd donated for the rock garden project. I looked closer and saw that it had blood—or something dark—on it and that the soil around it had been disturbed like it was picked up and put back. I pointed it out to him." She returned to her task.

"I'll keep that in mind if he resists me again," Bettina said with a satisfied smile. "His confidential informant isn't as confidential as he thinks."

The whistling kettle summoned Bettina to the stove, and soon the coffee aroma in the little kitchen intensified as boiling water dripped through the ground beans.

When they were seated at the table, steaming cups of coffee in front of them, Pamela said, "So the dark spot was really blood." She sampled her coffee.

"Really blood." Bettina scooped a spoonful of sugar into her cup. "And definitely *his* blood. That's been confirmed." She added cream to her cup and stirred the resulting mixture, now a pale brown. "And did you know"—she looked up—"fingerprints can actually be retrieved from rocks, and DNA too?"

"That should make it very easy to prove who killed him," Pamela said. "And soon, I hope. The 'Killer Aardvark' is giving the knitting club a very bad name in town."

Bettina had tasted her coffee and was studiously peeling the crinkled paper from her muffin. "Not so easy to prove," she murmured. She set the paper aside and sliced the muffin in half. "Half the volunteers who worked on the rock garden probably touched that rock, including about twenty kids from the high school."

"But if there's a suspect, and that person's finger-prints or DNA are on the rock . . ."

"Don't make me eat alone," Bettina said. "Get to work on that muffin." She herself was liberally spreading butter on both halves of her muffin. She finished her task. "Obviously, Clayborn's first thought was to talk to Brad Striker."

"The coach." Pamela sipped more coffee and set to work peeling the crinkled paper off her own muffin.

"The coach." Bettina nodded. "He had gotten him-self quite worked up about Jefferson's op-ed piece, and he was stomping around at the festival ranting about it to anybody who would listen."

Pamela nodded in return. "We heard him."

"Apparently some of his language was downright threatening, really vicious."

"Jefferson would already have been dead though. He was under the knitting club table all day." Pamela broke off a small piece of muffin and nibbled at it. "If you'd already killed a person, wouldn't it be dumb to advertise how much you hated him?"

"People with hot tempers don't always act ration-ally," Bettina said. "I've been to a few Aardvark games. Striker becomes completely unwound if the game isn't going well, hopping up and down on the sidelines and screaming, even obscenities sometimes. I'm surprised the parents of kids on the team don't complain." She picked up a muffin half and took a big bite.

"So Detective Clayborn talked to him and . . ." Pamela ate another piece of muffin and picked up her coffee cup.

Bettina finished chewing and pronounced the

muffin delicious. "Talked to him . . . and he has an alibi. He's married, and his wife says he was home Saturday night watching the sports channel. Of course, he could have sneaked out after she went to bed. But then there's the matter of putting the aardvark on the dead man's chest, which most likely happened during the parade." Bettina went on. "Several people saw Striker at the parade, and that cute Officer Anders was assigned to the parade. He says he's pretty sure Striker was there the whole time."

"He wasn't though!" Pamela set her coffee cup back on its saucer with a clunk. "He was heading back toward the library as I was on my way to the parade. It was about a quarter after eleven, and the parade had already started. I set out at eleven, and then I remembered I'd left the cash box behind, right out on the table. There wasn't anything in it yet, but I didn't want it to disappear. There was nobody at all in the parking lot when I retrieved the box, but I passed Brad Striker coming the other way on my way back up to Arborville Avenue."

"Interesting," Bettina said. "I wonder how many people Clayborn considers 'several.' Officer Anders, cute though he may be, is only 'pretty sure' about Striker being there the whole time." Bettina finished off the first half of her muffin and wiped her fingers on her napkin. "Maybe Striker's wife sleeps really soundly, and anyway does it really count if your alibi is your wife? Striker's brother is on the town council, you know," she said. "So a few strings might have been pulled. Clayborn is a decent guy though, and if the evidence was irrefutable—a witness, for example—I'm sure he wouldn't hold back. So far the only thing for sure is that Striker was furious at Jefferson."

"But there aren't any other suspects, are there?" Pamela asked.

Bettina shook her head. "No other suspects."

They refilled their cups and worked on their muffins, chatting about Penny's job and Bettina's grand-children. As Bettina rose to go, Pamela remembered that she had shortcakes for her. She handed them over with instructions to warm them so they could be buttered before piling on the strawberries and adding cream.

At the door, Bettina paused. "You're not going to try to talk me into climbing up that hill tonight, are you?" The weekly Knit and Nibble meeting was hap-pening that evening at Nell's house, in the section of Arborville known as the Palisades.

"If you're driving, I'll grab a ride," Pamela said.

"There's to be a new member," Bettina said. "Karen Dowling's friend."

"I wonder if she'll actually come." Pamela raised her eyebrows and twisted her lips into a wry expression. "Killer Aardvark, you know."

Chapter Five

Joe Taylor was gathering dead branches into a bundle as Pamela and Bettina parked in front of the substantial house where Nell and Harold Bascomb lived. The house was built of natural stone and perched on a steep lot, reached by a street that curved this way and that as it meandered up the hill that formed the backside of the cliffs overlooking the Hudson.

"Winter was hard on these guys," Joe said, waving toward a bank of viburnums. "Now they're all cleaned up and ready to grow." He deposited the bundle at the curb and with a cheery goodnight headed down the street.

"Hard worker," Bettina observed. "I wonder if Wilfred could use help in our yard."

They made their way up the stone steps, where Harold Bascomb greeted them at the door. "They're in the kitchen," he said, "and the new member is here already. Karen and Roland are on their way."

Pamela and Bettina ventured down the long hallway that led to the kitchen. The hallway was almost a gallery, lined with the curious art Nell and Harold had collected on their many travels. Before stepping through the kitchen door, they paused.

"We are really getting old," Bettina whispered to Pamela. Knit and Nibble's new member had purple streaks in her hair. She looked as young as Penny and was equally tiny, if not tinier. She and Nell were standing at Nell's kitchen table, and Nell was beaming delightedly at her visitor.

"Awesome." The young woman shook her head in amazement, her pretty face aglow. "I mean it—absolutely awesome. This is the most amazing kitchen I have ever been in. You are so, so lucky."

As young marrieds, Nell and Harold had moved into an old house with a kitchen recently redone to 1950s tastes—and the kitchen had remained the same ever since. The counters were pink Formica and the appliances were avocado green.

"And your amazing dishes!" The young woman gazed at the plates and cups laid out on the table, ready for the Nibble portion of the evening's meeting. "Do you know what people would pay for these on eBay?"

Nell's dinnerware dated from the 1950s too. It featured abstract shapes that suggested wildflowers and wheat, in now-faded shades of coral and gold. The plates and cups shared the table with a long, foil-wrapped object.

Nell looked up and noticed them in the doorway. "Come in, come in," she said. "Meet our new member, Holly Perkins."

"I'm so glad to meet you!" Holly's smile revealed perfect white teeth and created a small dimple in her left cheek. "I'm so excited about the club, and Karen has told me so much about all of you, and to come here tonight and get to know Nell is just . . . amazing."

"Hello!" Pamela and Bettina returned the greeting. "And, Nell," Bettina said, "how are you—after our experience?"

"None the worse for wear," Nell said cheerfully, "police interview notwithstanding. I'm tougher than you think." Indeed, Nell was tall and energetic, and only her white hair and wrinkled skin hinted at her age. She went on, "And if the whole thing hasn't scared Holly off . . ."

"Not for a minute," Holly said. "I can't wait to start my project."

They all chatted for a few minutes, then Nell picked up the foil-wrapped object and slipped it into the oven. "Cherry strudel," she observed. "It's even better when it's a little warm. I wanted to serve something healthier, like broccoli bars, but Harold prevailed."

"Does the Co-Op bakery make strudel now?" Bettina asked. "I never noticed."

"It's not from there," Nell said. "Harold went all the way up to the German bakery in Kringlekamack. The poor man ventured into the Co-Op yesterday and talked himself hoarse trying to defend the knitting club. The way rumors spread in this town is just ridiculous."

The doorbell chimed and they heard Harold's cheerful voice, and then Roland's, sounding peevish.

"I parked the Porsche on this side of the street," Roland said. "I couldn't find a sign with the alternate-side parking days."

"It's fine," Harold said. "They never check up here in the Palisades anyway."

"Are you sure?" The sharp edge to Roland's voice made him sound like he was conducting a cross-examination in court. "I don't want to get a ticket. I pay enough to this town in taxes as it is."

"Perfectly fine." Harold was a retired doctor, and his voice hadn't lost its soothing quality. "This side is legal until midnight."

Roland went on. "And why the police thought I would know anything about that . . . *incident* . . . at Arborfest is beyond me. Clayborn quizzed me for half an hour. Trying to earn his salary, I suppose."

The doorbell chimed again. "That has to be Karen," Nell said. "Shall we adjourn to the living room?"

Holly led the way, hurrying to Karen's side as soon as Nell had greeted her and made sure she'd survived her interview with the police. "I got here early," Holly said. "I was so excited I couldn't wait, and I met Nell and saw her amazing kitchen, and I met Pamela and Bettina . . ." She paused and beamed at Harold, and the dimple appeared. "And Harold, of course . . ." She seemed to run out of breath. Karen gave her a smile and quiet hello.

"How did you two meet?" Bettina asked, as people found seats, with Holly and Karen side by side on one of the loveseats that flanked the fireplace.

"The hardware store," they said in unison.

"My husband and I are restoring an old house too," Holly added. "Just up the block from Karen's, as it turned out, and we were both looking at paint samples."

"Holly has a great eye for color." Karen gave her friend an admiring glance.

Side by side on the other loveseat, Roland and Nell were pulling yarn and knitting needles from their knitting bags, though Roland's knitting bag was actually a briefcase. Nell examined her partly finished project, an olive-green rectangle about ten inches wide and, so far, two inches long.

"No more elephants?" Roland said. Nell's previous

project had been a whole herd of knitted elephant toys for the children at the Haversack women's shelter. The elephants had given the group the idea of making the aardvarks to sell at Arborfest.

"I'm taking a break from animals," Nell said. "This is to be a scarf for the day laborers. Harold is involved with a group that's collecting winter clothes for them."

Roland began casting on from a skein of pink angora yarn.

"Something new for you too, Roland," Bettina observed from across the room.

"Not so new," he said. "It's another sweater for Ramona." Ramona was the DeCamps' dachshund. "The first one turned out so well that Melanie begged me to make another. She picked out the yarn." Melanie was Roland's very chic wife. Pamela could only imagine that the choice of pink angora yarn for a dachshund sweater had been tongue in cheek.

Pamela was a bit at loose ends now that the aardvark project had been finished. She'd come to the meeting hoping for inspiration, and now she said, "I'll make a scarf too, Nell. If you have enough yarn for another, I'll get started right now."

Pamela and Bettina had settled onto the sofa that faced Nell's grand fireplace, built of natural stone like the house itself, and with an exposed chimney that dominated that end of the room. Where a fire would have burned in winter, a huge arrangement of dried flowers now took the place of logs. More travel souvenirs decorated the mantel, including a striking African mask and a pair of carved wooden puppets from Indonesia.

Bettina pulled her new project out of her bag, the beginnings of what was to be a stuffed cat for her new granddaughter, and flourished her knitting needles proudly. "I never thought I'd be able to knit," she said, "but now I can. All those years with the crochet." Bettina had been welcomed by the group despite the fact that her yarn creations were all crochet, until the time came to do the aardvark project.

"Oh!" Holly called from across the room. "Crochet seems like it would be much harder. I'd love to learn!" Her eyes glowed with admiration.

Total opposites, Pamela reflected, studying Karen and Holly. So curious that they should be such good friends—though she had to admit the same could be said about her and Bettina. Karen was quiet, and pale, and blond, with a sweet rosebud mouth that only occasionally curved into a smile, and a shy one at that. Holly was chatty, chatty enough for the two of them. Her dark hair (with purple streaks) framed a face with lively eyes and a mouth seemingly made to smile.

Just now she was smiling. "Are you going to tell them your exciting news—or let them guess?" she said, fingering the few inches of delicate white knitting that hung from one of Karen's needles.

"An interesting new project." Nell spoke up from the other side of the fireplace.

Karen blushed. "It's a sweater," she peeped in her tiny voice.

"A very small sweater," Nell said kindly. "Is it going to be for a very small person?"

"Yes," Karen said. "That's my news. Dave and I are going to have a baby, and we're thrilled."

"Well, that's wonderful!" Bettina set down her knitting and clapped delightedly. "Congratulations!"

"Yes," Pamela echoed. "Congratulations!" It seemed hardly any time at all since she had been a young married in a fixer-upper house and with a baby on the way. Now that baby was in college.

Roland seemed bewildered, as if he'd never been called upon to offer congratulations to an expectant mother. He looked from person to person, his gaze finally resting on Karen. "Very good news," he said, in a voice that might have been commenting on a favorable report from his stock broker. "An outstanding achievement."

Nell gave him a quizzical look but didn't say anything.

"And when is the baby due?" Bettina asked.

"December." Karen ducked her head, looped a strand of yarn around the knitting needle in her right hand, and began to knit.

"And, my goodness, Holly"—Bettina leaned forward on the sofa—"you are obviously *not* knitting a sweater for a baby."

From her bag, Holly had retrieved a pair of knitting needles thick as drumsticks. From one of them dangled the beginnings of a project knit from yarn so thick that it resembled rope, but rope twisted from a soft, pale fiber. "It goes very fast," Holly said, with one of her dazzling smiles. "I only cast on twenty stitches for this, and look how wide it is." It was at least twenty inches wide, and the individual stitches so huge that the effect was like knitting viewed through a magnifying glass.

"It's going to be this." Holly pulled a booklet from her knitting bag, opened it, and displayed a photo to the group. It showed a slender young woman with a dramatic, cropped hairstyle. She was wearing a black turtleneck, black leggings, and heavy black boots—topped off with a bulky white jacket knitted from yarn like Holly's. "Everyone wants to knit now," she said. "There are such amazing things to make."

Pamela focused on the scarf for the day laborers

and let her mind wander, summoning it back when it wandered too close to the events of the previous Sunday. At her side, Bettina whispered numbers. She was casting on for another piece of the in-progress cat, which was to be bright yellow. No one else spoke. Karen and Holly were both intent on their projects. Nell finished a row and held the growing length of fuzzy brown up for inspection. Roland picked up his skein of pink angora and tugged a longer strand of yarn free.

Bettina reached the number of stitches she was casting on and then was silent. For a long time there was no sound in the room but clicking needles. From the street the occasional passing car could be heard, or a chirping bug—Nell preferred open windows to air conditioning on all but the hottest nights.

"Killer aardvark," Roland said suddenly.

Pamela heard herself gasp. The sofa trembled as Bettina sat upright. On the loveseat to the left of the fireplace, Karen and Holly both lowered their knitting to their laps and stared across the room at Roland. Nell stared at him too, her gentle face distressed.

"Well, it's what we're all thinking, isn't it?" Roland said.

"We are," Bettina said sadly. "At least I am. I can't even go to the Co-Op anymore, and yesterday I was picking up my dry cleaning when a woman came out of Hyler's Luncheonette to tell me that she bought an aardvark for her grandson, and now he's afraid to even have it in his room."

"I've heard things too," Holly said. "Like somebody wants to collect all the aardvarks and have a bonfire. *Please!* Arborville *is* the suburbs, but—hello?—do people leave their brains behind when they move here?" She seized the strand of giant yarn that snaked across her lap and jerked it around her waiting needle.

"It's just a few people," Karen said in a soft voice, looking sideways at her friend. "Really."

"It's not just a few." Bettina stirred, and the sofa trembled again, sending Pamela's ball of yarn bouncing to the floor. Pamela bent to retrieve it. "It's everywhere I go," Bettina said, "and all over AccessArborville. Nobody's posting about anything else."

"Not quite true. Someone on Catalpa Avenue is giving away a bookcase," Nell observed.

"Well, hardly anything else." The words came out high-pitched and scratchy, hardly Bettina's voice at all. Pamela didn't know if Bettina was really angry or about to cry, or both. "And have you heard that there's a movement afoot to change the high-school mascot?"

"Oh, dear," Nell said. "They've been the Aardvarks forever, way back to when Harold's and my children were in school here, and even before. Varks! Varks! Go, Varks, go!" She laughed. "I can hear that chant like it was yesterday."

"What other animal starts with *A*?" Roland said. He rested his knitting in his lap and looked off into space, pondering the question.

"Armadillo?" Holly suggested.

"Sounds like something from Texas," Roland said. "Albatross?"

"Isn't that a sea bird?" Pamela asked. "We're not exactly a shore town."

"Antelopes?" Holly said with a laugh. "Though antelopes don't exactly come to mind when you think of football players."

"Do aardvarks?" Roland asked with a scowl.

"Not really. But armadillos maybe. Sort of bulky . . ." Holly shrugged.

"It won't be our decision," Bettina said, in that same unfamiliar voice. "But they'll think of something, I'm sure."

Roland scowled harder. "A new mascot will undoubtedly mean new uniforms, new signage, new everything. And who foots the bill? The taxpayer, of course." Nell suppressed a smile. "And meanwhile"—Roland's lean face was stern—"what, if anything, have our public servants actually done to solve this crime? Nobody's been arrested that I've heard of."

"True," Bettina said.

"I'd go after Brad Striker," Roland said. "He was certainly making his feelings about Randall Jefferson clear at Arborfest."

"He has an alibi," Bettina said. "He was home with his wife Saturday night. She's backing him up."

"Wives can lie," Roland said. "The *Register* said the murder weapon was a rock from the library rock garden. That means they can get fingerprints and DNA."

"The rock will have fingerprints and DNA from half the people who worked on the rock garden, including a bunch of high-school kids," Pamela said. "And it will have my fingerprints and DNA because I donated the rock."

"I doubt Brad Striker worked on the rock garden," Roland said with a laugh. "He's hardly the type. So if his fingerprints and DNA are on the rock . . ."

Holly was paying close attention to Roland's argument, the beginnings of her chunky-yarn project resting unattended in her lap like a pile of rope. Now she spoke up. "If he did it because he wanted revenge for the op-ed Randall Jefferson wrote, it would be dumb to make that obvious by putting the aardvark on the dead man's chest. Revenge of the aardvark? Wouldn't he want people to think the motive was anything but that and the killer anyone but him?"

"I agree," Pamela said. She was liking Holly Perkins more and more by the minute.

"The murder happened late Saturday night," Nell said. "The aardvarks weren't available in the booth till the next day. So the killer put the aardvark on Jefferson's chest several hours after he killed him."

"What if the killer made his own aardvark and had it with him when he clunked Jefferson with the rock?" Holly asked. Karen was watching her friend with a mixture of curiosity and admiration.

"It was one of my aardvarks," Pamela said. She felt her mouth twist into a rueful smile. "Detective Clayborn asked me to identify it."

"What if a different person put the aardvark there," Holly said. "Not the killer."

"Not logical," Roland said, as if refuting an argument in court. "That 'different person' would have had to know there was a body under the table, and anyway why would the 'different person' even want to do that?"

"Discredit the knitting club?" Holly said with a shrug. "Have you ever rejected anyone who wanted to join?"

"Oh, dear—we would never—" Nell began.

Bettina cut in. "That's just preposterous." She glared at Holly and then shifted her glare to Roland. Her voice rose an octave. "It's all very well to talk, talk, talk, but what are we going to do about this? I'm tired of not even being able to shop for groceries or pick up my dry cleaning in my own town."

Holly looked suitably chastened, but Roland's tense face relaxed slightly and he smiled. "That's an excellent point." He nodded at Holly, then let his gaze travel around the room. "*Have* you ever rejected someone who wanted to join?"

"Of course not." Bettina set her knitting aside and leaned forward. "We even let *you* in."

Roland's smile vanished. "If you meant that to be funny, it isn't."

Bettina pulled herself upright. "Maybe I meant it to be true." She gulped. "This is all so . . ." Her voice broke.

Pamela reached an arm around her friend and Bettina leaned toward Pamela's shoulder. Nell rose to her feet. "Let's all have some refreshments," she said, rubbing her hands together and mustering a smile.

"I'll help." Holly jumped up, and the knitting project sprang from her lap to the floor as if alive.

Chapter Six

"Are you okay?" Pamela asked Bettina as the others trooped toward the kitchen. She searched her friend's hazel eyes and watched as a few tears overflowed onto Bettina's cheeks.

"I love this town," Bettina said. "And it really hurts me that people just . . . jump to the conclusion that the knitting club had something to do with Randall Jefferson's murder." Her voice was calmer now, but mournful. "And the ridiculous thing is that nobody even liked him very much. Like Wilfred says, speak no ill of the dead, but I never heard a single person say they *liked* him. Sure, he was brilliant, an asset to the high school and a credit to the town and all that . . ." She sighed and shook her head.

"Maybe we can do a little research," Pamela said as they both stood up. She faced Bettina and rested her hands on her friend's shoulders. "There might be angles Detective Clayborn hasn't thought of."

By the time they reached the kitchen, Holly was placing slices of cherry strudel on dessert plates, exclaiming again about how much she loved Nell's vintage 1950s dinnerware. "And this silverware," she added, fingering a stainless steel fork. "Amazing!"

"May I?" Roland reached for a plate.

"There's ice cream too," Nell whispered. Indeed, an open quart of ice cream sat on a plate near the strudel platter.

"I'm not supposed to . . . my doctor . . ." Roland hesitated. "But just a spoonful."

Holly scooped a generous portion of ice cream onto Roland's strudel.

"You can be very argumentative," Roland said. "Did you go to law school?"

"The Haversack Academy of Hair Design," Holly said with a laugh. "My husband and I own a salon in Meadowside."

"There's tea," Nell said, "and coffee." A squat brown teapot waited on the counter, and an ancient aluminum percolator bubbled on the stove.

"And milk and sugar," Holly chimed in. She nodded toward a cream pitcher and sugar bowl featuring the same wildflower and wheat pattern that decorated the dessert plates and the cups and saucers. She had finished serving the strudel and was offering cups around.

Six pieces of strudel, swirling layers of golden-brown pastry and deep red cherries visible at their cut ends, waited unclaimed on plates. "Please—everyone—help yourselves," Nell said. "And the extra slice is for Harold. He always senses when food is being served."

"I smelled the coffee." Harold's voice came from down the hallway. "And I certainly want to taste that strudel I drove all the way to Kringlekamack for."

"Well!" Bettina's voice sounded normal again. "It certainly looks worth the drive—and, yes, I will take a bit of ice cream too." She and Pamela reached for plates and forks, helped themselves to ice cream, and waited while Holly poured coffee for them.

"We'll eat in the living room," Nell said. "Go ahead. I'll bring some napkins when I come."

Pamela and Bettina proceeded down the hallway, and Roland followed. Soon Harold joined them and perched on the fireplace's wide hearth. He and Nell could almost have been brother and sister. He was tall and rangy, with white hair, and eyes that were faded, but lively. Holly and Karen came next, Holly bearing a pile of well-worn, but clean and pressed, cloth napkins that she passed out before taking her seat beside Karen.

Nell was the last to arrive. She surveyed her guests before sitting down. "Does everyone have everything they need? Please speak up."

"Ummm . . . fine," Bettina murmured and picked up her fork. "Wonderful," she pronounced after a minute.

Pamela sampled a bite. Indeed, the strudel was wonderful—the pastry flaky and buttery, and the cherries a rich burst of sweetness balanced by a hint of tartness. She took a sip of Nell's percolator coffee. Almost no one else made coffee that way anymore, and it seemed extra intense and almost bitter, but in a way that made the strudel all the sweeter.

"This is the best strudel I have ever tasted," Holly pronounced, looking up from her half-eaten piece. "How did you know where to find it, Harold? You said you went all the way to a bakery in Kringlekamack."

Harold raised his head looking pleased with himself. "I've been going there for years, my dear," he said. "Probably since before you were born."

"And it's been there all that time," Holly said. "Awesome."

People ate in silence for a few minutes. Nell offered more coffee and tea, and hurried to the kitchen to fetch refills. Harold set his plate down on the hearth with a tiny clunk and glanced around the room. "But I hope I can go back to the Co-Op again someday—without having to defend the Arborville knitting club to all and sundry. And it doesn't help that Jefferson was our neighbor. I can barely put the recycling or the trash at the curb without somebody charging out of their house with some crazy theory."

"Randall Jefferson was your neighbor?" Holly's eyes were wide.

"Two doors down—the house on the corner where the cross street comes up the hill."

"Harold!" Nell's voice came from the hallway, its tone like a mother scolding a wayward child. "Don't bring Randall Jefferson up." She appeared at the entrance to the living room. "We are trying to have a pleasant evening."

Harold gave her a sheepish look and became very interested in the fresh cup of coffee she handed him. Roland accepted his coffee and said, "Insomnia for sure."

"Tea is coming next," Nell said, and headed back to the kitchen.

Holly jumped up and followed her. "I'll bring the milk and sugar out," she said.

Roland edged farther down the loveseat so he was just a few feet from where Harold perched on the hearth. "Did you know Randall Jefferson?" he whispered. The whisper, however, carried to where Pamela was sitting.

"Sort of," Harold whispered back. "As much as anybody could. He was a bit standoffish. But he seemed to trust Nell. He gave her a copy of his house key in case he ever locked himself out. Absent-minded professor, I guess, though he wasn't actually a professor."

Holly hurried back in with the cream pitcher and sugar bowl, which she set on the coffee table. Soon Nell returned with fresh cups of tea for herself and Karen. "Are you still talking about that?" she asked with a frown. "I told you we were trying to have a pleasant evening, Harold."

Harold cringed, but in a joking way.

"I mean it, Harold," she said, her hands trembling. A bit of tea slopped onto the ancient wood floor.

Pamela had never seen Nell so agitated before. A new topic of conversation was definitely called for. "You have a gardener," she exclaimed brightly. "Joe Taylor is working for you now."

Nell didn't exactly smile, but her face softened. She acknowledged Pamela with a grateful nod, delivered Karen's tea, and set her own on the coffee table.

Harold bounded up. "I'll wipe the spill," he said, and hurried off toward the kitchen.

"Yes, he is," Nell said in answer to Pamela's question. She settled in next to Roland on the loveseat. "Such an industrious young man."

"I think he does some work for the town too," Pamela said. "He was planting salvia in front of Borough Hall yesterday."

"He'd been living in California," Nell said. "Very different plants out there. He says he's had quite a learning curve."

Holly had been watching attentively, her expressive face mirroring Nell's distress and then brightening as the conversation took a more benign turn. "Who'd want to move here from California?" she asked. "Don't most people go the other way?"

"He told me he has family out here," Nell said. "And he's hoping to study at Wendelstaff College. Ornamental horticulture. Apparently their program is quite good."

Harold returned with a cloth and stooped to dab up the small puddle of tea near the entrance to the living room. Bettina set her coffee cup down and picked up her knitting. Holly began to collect empty plates, cups, and saucers as people retrieved their projects and set back to work.

A silence broken only by the click of knitting needles can be companionable. Tonight, however, the atmosphere seemed strained. Harold had finished his cleanup chore and left without saying a word. The topic of Joe the gardener had foundered. Perhaps, Pamela reflected, all that could be said had been said— but maybe she had just dropped the conversational ball. She could have enthused about Wendelstaff's reputation, or Joe's work ethic. She was pondering ways to get things started again when Bettina spoke up, observing that details for the Arborville Fourth of July celebration would soon be announced.

"The details will hardly be a surprise," Roland commented from his corner of the loveseat, "since the town does exactly the same thing every year."

"Oh, the details will be a surprise to me," Holly exclaimed from across the room. "It's my first summer in Arborville. There will be fireworks, I hope."

"Yes," Karen said, turning to her friend. "It's a big celebration, in the park where Arborfest was . . ." Her voice trailed off.

"Arborfest," Nell murmured, half to herself.

Her heart's sudden thud was so loud, Pamela

wondered if the whole group had heard it. She felt her fingers speed up in time with her pulse, and with each needle thrust she imagined herself attacking something. But what? The person who had disrupted the idyll of a small town's summer festival? Or the silly people in that very town who had nothing to do but gossip about a harmless knitting club? She had begun the scarf project just this evening, but six inches of knitting already hung from her needles. At this rate, it would be finished in no time.

She was roused from her meditations by Roland's voice. "Nine p.m.," he announced, consulting his handsome and obviously expensive wristwatch. "Time for me to pack up." He surveyed the first few inches of the pink angora doggie sweater he was knitting, smiled with satisfaction, and tucked the project into his briefcase.

"My whole back is finished!" Holly's giant chunky yarn had been shaped into a knitted rectangle so bulky and stiff it barely looked like it could be part of a wearable garment.

"So is mine, almost." Dangling from Karen's needles was a delicate white rectangle with the beginnings of armholes.

"Shall we?" Bettina said, and reached for her knitting bag.

"I'm ready to get going," Pamela said. "Just let me finish this row." She finished the row, but then she watched Holly and Karen pack up. She remained on the sofa, hand on Bettina's arm, as Nell escorted the two young women, along with Roland, to the door.

A few minutes later, Pamela and Bettina were standing at the entrance to the living room listening to the farewells at the front door, when Harold came creeping along the hallway. He twisted his face into a comical exaggeration of nervousness. "Is she still mad at me?" he asked.

The front door closed. They heard Nell's voice before they saw her. "Harold!" she called, then she joined them, took one look at his face, and burst out laughing. "Thanks for cleaning up the tea," she said at last, and slipped an arm around his waist. Old married couples, Pamela reflected. Not a bad way to grow old.

"We're on our way too," Bettina said. She took a step toward the entry, but Pamela pulled her back. She turned around and gave Pamela a puzzled look.

"Nell?" Pamela hadn't meant her voice to sound so tentative, but Nell seemed to sense that something serious was coming.

"What is it, dear?" She looked straight into Pamela's eyes.

"I want to go into Randall Jefferson's house." Pamela blurted it out. She knew Nell wasn't the type to be cajoled.

"What . . . ?" Nell pulled back, open-mouthed and wide-eyed.

"Harold said you have a key. I want to go into Randall Jefferson's house."

"Oh, no," Nell said. "You think you're going to figure out something that the police can't figure out. You may have gotten lucky that other time, but I'm not going to be party to your getting involved in something dangerous." Pamela watched Nell carefully, hoping she wouldn't get upset again. At least she wasn't carrying tea cups now.

"But you've always been adventurous, Nell—you and Harold. The trips, the volunteering in exotic places . . ." Pamela reflected that perhaps now she *was* cajoling.

"We were young then, and foolish sometimes," Nell

said. Bettina took another step toward the entry and Nell reached for her arm. "Harold," Nell said. "Let's show our guests to the door." Nell and Bettina proceeded through the entry. Harold took Pamela's arm, but he tugged her toward the hallway. There, dangling from a hook next to an African mask, was a solitary key.

"Take it," Harold whispered. "I like women who have guts." Pamela slipped the key from its hook and closed her fingers around it.

She joined Bettina at the door. They made their way down the steps that led through azalea and rhododendron bushes to the sidewalk. The night air was muggy but cool, and the bugs were louder outside. Pamela waited until they reached Bettina's car to open her hand and display the key.

"You got it!" Bettina whispered.

"Harold," Pamela whispered back.

"What a guy." She unlocked Pamela's door. "Let's throw our stuff in the car and nose around in there right now. According to Clayborn, the police are done. And I didn't notice any crime-scene tape as we turned the corner tonight."

"Not a good idea," Pamela said. "We'd have to turn on lights, and it would be obvious to the neighbors that somebody was inside. Better to come back tomorrow morning."

On Orchard Street, Pamela's porch light was on, welcoming her back to her little clapboard house. A bright window on the second floor told her that Penny was home.

Chapter Seven

Pamela's days started earlier in summer than in winter. On May mornings she often opened her eyes when it was barely six a.m., as the brightening sky made the white eyelet curtains at her bedroom windows glow. She was awake now, her mind letting go of a last dream fragment, displaced by the concerns of the day.

The key to Randall Jefferson's house! That was her first conscious thought. The second was that something didn't seem right. For more than half a year, the luxurious stretch with which Pamela greeted the day had triggered a stirring under the bedclothes. A warm shape would make its way along the side of her body, and then Catrina would creep out onto the pillow, her soft fur grazing Pamela's cheek. This morning, Pamela was alone. She sat up, swiveled around, and lowered her feet to the rag rug at the side of her bed. She crossed the room and took her summer robe from the hook on the back of the door.

"*Mo-om!*" It was Penny, out in the hall. "Are you up? I thought I heard you."

Was something wrong? No cat, and now Penny calling

for her mother quite a bit earlier than she usually rose. Pamela swung the door back, robe still in her hand.

"Look what I found." Penny stood barefoot, her light summer gown and tousled hair making her look like the little girl whose nightmares Pamela had once soothed. "Or rather, she found me," Penny added, cuddling Catrina against her shoulder. "She was in my bed when I woke up."

"I guess she's decided you're part of the family now," Pamela said, giving the cat a quick scratch between the ears. Catrina jumped out of Penny's arms and looked up expectantly at Pamela until she fetched her slippers and headed for the stairs.

In the kitchen, Pamela pulled on her robe and spooned a few dabs of cat food into a fresh bowl. She smiled as Catrina set to work on her meal. The next chore was starting water for coffee and setting out beans to grind. Then she interrupted her breakfast preparations to fetch the newspaper from the front walk—it would be hard to enjoy her toast and coffee while wondering about the day's coverage of the "Killer Aardvark" story.

She hurried back to the porch with the newspaper, extracted it from its flimsy plastic bag, and—holding her breath—unfolded it. Two large color pictures, but one showed the governor glowering at a crowd of reporters as a helicopter waited in the background, and the other, a group of Boy Scouts. Her eyes quickly skimmed the headlines, and she sighed with relief when none of them mentioned Arborville, aardvarks, or even murder. Perhaps there was something on an inner page, but new developments would surely have merited a front-page story.

"No," called a voice from the sidewalk. "There's nothing new today—and I guess that means Clayborn didn't have anything to tell them." Bettina hurried up the walk. Her face was bare of makeup, but she was dressed in a stylish outfit of linen pants and matching top in pale orange.

"You're up and out early," Pamela said as Bettina joined her on the porch.

"I'm excited!" Bettina said. "And you know why. I hope you put that key in a safe place last night."

"It's safe," Pamela said. "Come on in. There's going to be coffee. And you can say hi to Penny before she leaves for work."

"I'll talk to Clayborn later today," Bettina said as she followed Pamela into the house. "The *Advocate* already went to press for the week, but I'll tell him I can squeeze in another article if he has any news about the murder, to ease the minds of the worried citizens of Arborville who pay his salary."

In the kitchen, the kettle was whistling frantically, a plume of steam rising from its spout. "You go up and get dressed," Bettina said. "I'll make the coffee." She set about grinding the beans as Pamela retreated and headed for the stairs.

Pamela went first to her office, where she pushed the button on her computer and listened to the peeps and whirs that announced it was coming to life. Five messages waited in her inbox, but she opened only the one from her boss at *Fiber Craft*. "Thanks for the evaluations," she read. "That last one needs major editing, as you no doubt noticed, but you're right to point out that an article on weaving your own bed linens will be a big hit with the survivalists among our readership. Here are five more to look at. No hurry."

Pamela hadn't been serious and doubted *Fiber Craft*'s

readership extended to survivalists, but her boss didn't always get her jokes.

By the time Pamela returned to the kitchen, dressed in her summer uniform of jeans and a cotton blouse, Penny was settled at the kitchen table with a cup of coffee in front of her. The cut-glass cream pitcher and sugar bowl sat nearby. Bettina was standing at the counter holding a heel of bread. "This is the end—literally—of your whole-grain bread." She regarded it sadly. "The second-to-last piece and the third-to-last piece are in the toaster."

"I'll eat the heel," Pamela said. In fact, she wasn't very hungry. She was as excited as Bettina was about the adventure they had planned for that morning, and excitement always took away her appetite. "I knew the cupboards were getting bare," Pamela said. "I guess it's time for a trip to the Co-Op . . ." Her voice trailed off as she reached the end of the sentence. "Or some-where," she added, picturing herself fending off questions, and even accusations, as she browsed the Co-Op's narrow aisles or lingered in front of its tempting bakery counter.

"I could go," Penny said. "I don't think people would connect me with the knitting club."

"You have your bus to catch," Pamela said. She poured herself a cup of coffee but remained standing.

A muffled click announced that the toaster had finished its work. Bettina laid the two slices of toast on a cutting board and slid the cutting board onto the table, where butter, a knife, and napkins awaited. Then she slipped the heel into the toaster.

"Go ahead—both of you," Pamela said. She sipped her coffee, then opened the refrigerator to retrieve a jar of jam, which she set on the table.

"Are you still enjoying the job?" Bettina asked, as

she took a seat and began to spread butter, and then jam, on the two slices of toast.

"I love it," Penny said.

"And you're becoming quite the fashionista, I see."

"I've been going thrifting in Manhattan with Laine Larkin," Penny said. "She knows the best places." Penny was wearing a fetching green print dress with a demure white collar. She'd tamed her dark curls with a headband, revealing earlobes adorned with little pearl earrings.

Pamela joined them at the table when her toast was ready, and they chatted about Penny's job until Penny looked at the clock, jumped up, and hurried out. "I can go to the Co-Op when I get home," she called just before the door closed behind her.

"My cupboards are bare too," Bettina said. "Let's go to that big supermarket in Meadowside after we see what Randall Jefferson's house has to tell us."

"We'll take my car," Bettina said as they stepped onto the porch, "in case we need to make a quick getaway."

"You're not nervous, are you?" Pamela said with a laugh. "You were all set to do this last night. We'll go in, look around. What could possibly happen?"

"Nothing," Bettina said. "I'm just joking—and I don't want to walk up that hill."

It was the type of day that seems to promise only good things. The lawns were still green from the spring rains, a breeze softened the late May sun, and up and down the street, azaleas had come alive with colors that ranged from pale coral to deepest violet.

"Come in for a minute," Bettina said when they

reached the other side of the street. "I'll finish getting ready and grab my keys."

They stepped inside Bettina's comfortable living room to find Wilfred busy with lemon oil and a dust cloth. Woofus the shelter dog trotted in from the dining room, his toenails clicking against the floor. He headed toward Bettina but caught sight of Pamela and retreated nervously. "It's okay, boy," Bettina cooed, reaching out a hand. "You know Pamela." Woofus was a large shaggy creature who would have been intimidating but for his diffident air. He dipped his head gracefully and let Bettina stroke him. After a quick pat, he returned to the dining room and Bettina headed up the stairs. "Back in a minute," she called.

"That smells so nice," Pamela said, the lemony scent evoking scenes of domestic order and tranquility.

"Many hands make light work," Wilfred said cheerfully, sprinkling a bit of oil on his cloth and tackling a lamp table.

In a few minutes, Bettina was back, lipstick in place, a bit of eye shadow dabbed on her eyelids, and coral and gold earrings dangling from her ears. Wilfred looked over as she picked up her keys from a table near the door, his head cocked as if he was about to ask a question.

"I'll be back in an hour or so," Bettina said. Before he could speak, she added, "Nothing much—just a quick errand."

Randall Jefferson's house was an imposing structure, buff-colored stucco with half-timber details and a steep roof. It was made all the more imposing by its location on a hillside lot. Meandering slate steps led through drifts of shrubbery up to the front door, actually double doors, of well-cared-for wood with carved details and leaded-glass windows. Pamela and Bettina looked around to make sure no one on the block was out at this early hour and then climbed the steps.

Pamela twisted the key in the lock and pushed the right-hand door open. She and Bettina paused, and watched as the door swung back to reveal a shadowy hall paneled in dark wood. Pamela stepped inside first, treading hesitantly, glancing from right to left. Soft light spilled through an opening ahead. She tiptoed up to it. She could hear Bettina moving stealthily behind her. They gazed into a large room that opened off to the left. The light came through the windows, filtered through sheer curtains framed by heavy swathes of brocade.

"My, my," Bettina whispered. "He certainly did have a lot of nice things, though it's a bit much for my taste."

The room looked like it had been decorated many decades previously and not touched since. But the furnishings chosen then had been such good quality that the room could have been taken for a recent creation, the collaboration of a high-end decorator and a well-connected antiques dealer. The sofas and chairs glowed with velvety luster, and the graceful lines and elegant detailing of the wooden pieces—chests, cabinets, and tables—reminded Pamela of furniture she'd seen in museums. Paintings in ornate gold frames crowded the walls: impressionistic landscapes, renderings of flowers and fruit, and portraits of women in filmy dresses and large hats.

"It doesn't look like he really *lived* in this room," Pamela said. "Let's press on."

"This must be the dining room right behind us," Bettina said. Opening off the other side of the hall was an equally large room with similar window treatments, at least as much art, and an enormous, gleaming table with twelve chairs arranged in perfect symmetry. A collection of crystal decanters glittered on the sideboard.

"He must have had a den, or study, and bedrooms of course," Pamela said. "Shall we head for the stairs?"

The dark wood paneling continued up the stairs, which were extra wide with sweeping banisters on both sides, as if people had once descended grandly from the upper reaches of the house to greet their guests. At the top of the stairs they found themselves on a landing with six closed doors, three on each side, and a window on the back wall.

"Here goes nothing," Bettina said. She opened the nearest door and nearly shouted, "Good guess! It's his study." She flung the door back. A huge wooden desk, dark as ebony, dominated the room, its surface bare except for an expensive-looking pen set and a crystal bowl containing paper clips. Floor-to-ceiling bookshelves covered all four walls, interrupted by windows on two sides.

"No computer?" Pamela said. "I guess a computer wouldn't have fit with the style of the house."

"The police have it," Bettina said. "Clayborn told me. That's one of the first things they look at—who did the victim communicate with and so on. Maybe somebody who didn't like him. But nothing on it has pointed to any new suspects—at least so far."

"Lots of old photographs," Pamela said. She edged around the side of the desk to study an assortment of small photos, some framed in silver, others unframed and leaning haphazardly against books, interrupted by small knick-knacks. Meanwhile Bettina was scanning the other shelves.

"Hey, Wilfred reads this journal sometimes," she said. "The historical society has a subscription."

Pamela turned to see Bettina pointing at a row of slender volumes bound in unassuming gray. She tilted her head to read the words that ran along the length of the spine: *Studies in Eighteenth-Century American History.*

"The eighteenth century was a big deal in New Jersey," Bettina said. "George Washington's retreat and all of that." In fact, the oldest house in Arborville was a pink sandstone structure that had belonged to a Tory sympathizer during the Revolutionary War.

Pamela returned to studying the photographs, drawn to one that seemed to show the very house they were standing in, with a man and two children posing in front of it. Bettina began to page through one of the little gray volumes.

"Wow," she said after a few minutes. "Listen to this, from the Letters to the Editor section. 'The article about the role the Dutch farmers in the Hudson Valley played in the Revolutionary War, by *Mister* Randall Jefferson (esteemed I am sure by his colleagues at Arborville High School but by no one else), not only drew questionable conclusions but drew them from incorrect facts.' The letter goes on in that vein," she added, "and it's signed, Marcus Verteel, Ph.D., Professor of History, Wendelstaff College."

"Somebody who didn't like him!" Pamela said. "Good find! I guess Clayborn didn't think of looking through *Studies in Eighteenth-Century American History.* But given a letter like that, wouldn't it have made more sense if Randall Jefferson had murdered Marcus Verteel?"

"Maybe they fought," Bettina said.

"In the parking lot of the Arborville Public Library? With rocks?"

"Spur of the moment?" Bettina said. "Or maybe Jefferson had said equally mean things about Marcus Verteel. Maybe I can find the article Verteel thought was so terrible. Jefferson might have been taking apart some theory of his."

Pamela watched while Bettina squinted at the spines of the little volumes. "Here's the previous one," she said. "He lined them up right in order—very tidy."

Bettina pulled it from the shelf and opened it at random. As Bettina flipped pages back and forth, Pamela's gaze returned to the photo of the house. She supposed that she and Bettina were at that moment standing in the room behind the right-hand window on the second floor. She took a few steps and peeked out. She was gazing down into the front yard. If she craned her neck she could see Bettina's car, half a block distant. They'd purposely parked far enough away that no neighbor would wonder why Randall Jefferson, now dead, seemed to be entertaining visitors. And right below the window was a huge rhododendron bush, so huge she could have picked a few of its deep fuchsia blooms if the window had been open.

The rhododendron had to be very old. She checked the photo of the house again. In the spot now occupied by the giant rhododendron was a bush that reached to the knees of the man standing in front of the house. Possibly the same rhododendron. Judging by the clothes of the people in the picture, the photo had been taken decades earlier, maybe fifty years. The next time she ran into Joe Taylor, she'd try to remember to ask him how long rhododendrons lived.

Bettina was reading intently, her lips shaping an

amused smile. Marking her place with a finger and closing the volume, she looked up. "Randall Jefferson reviewed a book by Marcus Verteel," she said. "Something about George Washington's New Jersey battles—and he didn't like it at all. Listen to this." She opened the volume again and read, "Of course, who could expect a Belgian to truly understand the true meaning of the American Revolution, or anything American, for that matter? This so-called historian should go back to his own little country."

In her editing for *Fiber Craft*, Pamela came upon occasional cases where professional rivalries spilled over into print. She usually edited those parts out, or at least softened the language. Apparently the editors of *Studies in Eighteenth-Century American History* preferred to let the chips fall where they might.

"There's something by Marcus Verteel in this issue too," Bettina said, turning over a few pages. "An article, something about George Washington—I guess he's really into him—but along the way he says, 'I have skipped mentioning the ideas advanced by Randall Jefferson. Only a case of massive hubris would embolden a mere high-school teacher to imagine he had anything worthwhile to contribute to the topic of Washington's retreat on that fateful day.'"

"Well," Pamela said. "They hated each other. Definitely something to keep in mind. Are you going to tell Detective Clayborn?"

Bettina shrugged. "Maybe they just enjoyed throwing words at each other. It seems kind of tenuous. Of course, we don't know what this Verteel character is like. Maybe he's a Belgian Arnold Schwarzenegger. Or Clint Eastwood." She slipped the two little volumes back into place. "Shall we try another room?" she said.

"Look—" Pamela held out the photo. "It's this house, ages ago." She pointed to the knee-high shrub in the picture and then at the fuchsia blooms waving in the breeze just beyond the window. "And *this* is that giant rhododendron."

Bettina reached for the photograph. "Nice-looking kids," she said. "And the guy—pretty dreamy, in a British aristocrat sort of way." She fingered the edge. "Looks like there was somebody else in the picture too, but before Photoshop you just had to cut them off." She held the photo out toward Pamela. Indeed, the proportions were wrong. A four-inch by six-inch photo had been turned into a four-inch by five-inch photo. "Acrimonious divorce?" Bettina said, stepping toward the shelf. "Where does it go, anyway? Here, by the couple showing off their sailboat?"

"Down at the end," Pamela said. "Next to the graduation photo in the silver frame."

Back out on the landing, Bettina pointed at the doors one by one, chanting "Eeny, meeny, miny, moe . . . this one!" She skipped across the floor and pushed open the door to the other front-facing room. "He was a tidy man," she said.

They were gazing into a bedroom, as neatly made up as if ready for a photo shoot in a decorating magazine. The grand king-sized bed had an ornate carved ebony headboard and a matching footboard. A quilted brocade spread curved over a pair of carefully aligned pillows. Marble-topped night tables on either side held lamps made of Chinese vases.

"Maybe this is just the guest room," Bettina said.

"No, I think he really slept here, or someone did," Pamela said. "Look—there's a pair of glasses on the night table, and a book." She took a few steps across the carpet and picked up the book. "*Legacy of the Revolution*," she read. The cover showed a group of serious-looking men in powdered wigs conferring over a document. She held the book up for Bettina to see.

"Definitely his taste in literature," Bettina said. She was standing at the dresser now. "And look here—cufflinks." She displayed one in her palm. It was a golden oval, burnished rather than shiny, engraved with the initials RWJ.

"I guess he was wearing his second-best cufflinks the night he was killed," Pamela said.

Bettina set the cufflink down and advanced toward a door in the back wall. She opened it to reveal a row of hangers bearing jackets, pants, and faultlessly starched and pressed shirts. On the back of the closet door was a rack from which ties, mostly bow ties, dangled.

"No clues in here that I can see," Pamela said. "At least not so far. Should we go through the pockets of all his jackets and pants, do you think?"

"We could," Bettina said. "But he was so fastidious he probably never put anything away without checking the pockets himself."

"How about the wastebasket then?" Pamela said. It was an old-fashioned one made of tin and decorated with a flower pattern, tucked between the far side of the dresser and the window that looked out on the front yard. She leaned over it to peer inside. "Empty," she pronounced. She advanced farther into the room. In the far corner was a velvet-covered armchair, deep green, with a matching footstool. It was flanked by a brass floor lamp on one side and a little table on the other. The table held a stack of magazines.

"More reading material," Bettina said, joining her. "He had quite the cozy setup here." They thumbed through the magazines, copies of *The New Yorker*, with a few *Opera News* and *National Geographic*s mixed in.

"Shall we see what secrets lurk behind some of the other doors?" Pamela said. She surveyed the room again. "But that headboard really is something, isn't it?" she said. "You have to be standing at the foot of the bed like this to get the full effect—all those scallops and curlicues."

"Do you think he made his own bed?" Bettina asked.

"Who else would?"

"But he must have had a housecleaner to keep this huge place clean. I wouldn't want to dust all these curlicues." Bettina stepped toward the headboard to trace the elaborate pattern with a finger. Her hand strayed down to the quilted brocade. "This quilting makes for a very stiff bedspread," she observed, patting the hump that marked the nearest pillow. She continued patting, in widening circles. Then she paused and turned toward Pamela with a half smile of discovery. "Something's under here," she said.

She probed against the headboard for the edge of the spread and peeled it back, revealing a pillow sheathed in fine, smooth cotton. The pillow almost, but not quite, hid the tip of a knitting needle resting on the smooth edge of the matching sheet. Bettina thrust the pillow aside.

"Well, well, well," she said. "What do we have here?"

Chapter Eight

The question could have been answered in a number of ways.

There was dubious taste, particularly in the context of the refined surroundings. There was ambition, though directed at a creation a bit beyond the creator's abilities. There was neon-orange mohair yarn, shading into neon chartreuse.

"My, my!" Pamela lifted it from the smooth sheet where it rested, nestled beside a fat skein of yarn and a knitting needle with the beginnings of a narrow knitted strip dangling from it. The object resembled a stocking cap, but with long, floppy ears attached. "This is quite something," Pamela added. It was indeed, but the knitted surface was marred by occasional bumps and holes, suggesting the knitter had purled when knitting was called for and knitted when purling was called for, as well as dropping the occasional stitch.

"What do you think *this* is going to be?" Bettina picked up the needle with the dangling strip. "And where's the other needle?"

Pamela slipped her hand between the mattress and the headboard and brought up a mate to the needle.

Her gaze wandered to the night table on the other side of the bed. "So he read *Legacy of the Revolution* while she clicked away on her knitting needles."

"Definitely the odd couple," Bettina said. "Do you think he made her hide her project under the pillow during the day because it didn't go with the décor of the room?"

Pamela shrugged. "That's a good question, but the more pressing question is—"

Bettina chimed in and they both spoke at once. "Who is she?"

"No women's clothes in the closet . . ."

"But—" Bettina hurried toward the landing, and Pamela heard a door open. "No women's things in the bathroom," Bettina called back, her voice echoing off tiles.

Pamela joined her, and they opened all the drawers in the vanity just to make sure. Then they checked the other doors on the landing. One opened to a set of stairs. "Probably the attic," Bettina observed.

Behind the other two doors were rooms furnished for children, with single beds, low bookcases, and desks suitable for doing homework. No personal traces remained, and the book titles suggested that the bookcases now held the overflow from the substantial library in the study rather than books a child, or even a teenager, might read. The closets and dresser drawers were empty.

"He grew up in this house," Bettina said. "I wonder which bedroom was his."

"The one he's using now is probably where his parents slept," Pamela said. "With such a big house all to himself now, why *not* move into the biggest, nicest room?"

"Would you want to live in the house where you grew up?" Bettina asked.

"I'd be remembering things every time I turned a corner," Pamela said. "Things that happened when I was ten. I'm not sure I'd like it." She paused. "Of course . . . now . . . I remember things about Michael."

Bettina squeezed her hand. "Let's tuck that amazing creation back under the pillow and pay a visit to Nell."

They'd gotten up and out so early that Nell was still drinking her morning tea when she answered the door. "Good morning," she said, looking surprised but with a cordial smile. "What brings you two up here at this time of day?"

Before Pamela could open her mouth (to say what, she wasn't sure), Bettina spoke. "A walk," she said. "Climbing that hill is such good exercise, and it gets too hot later." She ignored the amazed look Pamela gave her, and Pamela reflected it was a good thing they had parked in the next block. "And so," Bettina went on cheerily, "here we were walking along, and we stopped to catch our breath and realized we were standing right in front of your house. And we thought, let's say hello and tell Nell what a lovely session of Knit and Nibble she hosted last night."

"There happens to be some strudel left," Nell said with a laugh. "And I know you're both coffee drinkers, so I'll put some on."

"What are you up to?" Pamela whispered as they followed Nell down the hallway that led to her kitchen.

"Watch and see," Bettina whispered back.

Fifteen minutes later, they were sitting at Nell's kitchen table, forking the last tasty strudel crumbs from the wildflower-and-wheat patterned dessert plates and sipping Nell's percolator coffee from the wildflower-and-wheat patterned cups. They had been chatting about the knitting group.

"Such fun to have young people joining," Bettina said. "Karen and Holly—and just starting married life here in Arborville. Wilfred and I have been so happy in this town."

"Harold and I too," Nell said, then her lips tightened. "Until recently, that is."

"Every town has gossips," Pamela said, trying to sound comforting, but Bettina didn't seem interested in taking up the gossip thread.

"You and Harold have lived in Arborville as long as anyone," Bettina said, "even longer than Randall Jefferson."

"He moved away and then came back. When both his parents were gone, he inherited the house." Nell picked up the strudel knife. "A bit more?"

Bettina nodded as Nell slid another slice of the cherry-streaked pastry onto her plate. "I guess you never got to know him too well," she said. "But when you're such a close neighbor, you learn things about people even if you almost never actually talk to them."

"I can vouch for that," Pamela said. "Though what you think you've learned doesn't always turn out to be true. I thought my new neighbor was a complete womanizer—and with a taste for women half his age. Then it turned out the women coming and going were his daughters."

"I need to refresh my tea," Nell said, rising to her feet and turning toward the stove.

Bettina gazed at Pamela with wide eyes. "Bingo," she mouthed.

"What's going on?" Pamela mouthed back.

"Did you ever see women coming and going at

Randall Jefferson's house?" Bettina asked. What an actress, Pamela thought to herself, making the question sound so offhand. But she was almost equally delighted—she'd always known Nell was hard to fool—when Nell turned back around and shook a finger at Bettina.

"I know what you're up to," she said. Shifting her gaze to Pamela, she added, "And you too, I suspect." She set her tea cup on the table and sat back down. "I will not be a party to this. The police will solve the crime. You two will not get involved."

The back door opened, and they heard footsteps in the mudroom. From the same direction came Harold's voice calling, "It's me, but I've got more bags to fetch from the car."

Nell interrupted her scolding to call back, "I'm in the kitchen." She focused on Bettina again. "And anyway, I am not a nosy person—you know that—and I'm not a gossip. And even if I was, it would be hard to keep tabs on Randall Jefferson's visitors with two houses between us and him, and his house on the corner with his driveway on the side street. So you're not going to enlist me in your sleuthing, and if you have any sense at all, you're going to drop this right now."

Pamela was feeling quite chastened, at least when it came to getting Nell's help on this particular issue, but Bettina persisted.

"I've been keeping in touch with Detective Clayborn," Bettina said, "reporting on the case for the *Advocate*. He hasn't said anything about pursuing the romantic angle—jilted lover taking revenge, that sort of thing. So if you've seen any signs that Randall Jefferson had a lady friend—"

"I haven't," Nell interrupted. "And I'm sure Detective

Clayborn knows what he's doing." She raised a hand to her forehead. "Where was I?"

"You had just refreshed your tea," Pamela said.

"Oh, yes." Nell mustered a smile. "So I had. And how about you two? There's more coffee."

"I'm good," Pamela said.

Bettina nodded and added, "Thank you for the strudel. We should be going, and I'm sorry we upset you."

Harold's voice carried in from the mudroom again. "Successful trip," he called, then he appeared in the doorway carrying two bulging canvas bags. "I went to the wholesale food place along the tracks in Haversack. We like to support the Co-Op, but after that experience Monday, I've been steering clear." He swung the canvas bags up onto the table. "This is only half of it. I've got more bags to fetch from the car." Harold was dressed for the spring day in a well-worn pair of khaki pants and a faded sports shirt.

"I thought you *were* fetching them," Nell said.

"I heard Pamela's and Bettina's voices. Had to say hello." He smiled and raised a hand to push back the unruly lock of white hair that had strayed onto his forehead.

"Hello," Pamela said, and Bettina echoed the greeting.

"So . . ." Harold nodded briskly. "Good to see you. Enjoy the rest of your day."

Nell saw them to the door. No sooner had they reached the sidewalk than Harold hurried toward them from the driveway. The trunk of his car stood open, and two canvas bags sat on the dark pink paving stones that made up the driveway's surface. A bunch of celery protruded from one.

"Nell used to be the one who was always telling people to question authority," he said. "I still believe it. Detective

Clayborn probably knows what he's doing, but I admire initiative. So . . . to answer your question . . ."

Pamela laughed and reached out to squeeze his arm. "You were in the mudroom the whole time listening."

Harold grinned delightedly at his own mischief. He pointed a bony finger at the next house over. "This woman here knows everything that goes on in this block. Nell won't talk to her anymore, but sometimes she nabs me and it's hard to escape." He leaned close and whispered, more for comic effect than because anyone might be listening. "Randall Jefferson did have a lady friend, at least according to my informant. She came and went at night. Almost every night."

"Wow!" Bettina opened her eyes so wide Pamela could see white around her irises.

"Figure out a way to talk to her," Harold said, bony finger still aimed at his informant's house. "It won't be hard—the hard part will be getting away. She walks a dog, every day. She'll probably be out any minute. Past here, down to this corner, heads down the hill, and circles back up past Randall Jefferson's house. I've seen her as far away as Arborville Avenue."

"How will we be sure it's her?" Pamela said.

"Poodle," Harold said, bending down and letting his hand hover about six inches from the ground. Springing back up with a wave, he returned to his grocery bags.

Pamela and Bettina turned to each other. "Woofus!" they said in unison. "And we'll be fellow dog walkers stopping for a chat," Pamela added.

They hurried back to the car, and in a few minutes they were pulling up to the curb in front of Bettina's house. "I've got to change my shoes if we're actually going to be climbing that hill," Bettina said. She had started out that morning in a delicate pair of high-heeled sandals that matched the pale orange of her outfit. "And, of course, I've got to round up Woofus. Do you want to come in?"

"I'll wait out here," Pamela said. The rhododendron bushes along the front of Bettina's house were in full bloom. Bettina's neighbor was gathering roses from a sprawling rose bush that had climbed nearly to the roof of her neat brick house.

Bettina's front door opened and Woofus nosed out, stopping at the edge of the porch and twisting his head back toward the house. A leash stretched from his collar to the doorway, and in a few seconds Bettina stepped through the door, leash in hand and the fancy sandals replaced by flats.

Pamela joined them on the sidewalk. Woofus dipped his head and gazed up at her, then retreated as far as his leash would allow. "Come on, boy," Bettina cooed, and Woofus lurched ahead, pulling Bettina with him.

Grand trees lined Orchard Street, planted between the sidewalk and the curb long ago. The trees were in full late-spring leaf now, some with branches that reached halfway across the street to meet branches from the other side. Here and there the sidewalk had been pushed up by giant roots. In some spots, the remedy had been to replace the broken patch with fresh concrete, creating a path that interrupted the straight line of the sidewalk to detour in a wide arc around the base and roots of the offending tree.

"Shall we continue on Orchard?" Bettina called when she and Woofus reached Arborville Avenue. "Or circle around so we're going up where Harold said the gossipy dog walker usually comes down?"

"Let's try that," Pamela said when she caught up with them at the corner. They walked along Arborville Avenue for a few blocks, but then turned and headed up the hill right before they reached the commercial district. "I miss the Co-Op," Pamela said. "Especially that good bread and the crumb cake."

"We'll get this figured out," Bettina said, pausing to catch her breath. The stretch from Arborville Avenue to the next cross street was especially steep. "Then things will be back to normal. Once the killer is identified, people will have no reason to think Knit and Nibble had anything to do with what happened at Arborfest." They were moving again, Woofus leading the way but making sure to sniff the base of each tree they passed. "I think we're really onto something," Bettina added. "What better motive than rejected love?"

"It has to have been an odd relationship," Pamela said. "She wasn't allowed to keep any of her personal things there—yet obviously she shared his bed." They'd reached another cross street. She scanned the sidewalk that stretched ahead, rising, but less steeply, empty of people as far as she could see. Harold and Nell's house—and the house of the gossipy dog-walking woman—was four blocks farther up. Pamela went on, musing, "Of course, it could have just been a . . . business . . . arrangement."

"A delicate way to put it," Bettina said. "I was thinking that too—but knitting in bed is so *domestic*. If I was in that . . . business . . . I don't think I'd linger."

"No," Pamela said. "So we're back to rejected love. Him rejecting her. She loved him, and she hung in there, hoping and hoping that eventually he'd see the light, that he'd care for her the way she cared for him."

"But he was *cold*." Bettina stamped her foot as if personally angry at Randall Jefferson. Woofus gave an alarmed start and hopped away. "Cold—and so formal."

"She probably thought he was brilliant though, like having a crush on a professor in college."

"But then, finally, she's fed up," Bettina said, furrowing her brow and gesturing dramatically, as if making a case in a courtroom. "She's waiting on his doorstep at the appointed time. It's Saturday night—the night he begrudgingly lets her pretend it's date night. Maybe she brings food—or cooks dinner for him. She's been looking forward to Saturday night all week." Bettina's eyes flashed. "But he's not there. She knows where he is—at the library, because he cares more about his research than he cares about her."

They had stopped walking. Pamela took up the story, as Woofus investigated a bed of petunias along the sidewalk. "She drives down the hill to the library. People are leaving after working on their booths, but she's just arriving. She sits on that pretty wooden bench near the rock garden to wait for the library to close. He comes out. He's puzzled to see her there, but he joins her on the bench. She's restrained at first—they seem to just be a couple enjoying the spring night."

"The library empties out," Bettina chimed in. "People wander away. Nobody is left near the library but them."

"He becomes angry." Pamela's delivery wasn't as dramatic, but Bettina nodded enthusiastically.

"Why are you following me around?" Bettina growled, acting Randall Jefferson's part and scowling ferociously.

"I love you," Pamela whispered.

"Well, I don't love you," Bettina growled. "You knew the ground rules when we started."

"But I—" Caught up in the story, Pamela felt her throat tighten.

"And then—" Bettina clapped her hands. "She picks

up the rock and *bam.* That's it. Under the table he goes." Woofus's leash dropped to the ground.

"What about the aardvark?" Pamela asked.

"We'll figure that out later," Bettina said. "First things first. Let's find that poodle."

Chapter Nine

Suddenly distracted from his investigation of the petunias, Woofus raised his head. His shaggy ears quivered. He spun around, then careened past Pamela and Bettina, trailing his leash behind him. Bettina started after him, heading down the block they'd just come up. A furious yipping drew Pamela's attention in the opposite direction. Emerging from the cross street and heading toward the petunia patch was a tiny white poodle straining at his leash. Holding the leash was a small, sturdy woman with gray hair pulled into an untidy ponytail. An oversized pair of sunglasses perched on her nose.

A boisterous laugh erupted from her wide mouth when she caught sight of Woofus. He was cowering at Bettina's side, regarding the scene from the other side of the street. Bettina had recovered the end of the leash, and her free hand was resting on the nervous dog's head.

"It's the big ones that are the biggest sissies," the woman said. "My little Rambo here doesn't let anybody push him around." She followed the statement with another laugh, equally boisterous.

Pamela's first impulse was to retreat across the street too, but it was clear they'd met the very person they'd set out to find. She arranged her lips in her social smile and said, "My, what an adorable dog—and so brave."

Within moments, Bettina had joined her, though Woofus lingered a good ten feet away, the leash stretched to its maximum length.

"I thought I knew all the dog walkers," the woman said. "Are you new in town?" She took off the sunglasses and studied Bettina, then turned to examine Pamela, grinning suddenly. "Aha!" she said. "I see why you're hiding out. You're the knitters, aren't you? Looking for a neighborhood to walk where you won't be recognized."

Pamela and Bettina looked at each other. Before either could respond, the woman spoke again. "Don't worry—I'm not one of those gossips. No, sir, not me. Nobody's business, that's what I say." The poodle was gazing up at her. She leaned down and, in a high-pitched singsong voice, addressed the dog. "Nobody's business, is it Rambo? Nobody's business at all."

"It's pretty up here," Pamela ventured, "but so steep."

"Oh, it is that," the woman said, spinning around to face up the hill. "Heading this way?" She took off at a trot and the poodle followed, its tiny legs moving so fast they were almost a blur.

Pamela fell in line behind the poodle. She could hear Bettina panting behind her, and the jangle of Woofus's leash, but her own long legs allowed her to gain on the small woman. By the time they reached the next cross street, they were walking side by side.

"Have you lived up here long?" Pamela asked.

"Forever," the woman said. "People come and go,

but we've just stayed." She launched into a catalogue of all the houses she and her husband had looked at before settling on the one they bought. "Thirty years ago. Seems like yesterday. People come and go, yes, come and go, but we came, and we're still here."

They'd covered three more blocks. Now they paused at the corner of Harold and Nell's street. Pamela herself was feeling a bit winded, but the small woman showed no signs of having just climbed one of Arborville's steepest hills. In fact, she let loose another of her boisterous laughs. "They come and go," she crowed delightedly. "Yes, indeed they do. And *he* just went." She pointed down the block toward the corner where Randall Jefferson's house was situated.

Pamela looked around for Bettina, but she was too far away to help make use of this promising opening, and Woofus was lagging even farther behind. "Oh, my," Pamela said, touching her fingertips to her lips. "That's not where Randall Jefferson lived, is it?"

"The very house."

"Did you know him?" she asked, glancing around to check on Bettina's progress up the last stretch of hill.

"We're two doors away." She gabbed Pamela's arm. "See, the gray shingle house, and his house is the big buff stucco one on the corner."

"Neighbors," Pamela said.

"He was quite the character, I'll say that. Standoffish, not friendly at all, but living that close to somebody, you get to know them anyway."

"All alone, in that big house," Pamela murmured. Bettina was so good at getting people to say what she wanted, but she was still half a block away. Pamela glanced around again and beckoned discreetly.

Bettina called, "Coming!" Woofus bounded ahead,

Rambo yipped, and Pamela almost missed hearing the small woman say, "Not so alone."

"Not so alone?" Pamela was not actually as surprised as she pretended. "Do you mean he had a lady friend?"

"I guess you could call her that," the small woman said. The expression on her face combined amusement and skepticism. Pamela wondered whether the word in dispute was "lady" or "friend." Or maybe both.

Bettina arrived, with Woofus still ten paces behind and straining at his leash to keep as much distance between himself and Rambo as possible.

The small woman went on. "She came and went, always at night. Stayed maybe an hour, sometimes less, sometimes more." Pamela was wondering how to bring Bettina up to date on this promising revelation, but the small woman saved her the trouble. "People aren't what they seem," she announced. "Randall Jefferson—to look at him you'd think he was the perfect gentleman, but I could tell you things . . ."

Bettina widened her eyes and suppressed a grin, then she turned to the small woman. "It's obvious you're a very observant person," she said.

"Well . . ." The small woman acknowledged the compliment with a nod. She stretched her lips into a satisfied smile. "I couldn't see much. Like I was telling your friend, it was always dark when she paid her . . . visits. But sometimes she parked near the streetlight. We don't get much traffic up here, so when you hear a car in the middle of the night, naturally you get curious. Not his type at all, I wouldn't have thought. Of course, he wasn't taking her to the opera. Or anywhere, for that matter, but he's devoted—*was* devoted, I should say—to the opera, you know—reads *Opera News* faithfully. We get his mail sometimes. Anyway, she had red hair, but not a normal color, if you know what I mean."

Bettina raised a hand to her own hair, which was a color she herself described as "not found in nature."

"Oh, yours is very attractive." The small woman reached out and patted Bettina's arm. "But I mean *red*, and long, and curly, and all over the place. And the clothes! Capes, and boots, and long skirts like a gypsy, and sandals, even in the winter."

Rambo had been nosing enthusiastically at a cluster of ferns surrounding the base of a huge maple tree. Meanwhile Woofus had gradually crept up the hill and stood huddled against Bettina's leg. Now Rambo looked around as if satisfied with his explorations among the ferns. He bounded across the stretch of lawn between the maple tree and the sidewalk and lunged at Woofus, yipping furiously.

Woofus reared back, then dashed in front of Bettina and headed down the hill, jerking Bettina's arm across her body until the leash stretched tight and slipped out of her hand. It trailed along the sidewalk, bouncing and jangling. Bettina paused a minute to get her balance, then took off after Woofus, calling to him to watch for cars.

"I guess I'd better go too," Pamela said, raising her voice over the yips. She danced to the side as Rambo, ignoring the tug on his collar as his mistress held fast to his leash, tried to pursue Woofus down the hill.

"You just hang in there," said the small woman—or yelled, actually, since Rambo was still yipping furiously. "Don't let those gossips get you down. The police will have this solved in no time. My money's on the football coach. He'd be locked up right now except his brother's on the town council. Of course his wife is going to say he's not a murderer."

Pamela caught up with Bettina and Woofus a few blocks above Arborville Avenue. Bettina had lowered herself to the curb and was panting and fanning herself, while Woofus hovered nearby, occasionally dipping his head gracefully to nudge her arm with his muzzle.

"I wonder if Detective Clayborn knows about the red-headed woman," Pamela said, joining Bettina on the curb.

"I expect so," Bettina said. "I think the police interviewed the neighbors. Our talkative friend might even have been able to provide him with a license plate number."

"Do you think he's followed up?" Pamela asked.

Bettina shrugged. "Probably not. As far as he knows, there's nothing but a gossipy neighbor to connect her with Jefferson. So she parked on his street? So what?"

Pamela nodded. "Because he doesn't know about the knitting project under the pillow. Are you going to tell him?"

"I'd have to tell him how we found out about it, wouldn't I?" She ran a comforting hand over Woofus's shaggy back.

"I guess you would."

"So, no." Bettina pulled herself up and gave Woofus's leash a shake.

Meadowside was the next town south of Arborville, different from its northern neighbor only in being slightly larger and boasting a giant, fluorescent-lit supermarket with wide aisles and a huge parking lot. Convenient as the Meadowside supermarket was—and often even cheaper—most of Arborville's residents preferred their own quaint Co-Op Grocery where you could always count on running into someone you knew and coming home with both a supply of groceries and an update on doings around town.

Pamela and Bettina were quite aware of the doings around town that had been providing fodder for Co-Op shoppers for the past few days. It was for that reason Bettina was now pulling into the Food Plus lot.

"It's Wednesday," she said, "so that means meatloaf, and Wilfred made up a list for me. Tomorrow he'll do some chili, and Friday will be pizza from When in Rome . . ." She glided into a spot, switched off the ignition, dropped the keys in her purse, and pulled out a small sheet of paper. "Then there's the barbecue on Sunday, but I've got time to figure that out." Bettina hosted a "Welcome Summer" barbecue every year and had been planning this one for several weeks.

"I'll bring something," Pamela said. "How about deviled eggs?" She reached into the back seat for the canvas bags she'd brought along.

They discussed the menu for the barbecue as they strolled toward the wide glass doors of the supermarket, pausing along the building's brick façade to collect carts.

Half an hour later, they had loaded their groceries into Bettina's trunk and were heading home. Pamela had bought bread, as close to the Co-Op whole grain as Food Plus offered, and cheese and eggs. She'd stocked up on salad ingredients and fruit and bought some already-cooked shrimp at the Food Plus fish counter. Tonight, she'd make a green salad with oil and vinegar dressing and toss the shrimp in. Then maybe there would be toast with grated cheese on top, melted under the broiler, and some sliced tomatoes— though only grocery-store ones—on the side. The next night could be omelets, and maybe she'd borrow Bettina's idea of pizza for Friday. Or if Penny had dinner plans, she'd make another salad.

At home, groceries put away, Pamela climbed the stairs to her office. Catrina had lately taken to napping on the computer keyboard, and was sprawled across Pamela's desk now, a sleek swathe of glossy black fur. She allowed herself to be gently lifted to the floor and wandered off toward the door, tail waving gracefully.

The article on weaving one's own bed linens waited on her computer, along with her boss's instructions to do whatever she needed to do to bring it up to *Fiber Craft*'s editorial standards. She'd get to it soon, but first she had another task, unrelated to her professional duties.

She opened the Google search page and keyed "Wendelstaff College" into the waiting rectangle. The Wendelstaff College website came up with an image of the central quadrangle, crisscrossed by paths and flanked with ivy-covered buildings. She clicked on the "Departments" tab and located a description of the history department with a list of faculty—among them the person she was interested in: Marcus Verteel.

Marcus Verteel had his own page, complete with a list of his degrees and his many publications—including articles in *Studies in Eighteenth-Century American History*. Most interesting to Pamela, however, was the fact that his page also featured his picture. He might have been a formidable adversary in print, but . . . in person?

Marcus Verteel's photo showed a man of at least sixty, with neatly combed white hair, a well-groomed moustache and goatee, and little rimless glasses. A person can perform amazing feats when adrenalin is surging, but—she studied the image of the mild-looking professor—could he have picked the yam-shaped rock out of the rock garden and used it to murder Randall Jefferson?

She was so caught up in untangling the syntax of the woman who wove her own bed linens that Penny had crept all the way up the stairs before Pamela was aware how late it had gotten. "I fed Catrina," Penny said. "She was getting quite desperate. And," she added, "I brought some food for you. From the Co-Op."

Pamela turned. Her daughter was standing in the doorway, her dark hair setting off her blooming com-plexion, and still dressed in the green-print dress and pearl earrings she'd worn to work. Pamela saved her in-progress editing and closed the file. She arched her back and stretched, then turned off her desk lamp and followed Penny down the stairs and into the kitchen.

"Whole-grain bread," Penny called over her shoul-der. "I know you can't get the kind you like anywhere else. And I got some good cheese." The groceries were arranged on the kitchen table—the crusty bread on a cutting board with the cheese, a buttery-yellow wedge of Swiss patterned with random holes. "And this," Penny said, holding out a white bakery bag, "is crumb cake."

"Thank you!" Pamela reached out to give her daugh-ter a hug. "Bettina and I went to Food Plus, but they don't have the right bread, or the really good cheese. Or the crumb cake."

"Mom?" Pamela still held her daughter in a hug and couldn't see her face. But her voice sounded suddenly mournful. Pamela stepped back. Penny grabbed her mother's hands. "It's good you didn't go to the Co-Op today." Pamela felt a twinge of alarm. Penny's pretty mouth twisted and she bit her lip. "There's a big box out in front. People are putting the aardvarks in it."

Chapter Ten

"No good deed goes unpunished. That's all I have to say." Wilfred returned his coffee cup gently to its saucer and stood up. He walked to the porch railing and gazed over the hedge that separated Pamela's yard from the church next door. "That young man is doing a nice job over there," he observed in a more cheerful voice. "Very industrious."

Joe Taylor was tidying the shrubbery that edged the slate path from the sidewalk to the church steps.

But Bettina wasn't ready to let the subject drop. "Dumping the aardvarks in a cardboard box in front of the Co-Op—after all the work we did on them! And I suppose people will want their money back!" She leaned forward in her chair, and the plate with the remains of her crumb cake nearly slid off her lap.

"Dear wife, dear wife—" Wilfred retreated from the porch railing to stroke Bettina's shoulder.

"We already gave the money to the athletic program," Pamela murmured. "I'm sure people will see the money they paid for the aardvarks as a donation to the high school, even if they don't want to keep the aardvarks."

"Children are afraid of them now." Bettina tightened her lips in disgust.

"Only because the parents are making such a fuss," Wilfred said soothingly. "I'm sure the children would keep them if it was their choice."

"There's more crumb cake," Pamela said. "And coffee."

If not for the depressing topic of conversation, the morning would have been idyllic. The weather continued to prove that May was the perfect month, and where better to enjoy it than on an expansive porch? While sipping coffee and nibbling on crumb cake? Lawns were still the tender green of late spring, shrubs were in flower, and trees were in full leaf, easing the sun with wide swathes of shade. A breeze brought the smell of cut grass from somewhere down the block.

"No more for me," Wilfred said. "A dollhouse awaits me in the basement." He was dressed for his project in his customary outfit of plaid shirt and bib overalls.

"It's more than a dollhouse," Bettina said. "He's making a replica of the Mittendorf House." The Mittendorf House was a local attraction. Built of pink sandstone and dating from the eighteenth century, it had been confiscated from a Tory sympathizer and presented to one of Washington's generals. She poured a splash of coffee into her cup and added cream and sugar.

"It's to be displayed by the historical society next year at Arborfest," Wilfred said modestly.

"That reminds me," Pamela said as Wilfred headed down the front walk, "I looked up Marcus Verteel on the Wendelstaff website after I got home yesterday."

"And . . . ?" Bettina's coffee cup was poised halfway to her lips.

"He's definitely not a Belgian Arnold Schwarzenegger,"

Pamela said. "He looks like he's sixty, at least, with white hair and little rimless glasses. I really doubt he'd be capable of killing someone with a rock."

"But Randall Jefferson wasn't much of a physical specimen either."

"True." Pamela leaned back in her chair and gazed out at the scene before her. She checked her watch. "Such a pretty morning," she sighed, "and so much to do for the magazine." She leaned toward Bettina. "You've probably got an assignment for the *Advocate* too."

Bettina nodded and murmured, "Big doings at the senior center."

"This coffee is awfully good though," Pamela said. "Shall we dawdle just a bit longer? I'll make another pot. And there's still some crumb cake left."

A square of the cake, fine buttery sponge topped by streusel crumbles with a hint of cinnamon, remained on the small gold-rimmed platter.

"I won't say no." Bettina sliced off a narrow sliver of the cake and coaxed it onto her plate.

Inside, Pamela ground beans and set water to boil, taking up her usual position at the counter while she waited for the kettle to whistle. From that spot, the view through her kitchen window was of Richard Larkin's side door and his trash and recycling containers. The Bonhams, who had owned the house until the previous fall, had been meticulous about maintaining their yard. A neat row of well-groomed shrubs had distracted the eye from the more utilitarian uses of the space. Now the foliage sprawled in a shapeless jumble, interrupted by an occasional stand of bare twigs, skeletons of shrubs that hadn't made it through the winter.

And Miranda Bonham's perennial border! If Pamela stood on tiptoe, leaned close to the window, and looked as far to the right as she could, it had been visible in all its English-garden glory. Now it was in a pitiable state, fading peony petals scattered around iris stalks whose blooms had dried into hard little knobs, rampant vegetation that should have been tamed with its first reappearance in March, and weeds.

The whistling of the kettle brought her back to her own kitchen and the task at hand. A few minutes later she was stepping back onto her porch with a fresh pot of coffee.

"Something's going on next door," Bettina said. In fact, cars were easing into spots along Pamela's curb and farther up the street, and soberly dressed people were making their way along the sidewalk. "A few of the teachers from the high school walked by while you were inside," Bettina added, turning away from the porch railing that faced the church.

"Randall Jefferson's funeral?" Pamela set the coffee down on the small table that matched her wicker porch chairs.

"Yep!" The voice came from behind the hedge. Joe Taylor's head popped up above the glossy dark green leaves. "You guessed it. Time for the gardener to be on his way." He vanished again, reappeared at the end of the hedge, and strolled jauntily up the sidewalk toward Arborville Avenue.

"So handsome," Bettina said. "I wonder if Penny would be interested in him. A little summer fling at least, while she's home from college."

"I'm not sure she's interested in flings," Pamela said. She poured coffee into their cups.

"Now that I think of it, Jefferson's funeral notice was in the *Register*." Bettina scooped a spoonful of sugar from the bowl. "I saw it before we knew about the knitting woman with the red hair, so there didn't seem too much reason to be interested. But now . . ."

She rearranged her chair so she was facing the street. "Let's see if she shows up."

"It would be very helpful if we could talk to her," Pamela said.

"Here come a few more high-school teachers." Bettina pointed at a pair of women climbing out of a car. "And it looks like the hearse has arrived."

A long black vehicle with a squared-off back and curtained windows had pulled up directly in front of the church. Pamela sipped her coffee and watched as two men in black suits opened the back and lifted out two large flower arrangements in shades of red, white, and blue. They carried the arrangements up the slate path toward the stone steps and the heavy wooden church doors, now standing open. People were converging on the church from various directions, and a low hubbub of voices reached the porch.

No one sounded particularly grief stricken. Many in town perhaps felt duty bound to pay their respects to Randall Jefferson and saw the funeral as a social occasion as much as anything. Some voices were downright cheerful, greeting old friends. But Pamela swiveled her head in surprise when from the sidewalk came a voice fairly bubbling with laughter, asking, "Are you here to make sure he's dead?"

The speaker was a jovial-looking string bean of a man with dark, wild hair. He was talking to an older man, equally tall and thin, but with white hair, a white moustache, and a white goatee. His little rimless glasses reflected the bright May sun.

"He's dead," the older man said flatly. "I am sure of that." His voice was slightly accented, in a courtly, European sort of way.

Pamela touched Bettina's arm and nodded toward where the two men stood, right at the end of Pamela's front walk. She whispered, "That's Marcus Verteel. He looks just like his picture on the Wendelstaff website."

"Jefferson was making a lot of progress with that study of shifting loyalties among the Dutch farmers in the Hudson Valley," the other man said. "Remarkable, considering he was only a high-school teacher. But anyway"—he winked—"now you won't have to worry about him grabbing all the glory before your book comes out."

"No, I will not," Marcus Verteel said with a tight little smile. "I definitely will not." They resumed walking.

Pamela and Bettina stared at each other, amazed.

"He may not be the Belgian Arnold Schwarzenegger, but he's pretty tall, and he looks like he's in good shape for his age," Bettina said.

"And he has more reason for wanting Randall Jefferson out of the way than we thought," Pamela added. "He was afraid Randall Jefferson would scoop his book idea."

"I'll tip Clayborn off," Bettina said. "I'm seeing him tomorrow morning."

"But we only found out about Marcus Verteel because we sneaked into the house. Detective Clayborn isn't supposed to know about that."

"Not a problem," Bettina said. She sliced off another sliver of crumb cake and eased it onto her plate. "I'll say Wilfred just told me there've been rumors in the historical society. He knows Wilfred is a member."

The sidewalk was empty now, except for a group of men in dark suits standing near the hearse. Pamela checked her watch. "Ten a.m.," she said. "They'll probably be starting."

One of the men opened the back of the hearse and reached inside. Out glided a shelf with a gleaming dark brown coffin on it. The other men came forward and grabbed polished bars along the sides of the coffin, three men on one side and three on the other. They stepped over the curb and made their way along the slate path and up the church steps. A few of the men looked very young, students perhaps, Pamela thought. Some of the few students who appreciated Randall Jefferson's knowledge and rigor.

"Shall we?" Pamela said. She drained her coffee cup.

"Shall we what?" Bettina gave her a puzzled stare.

"Join the mourners. The red-haired knitting woman might be in there. We might not have noticed her arriving. Marcus Verteel seems a likely suspect, but what if he didn't do it? We'll just quietly peek in from the back. People won't notice—they'll be paying attention to the service."

"What will we do if she's in there?" Bettina asked.

"Mingle as people leave the church. We'll find some reason to talk to her." She surveyed Bettina, who was wearing a smart aqua shirtdress. "You look fine for a late-spring funeral. Lots of the people we watched arriving were dressed casually. I'll just run inside and change out of jeans."

The heavy wooden door creaked slightly as Pamela pulled it toward her. The church entry was cool and shadowy, and empty. Everyone, even the ushers, had taken seats. Lighter doors, with little windows in them, separated the entry from the main body of the church. Pamela bent toward one of the windows, Bettina stood on tiptoe to look through the other.

Few people wore hats to church anymore, even to funerals, so it was easy to study the heads arranged in the pews before them. Most people were facing the pulpit to the left side of the altar, a few were looking down. The minister's voice carried as a low murmur.

"There's some red hair in the second pew on the right," Bettina whispered.

"Blondish red," Pamela whispered back, "and I wouldn't describe it as curly, or all over the place."

"No," Bettina agreed. It was trimmed in a cute pixie cut, in fact, and when the owner of the hair turned her head slightly, she proved to be still in her teens.

"A relative, perhaps," Pamela whispered.

They stood there a few more minutes. Pamela made a point of counting the heads, to make sure she'd given each one adequate study. But when she reached number thirty-one, a gray but very chic bun on the far left in the last occupied pew, she turned to Bettina and whispered, "No luck."

Bettina's voice, bursting with excitement, rang out in the silent room: "The police have arrested Brad Striker!"

It was late Friday afternoon. Pamela had spent the last hour in the seventeenth century, immersed in a discussion of Jacobean crewel designs, but the announcement pulled her back to the present. She'd ignored the phone, but now she picked up and exclaimed, "Bettina, it's me. I'm here."

"I thought I was talking to voice mail." Bettina laughed.

"You were, but now you're talking to me. Brad Striker's been arrested? Where did you hear this?" Pamela rolled her desk chair back and swiveled away from the computer screen.

"Straight from the horse's mouth. Clayborn. I'm

sitting in my car in the police department parking lot. I'll be over in five minutes. It's about quitting time for you anyway, isn't it?"

Pamela finished the paragraph she'd been in the middle of editing and made a note of where she left off. She saved the file and turned off the computer.

Downstairs, Catrina was sitting expectantly in the corner of the kitchen where her dinner customarily appeared. The doorbell rang just as Pamela was stooping to deliver a clean bowl with a few scoops of cat food. Catrina was weaving excitedly from side to side while watching the bowl descend.

Bettina began talking before she even stepped over the threshold. "All day with the Arborville grandchildren," she said breathlessly, and, indeed, she did look a bit disheveled. "But," she went on, "I got away just in time to nab Clayborn while he was walking to his car. It will be in the *Register* tomorrow, so no big scoop for me, but—"

"Come in, come in," Pamela said, stepping back and motioning Bettina through the door. "Tell me everything."

"First, I need water." Bettina headed for the kitchen. Pamela followed and filled a glass at the sink while Bettina settled at the table.

"What changed?" Pamela said. "Why arrest him now and not last Monday?" She set the water in front of Bettina, who took a long swallow.

"He had an alibi, and now he doesn't," she said. "His wife came forward to say he actually *wasn't* home with her Saturday night." Bettina raised her eyebrows and pursed her lips in an expression that invited Pamela to appreciate the interesting implications of this news—at least as it applied to the Strikers' marriage.

"Something happened between them," Pamela said. "She was trying to save him, and now she isn't."

Bettina nodded. "So the murder is solved. People can take their aardvarks back, or at least stop blaming Knit and Nibble."

"It's still odd that he'd want to link the murder with the athletic program—and himself—by putting the aardvark on Jefferson's chest," Pamela said.

Bettina frowned. "You did say you thought you saw him walking back to the parking lot during the parade."

"I did," Pamela said. A little wrinkle appeared between her brows. "But would he have taken *two* aardvarks? And put one on Jefferson's chest and hidden the other . . . somewhere . . . to save for his next victim?" The wrinkle between Pamela's brows deepened. "Who would his next victim be? The editor of the *Advocate*?"

Bettina held her head and groaned. "I've had too busy a day to think about all that now. Let's talk about the menu for Sunday."

Pamela jumped from her chair. "Speaking of food . . ." She opened the refrigerator and placed the wedge of Swiss cheese Penny had brought from the Co-Op on a cheese board. Then she plucked an apple from the fruit bowl on the counter, quartered and cored it, and arranged the pieces next to the cheese. She carried the cheese board to the table, along with napkins and a knife.

"People have already told me they'll bring things," Bettina said, slicing off a thin wedge of cheese. "Wilfred's cousin is bringing some of his homemade sausage to go on the grill. I invited all the people from Knit and Nibble, plus spouses of course. Roland and Melanie are going to Cape Cod this weekend, and Holly has a family event. But Nell and Harold will be there, and Nell is making a corn and bean salad."

"I *will* make the deviled eggs," Pamela said.

"Karen Dowling is bringing chocolate chip cookies, and Richard Larkin is bringing a watermelon."

"You didn't invite him!" Pamela slapped the table.

"Why not?" Bettina said. "He's a neighbor. And his daughters will be there too. One of them is making some kind of salad with a funny name. I hope Penny is coming."

"She's planning on it," Pamela said. "But really, Bettina. I'm not interested in Richard Larkin."

"If you just got to know him a little better. Wilfred thinks the world of him—he's always so interested in the dollhouses when he and Wilfred have their chats."

Pamela sighed and picked up the knife to cut a slice of cheese. "We'll need more food for all these people," she said.

"There'll be plenty of food," Bettina said. "Wilfred is grilling chicken with some of his special barbecue sauce. And the Arborville children are coming, and the grandchildren. My daughter-in-law is making potato salad. I'll get rolls for the homemade sausages. Wilfred said the farmers market in Newfield has good tomatoes already, so we'll have a platter of sliced tomatoes." She paused and reached for a piece of apple. "But maybe we *will* need another dessert. Watermelon isn't very filling, and I don't know how many cookies Karen is bringing."

"I can bring a dessert, besides the deviled eggs," Pamela said. "Maybe my lemon bars. They're good for a crowd. Can Wilfred get me some lemons when he gets the tomatoes?"

"Of course," Bettina said. She checked her watch.

"I should go. No cooking tonight because Friday is pizza, but Wilfred will want an update on the grand-children."

She was just about to rise when the sound of an opening door came from the entry and Penny called, "I'm home."

"In here," Pamela called back.

Penny bounced into the room, her blue eyes lively and her smile wide. "Guess who was on the bus tonight," she said. She was wearing another of her thrift-store outfits: a purple minidress that skimmed her young curves and had been made suitable for work by the ad-dition of matching tights.

"I'll bite," Bettina said with an answering smile. "Who?"

"You might not know her," Penny said. "But Mom will remember. Candace Flynn. She's working in the city now."

Candace Flynn had been the bane of her teachers at Arborville High, a rebellious creature who de-lighted in flouting rules and had attracted a small group of like-minded followers. Penny had always been an obedient child, but in the years that followed her father's death, she'd seemed even more deter-mined not to cause her mother extra heartache. So Pamela had never worried that the example of Can-dace Flynn would lead Penny astray. When college ac-ceptances began to come in, with Penny and her friends looking forward to the next chapter of their lives, Candace Flynn had seemed destined to a future working in retail at the mall, if even that.

"What's she doing?" Pamela asked.

"I don't know." Penny shrugged. "She didn't say. But she still lives in Arborville, and she knew all about Mr. Jefferson being killed, and what a mystery it is and

everything, and how everybody's talking about it."
She reached for an apple slice.

"It's not so much of a mystery anymore," Bettina
said. "Brad Striker's been arrested."

"Candace Flynn knows everybody thinks he did it,
but she said he couldn't possibly have." Did Penny's
smile suggest the tiniest hint of gloating?

"And you know this because . . . ?" Pamela had
always encouraged Penny to think critically.

"He was with her Saturday night."

"Wow!" Bettina clapped her hands and smiled delightedly. "I guess I know something Clayborn doesn't."

But Pamela had always encouraged herself to think
critically too. "Are you sure this is true?" She leveled a
stern look at Penny. "Candace always liked attention.
She could have just been angling for a reaction."

"It's true, Mom. At least, it's true that he could have
been. They were . . . sort of together . . . when she was
still in high school. She was a cheerleader, remember?"

"Oh, my!" Bettina's smile faded. "The football
coach, and a cheerleader, and she probably wasn't
eighteen yet."

"Nobody was supposed to know," Penny said. "But
people sort of did. But maybe they weren't . . . you
know . . . then. Maybe they were just friends."

"And now she's eighteen, or more, and it sounds
like they've moved beyond friendship." Bettina nodded
slowly.

"But he's married," Pamela observed.

"He was married *then*," Penny said. "And I've got to
change. Lorie Hopkins and I are eating at the Golden
Pagoda, and then we're going to hang out at her house."
She stooped to give Catrina a quick pat and a few
seconds later Pamela heard her feet on the stairs.

"What do we do?" Pamela said. "If he's really not guilty, but Candace Flynn is his alibi . . . ?"

"His wife must know about Candace Flynn," Bettina said. "That's why she retracted her story that he was home with her Saturday night. She's probably furious— so furious that she doesn't care if he goes to prison for a murder he didn't commit."

"If Candace Flynn really cares for him, she'll give him an alibi, won't she?" Brad Striker certainly hadn't made a good impression on Pamela at Arborfest, but she liked to think that life was basically fair.

"If his wife already knows about Candace Flynn, there's no secret to keep anymore." Bettina checked her watch again. "I've really got to get going." She stood up.

Pamela carried the cheese board to the counter and slipped the rest of the cheese into a zipper bag. She paused in mid-zip and turned toward Bettina. "When Penny talked to Candace on the bus, nobody except you, the police, and Brad Striker knew that he'd been arrested. It will be in the *Register* tomorrow. So we'll see what happens with Candace."

"She'll say something and they'll let him go," Bettina said. "That's my bet."

Pamela finished zipping the cheese into its bag and opened the refrigerator. "So we're right back where we were," she said. She tossed the cheese onto a shelf and slammed the refrigerator door.

"I told Clayborn about Marcus Verteel," Bettina said. "He seemed noncommittal."

"There's always the red-haired woman."

Bettina left, and soon Penny was out the door, dressed for the evening in jeans and a T-shirt. Pamela checked for new messages from her boss at *Fiber Craft*, resisted the urge to visit AccessArborville for the latest twist in the KILLER AARDVARK thread, and deleted an email offering coupons from the hobby shop at the mall.

Downstairs she made a salad, and got the Swiss cheese out again. After this simple dinner she settled onto the sofa. It was just time for her favorite British mystery program, and she had knitting to do. The scarf project she'd started at Nell's on Tuesday had been growing all week, and if she could add a few more feet it would be ready to present to Nell at the next Knit and Nibble session. As soon as her needles began clicking, Catrina appeared, wending her graceful way in from the dining room, tail aloft. She hopped lightly onto the sofa and curled up against Pamela's thigh.

Chapter Eleven

Someone was in the kitchen making coffee, but it wasn't Pamela. She was still in bed. She rolled over, pulled her tangled bedclothes smooth, thrust her arms back until her knuckles tapped her bed's brass headboard, and stretched. Near her knees, something stirred. A warm presence made its way gently across her belly, and Catrina's face emerged from under the edge of the sheet.

Pamela twisted her head to glimpse the clock on her night table. Eight a.m., early to rise for a Saturday. She could close her eyes for a few more minutes. But the coffee—undoubtedly Penny's doing—smelled so alluring. And the light behind the white eyelet curtains hinted at a day in which time spent in bed would be time wasted. Besides, she recalled, as the last remnants of dreams retreated and the day came into focus, this particular Saturday was the fourth Saturday in May.

Arborville, as Roland often pointed out, could be very predictable. The town had many churches, and the churches had fundraisers, and the town calendar allotted dates to bazaars, fairs, sales of all kinds, pancake breakfasts, spaghetti dinners, and even bingo. The fourth Saturday in May had been, as long as anyone could remember, the day St. Willibrod's church held its annual rummage sale. Hanging above Pamela's dresser, and visible from where she was lying, was a treasure she'd discovered there the previous year, a mirror whose frame had been decorated with antique buttons of all shapes and colors.

"You're awake early for a Saturday," Pamela said as she entered the kitchen. Penny was sitting at the table dressed in jeans and a frilly blouse that made her resemble the heroine of an old-fashioned romance, at least from the waist up. She was eating a piece of toast. The *Register* lay before her, front page uppermost. A cup of coffee sat near it and a whole carafe waited on the counter.

"I'm meeting Laine in the city," Penny said. "She's going to show me her dorm at NYU, and we're going thrifting in Brooklyn. Then we're coming back to Arborville, and Sybil is coming back too, and they'll be at the barbecue tomorrow."

Pamela was listening to her daughter, but her eyes were on the *Register*. Penny noticed.

"It's all in here," she said. "About him being arrested for killing Mr. Jefferson, that is." She shrugged. "What do you think will happen? Candace can't just let him go to prison."

"I don't know," Pamela said. "He wouldn't keep quiet, I don't think, if Candace could be his alibi now."

Penny fixed her eyes on her mother in an intense way that made looking away seem impossible. "You and Bettina aren't getting involved in this, are you?" she said.

"Why would we?" Pamela gestured toward the newspaper.

"He's not guilty, Mom. So that means somebody else is."

After Penny left, Pamela reached a cup and saucer from the cupboard and slipped a piece of whole-grain bread into the toaster. A few minutes later, coffee poured and toast buttered, she settled at the table and pondered the front page of the *Register*. A headline in type larger than any other on the page announced ARREST MADE IN ARBORVILLE MURDER. In smaller type beneath it were the words FOOTBALL COACH IN CUSTODY. A *Register* photographer had obviously been on hand to get a picture of Brad Striker being escorted to a waiting police car. The pleasant little house in the background was one she had often walked past on her rambles around town.

The article didn't add anything beyond what Bettina had reported, and mercifully it avoided using the phrase "Killer Aardvark." It featured a quote from Detective Lucas Clayborn to the effect that the murder had arisen from a personal grudge, smart police work had resolved the case, and the residents of Arborville had never been in danger. "Smart police work," Pamela murmured to herself. She liked Detective Clayborn, and she felt bad that he was going to be on the front page of the *Register* probably quite soon, admitting that Brad Striker was not the murderer after all.

* * *

St. Willibrod's was on Arborville Avenue, but at the north end of town. Pamela contemplated taking her car. What if she found so many treasures that she couldn't carry them all home? And if she walked, she'd have to go on foot through Arborville's commercial district, risking the possibility of unpleasant conversations about what people would probably never cease calling the "Killer Aardvark." Of course, she'd risk unpleasant conversations at the rummage sale too, but she wasn't about to skip one of her favorite treasure hunts. At least maybe some attention had been deflected from Knit and Nibble by the arrest of Brad Striker, unwarranted though his arrest was.

She hesitated on the porch, keys in hand, car waiting in the driveway. But the day was perfect again, the bright green lawns darker where trees cast their shadows, the sun softened by a breeze that stirred the branches. She'd walk, but she'd take a roomy canvas bag.

Back in the house, she collected a bag from the closet in the entry. As she was doing that, the phone rang. She paused long enough to hear a voice tell her voice mail that a truck would be on Orchard Street the following week collecting used furniture. Halfway out the door, she noticed that the paper recycling basket was about to overflow, so she detoured around the side of the house to dump the contents into the recycling bin.

Thus it was that she was heading down her driveway when a voice addressed her from the hedge that separated her house from Richard Larkin's.

"Hello," the voice said. "Could I ask you something?" She looked up to see Richard Larkin's head projecting above the foliage. He looked different somehow, not so shaggy. Perhaps he'd gotten his hair cut.

"Um . . . sure." She squinted up at him. He was very tall and the sun was right behind him.

"I . . . could you come around here?" He took a few steps toward the sidewalk. Pamela proceeded down her driveway, and they met at the end of the hedge.

"There's a plant here on the porch." He waved toward Miranda Bonham's ceramic planter, which sat next to the front door. "It *was* a plant, at least." Just visible over the scalloped edge of the planter were a few spiky stalks bearing shriveled brown nubbins. "So many things are coming up all over the yard. I thought it would turn green again, whatever it is."

"Oh!" Pamela laughed. "Miranda always had marigolds there in the summer. These are the remains of them. Marigolds are annuals. When they're gone, they're gone. They'll never come back. Not like perennials."

"Oh." His face could look very stern, despite his gentle mouth.

"You can plant new ones," Pamela said. "That's what people do. Just go to the garden center. They don't have to be marigolds. Buy anything that you think looks nice." A beat or two passed before he nodded, as if he hadn't really been paying attention despite his intense gaze. "So," she said brightly, taking a step. "I'm off."

"I'm going to have help," he said. "I've hired Joe Taylor."

Arborville's commercial district, all two blocks of it, was busy. From across Arborville Avenue, Pamela could see the usual Saturday morning cluster of people gathered near the bulletin board on the Co-Op's façade, catching up on the week's gossip before proceeding into the store to do their shopping. Shoppers who had completed their task pushed carts loaded with groceries along the sidewalk to cars angled into the parking spots along the Co-Op's stretch of curb. Pamela caught a glimpse of the cardboard box set up to receive the discarded aard-varks and averted her eyes. She hurried on, past a bank, Hyler's Luncheonette, several shops, the Chinese takeout, and When in Rome Pizza, staring fixedly ahead, as if in too much of a hurry to notice if she passed a familiar face.

St. Willibrod's possessed a large church hall, built much later than the venerable church itself and in a style that had been modern in the 1950s. A hand-lettered sign on the heavy glass doors announced: RUMMAGE SALE TODAY—ALL WELCOME. Pamela felt the little thrill she always felt when rummaging. Perhaps a treasure was waiting to be discovered, and even if she came away with nothing, she enjoyed imagining the previous lives of the curiosities set out for sale.

Inside, the hall was bright with fluorescent lights. Indistinct conversations echoed in a low buzz. Long tables set end to end stretched along both sides of the room, with an island formed from more long tables in the center. Some of those tables held baked goods.

Pamela veered to the left, where the closest table offered a jumble of china, glassware, and curious objects. She browsed among bowls with gilt edges, sets of wine glasses suitable for parties of three, African wood carvings, crystal paperweights, and small boxes with exotic motifs rendered in brilliant colors. A small brass cat, perhaps a doorstop, caught her eye and she scooped it up.

She made her way slowly around the room. A few

people greeted her, but no one said anything about the murder or the aardvarks. Perhaps the knitting club's connection with the murder had been diluted, at least temporarily, by the news of Brad Striker's arrest. She examined a beaded handbag as a part of her mind tussled with the issue of Brad Striker's yet-unrevealed alibi. It inevitably *would* be revealed, she was sure, and what would happen then?

The handbag was too beautiful not to rescue. She opened the clasp and looked inside. The silk lining was frayed, but it could be replaced—or the fraying could just be ignored. As she pondered these alternatives, a voice came from behind her.

"So—they arrested the football coach, huh? What do you think about that?" Pamela turned. It was the small woman she and Bettina had met on Wednesday, the neighborhood gossip that Harold had recommended they seek out for details about Randall Jefferson's lady friend. "I guess even having a brother on the town council can't keep the law from catching up with you." She grabbed Pamela by the arm and let loose with one of her boisterous laughs.

Pamela wasn't sure what to say. She certainly wasn't going to tell the small woman that Brad Striker would undoubtedly be released as soon as his girlfriend came forward with the true story of his whereabouts Saturday night. But she was saved from having to say anything. Still clinging to Pamela's arm, the small woman focused on the beaded bag. "So you like this old stuff too?" Another laugh erupted from her wide mouth. "Of course, why else would you be here?" She surveyed the room, then squeezed the arm she still clung to. "Well, I'll leave you to it." But before she turned away, she raised herself on her toes to lean toward Pamela's ear and whisper, "Do you believe in ghosts?"

Pamela didn't, but she was too startled to answer.

"Either that, or Randall Jefferson had a double." The small woman drew back, her face serious now. "I saw him last night, walking down the street that runs along the side of the Jefferson house." The expression on her face made it clear that she expected an answer.

Pamela searched her mind for an appropriate comment. At last she said, "Really? Did you talk to him?"

"I was too far away," the woman said. "I was coming up the hill with Rambo. Rambo didn't bark—that's what made me realize I probably wasn't seeing a real person." Giving Pamela's arm one final squeeze, she added, "I'm not afraid of ghosts. I believe that we can all coexist." And with that, she wandered off toward the baked goods.

Bettina should be told about this interesting development, that was certain, though Pamela doubted the small woman had seen a ghost or even Randall Jefferson's double. In the dark, and to a suggestible imagination, any tall middle-aged man in a suit could look like any other tall middle-aged man in a suit.

"Do you want me to hold those while you look around some more?" The question came from a kindly looking gray-haired woman standing behind the table where Pamela was browsing. Pamela nodded and handed over her finds. The woman reached out for the brass cat, handling it as if it was a live creature. "I'm glad this beauty is getting adopted," she said with a smile. "And this little purse. What stories do you think it could tell?"

Pamela detoured around the baked goods. The tables along the other side of the hall held knitted and crocheted items, both old and new, along with piles of fabric. Pamela herself was not a sewer, but she had plenty of unused yarn she'd bought because it was beautiful and she'd certainly do something with it someday. So she understood how three yards of cotton fabric that featured blue oranges on a bright yellow background could end up unused on a rummage sale table, stacked with fabrics in colors and patterns equally antique.

The next table, though, held offerings of genuine interest. The woman presiding over it led a crafts program for the senior center. Pamela recognized her from articles Bettina had written for the *Advocate*. A few cuddly crocheted toys—not aardvarks though—shared space with a group of knitted and crocheted scarves and another group of hats and mittens.

"Some are new—newly made by our seniors group, that is," she said, "and some are donated."

Pamela moved a few hats out of the way to examine one with a ruffled border. When she lifted that hat, another was revealed, and she was so startled that a tiny squeal escaped from her lips.

"Are you all right?" The woman presiding over the table leaned across it and reached a hand toward Pamela.

"Fine! Yes, I'm okay," Pamela said. "It's this hat." She exchanged the hat with the ruffled border for the one that had been hiding under it.

"Oh!" The woman laughed. "It was a donation. I almost didn't set it out, but if people don't see their donations here, sometimes they don't donate again."

Pamela held it in both hands. Neon-orange mohair shaded into neon chartreuse and back again to orange. From the rounded top of the hat rose two ears, so

large they flopped over like dachshund ears. Dangling
from the back was a tail. The knitter had not been an
expert. Bumps and holes marred the knitted surface.

She'd seen a hat just like it before, of course, under
the left-hand pillow on the bed in Randall Jefferson's
bedroom. All that had been missing was the tail. But a
tail—she now realized—had been in progress on the
needles that accompanied the hat, undoubtedly just
such a tail as the one that now hung between her hands.

"I'll take it," she said. "How much?"

"You really want it?" The woman seemed amazed.
"Well . . . whatever you want to pay is fine. I didn't think
anyone would buy it." Pamela took out her wallet and
handed over five dollars. "I'll get your change," the
woman said.

"That's okay." Pamela waved a hand. "Please keep it.
It's for a good cause. I have my own bag." She tucked
the hat into the canvas bag she'd brought. "I wonder
though . . ." she paused. "Can you tell me who donated
it? I'd love to get the pattern."

The woman blinked a few times. "Well, I suppose if
it was made with different yarn, and the person was a
better knitter . . . to each his own." She frowned and
folded her hands under her chin. "Who donated it?"
The frown deepened. "I think it was Nancy, from the
library. Nancy Billings."

"Does she have red hair?" Pamela asked, feeling her
heart speed up the way it had when Harold Bascomb
showed her the hook where Randall Jefferson's house
key was hanging.

"I suppose so," the woman said, still frowning. "I
suppose you could say she has red hair."

Pamela still had to pay for and claim the brass cat
and the beaded purse. She detoured around the baked

goods tables once again. She was tempted to pick up a dessert for the barbecue, but she'd promised Bettina she'd make lemon bars, and Wilfred had probably already bought lemons for the project.

She handed over ten dollars for her rummage treasures and tucked them in with the curious hat. Then she set out to visit the library.

Chapter Twelve

If a woman had wild, flyaway red hair, would you just say you *supposed* she had red hair? Pamela wasn't sure. Nancy Billings might be the person who knitted the hat—though Pamela didn't think she'd ever noticed anyone who dressed like a gypsy working in the Arborville Library—or she might not. But if she'd donated the hat, she'd have a lead to the actual knitter—hopefully. She was definitely worth talking to.

Pamela hadn't been near the library since Arborfest the previous Sunday. Now she turned off Arborville Avenue onto the cross street where the library was located and turned again to follow the sidewalk that led along the library's side. The main entrance faced the parking lot, the very parking lot where she'd found Randall Jefferson's body less than a week ago. Pamela skirted the rock garden, casting a glance at the pretty wooden bench where she'd waited to be interviewed by Detective Clayborn. A gap yawned in the border of the rock garden where the yam-shaped rock had reposed.

Inside the library, Pamela scanned the room, looking for a woman with red hair. But a Saturday in the late spring was a slow day for the library. A few retirees dozed with magazines in the chairs near the windows, and no one was on duty at the reference desk. Pamela was surprised to see that the display devoted to the high-school athletic program had been left up, given that it was devoted to the exploits of the Aardvarks— and aardvarks were currently in such bad repute. But the town did love its sports. Nineteen eighty-five must have been a thrilling year, evidenced by a yellowed clipping from the *Advocate*, dated November 16, 1985, which announced: Aardvarks Win State Championship— Victorious in Final Seconds.

Pamela approached the circulation counter, where a young woman she recognized as one of Penny's class-mates from the high school was stationed.

"Home from college for the summer?" Pamela asked, searching her memory for the young woman's name. The young woman hadn't been one of Penny's friends, but she hadn't been one of the reckless girls who admired Candace Flynn either.

"Yes." The young woman nodded, adding a giggle. "Can I help you?"

"Is Nancy Billings here today?"

Now the young woman shook her head no. "Monday," she said. "Nancy doesn't come in on weekends."

"Does she have red hair?" Pamela asked.

The young woman shrugged. "Not exactly."

"Not wild, flyaway red hair?" Pamela waved her hands around over her head.

The young woman gave Pamela a curious look. "Why?"

"I'm looking for someone with wild, flyaway red hair." Pamela tried to say it as if this constituted a per-fectly normal errand. "Thank you," she added. "I'll come back on Monday."

She lingered at the display again on her way out. Football did rattle the brain, but a photo from the victory year showed a sturdy young man that the caption identified as BASCOMB, #12 posing with his helmeted cohorts: STEWART, #17; ARMSTRONG, #76; JEFFERSON, #43; CARROLL, #29; AND LINDLEY, #34. Nell couldn't have been happy about her son's chosen sport, Pamela reflected, but she and Harold must have felt he was entitled to make his own choices. As far as Pamela knew, the Bascomb children had grown up to have successful careers and nice lives, so not too rattled, despite the sport.

Catrina wasn't at all interested in the brass cat doorstop. She didn't even seem to recognize it as a fellow cat. Pamela set it on the stairs. The door to her bedroom tended to swing closed of its own accord, and a doorstop would be useful. In the kitchen, she switched on the light over the table and laid out her other finds: the beaded bag and the orange and chartreuse hat with ears and a tail. The two objects could hardly have been more different. The bag was so delicate, with iridescent beads shaping a pattern of pale pink roses with pale green stems against a background of pearly white. It hung from a tarnished but still silvery chain and had a tarnished but still silvery filigreed frame and clasp. And then there was the hat—with its bumps and holes and floppy ears and trailing tail, its colors and a fuzzy texture evoking a curious form of plant life.

The sound of feet on the porch distracted Pamela from her study of the hat. "Hello!" boomed a cheery voice, accompanied by a tapping. From the door that led from the kitchen to the entry, Pamela could see a bulky shape behind the lace that curtained the oval window in her front door. She hurried to open the door.

Wilfred stepped in, followed by Bettina. Wilfred carried a plastic bag, lumpy and full to nearly bursting. "Lemons from the farmers market in Newfield," he announced, holding the bag aloft. The fruit showed pale yellow through the plastic of the bag, and the citrusy smell was sharp.

"Bring them in here," Pamela said, retreating to the kitchen.

Wilfred set the lemons on the table and gave Pamela a courtly bow. He turned to Bettina and bowed again. "I have delivered your parcel, dear wife," he said, "and I will be on my way."

"Thank you!" Pamela followed Wilfred to the kitchen door. She turned around to see Bettina staring at her, wide-eyed.

"You went back to the house?" Bettina asked, picking the hat up with two fingers.

"It's another one," Pamela said, relishing her friend's amazement. "Notice the tail."

Bettina stroked the tail. "The ears look like dachshund ears," she said. "But do dachshunds have tails this long? I'm trying to picture Roland's dog."

"I'm not sure," Pamela said. "But I'm on the trail of the person who made this. I found it at the St. Willibrod's rummage sale this morning." She described the crafts table and her visit to the library in search of Nancy Billings, adding the caveat that Nancy Billings—though possibly a redhead—might not herself have the wild red hair that the small woman had described.

"This is a huge discovery," Bettina said, clapping her hands with delight. "Both the hats have to have been made by the same person. And Monday we'll know who that person is. The rejected lover who finally had enough."

"That dog-walking woman was at the rummage sale," Pamela said. "And she thinks Randall Jefferson is still hanging around—but in ghostly form."

Bettina laughed. "She gave us a good lead to the red-haired woman," she said. "But I'm not sure what we can do with this ghost idea."

"She said it was nighttime when she saw him," Pamela said. "It could have been any man in a suit, really." She paused. "But she did say Rambo didn't bark—and we know he's a barker."

After Bettina left, Pamela made a grilled-cheese sandwich and ate it while browsing through the rest of the Saturday *Register*. She checked her email, got a load of wash started, and vacuumed and dusted the whole downstairs, pausing at one point to transfer the wash to the dryer.

Just as Pamela was putting the vacuum away, Penny came in carrying two huge plastic shopping bags. The day's thrift-store finds—which included a circle skirt printed with poodles, berets, and glasses of red wine, plus a matching red patent-leather belt—had to be examined and commented on. Pamela showed off the beaded bag and the brass cat doorstop, which still waited on the stairs to be transferred to its new home. She'd tucked the curious hat away because she didn't want to have to explain to Penny why it had caught her eye.

Penny was off again a few minutes later, but just next door, to order pizza and spend the evening watching TV with Laine and Sybil. Pamela set eggs to boiling for the deviled eggs she'd promised Bettina for the barbecue. A twinge in her stomach told her that she was ready to think about dinner too. And Catrina wandered in, seated herself on her haunches with her tail enfolding her forepaws, and gazed up at Pamela looking expectant.

"Yes, yes, I know it's that time," Pamela said, and opened the refrigerator. A half-empty can of cat food sat on the top shelf, along with some of the cooked shrimp from the foray to the Meadowside supermarket. Pamela served Catrina her dinner, then chopped the shrimp up, mixed in celery and mayonnaise, and ate the result between slices of toasted whole-grain bread.

After dinner, she transferred the boiled eggs to a dish. There would be plenty of time to devil them in the morning, but the lemon bars would be made tonight. The lemons waited on the counter in a favorite old green bowl, many more than she'd need for the recipe, but lemons kept a long time, and there was always lemonade.

But the first step was to make the crust. Pamela measured flour and confectioners' sugar into a mixing bowl, blended them with a wooden spoon, and used her fingers to work in butter until the mixture resembled fine, buttery crumbs. She emptied the bowl onto a sheet pan that she'd lined with foil, and compressed the buttery crumbs into a thin layer with her buttery fingers. The sheet pan went into the oven, and she washed her hands.

She selected a few particularly large and glossy lemons from the bounty Wilfred had brought. The recipe called for a tablespoon of grated lemon zest, so she set to work scraping one of the lemons against the tiniest prongs her old aluminum grater offered, enjoying the bright, tangy odor of the lemon oil. The zest accumulated slowly, but soon she had a spoonful of zest and a bare lemon. Meanwhile the kitchen filled with the tantalizing aroma of buttery sweetness.

Pamela's lemon squeezer was decidedly low-tech—a shallow glass bowl with a ribbed dome rising from the center. One pressed a lemon half onto the dome and twisted it this way and that. The result was juice, in the channel that ran around the dome, and a hollow lemon half. The bare lemon, plus two others, yielded the two-thirds cup of juice the recipe called for. Pamela washed her hands again, and opened the oven to check on the progress of the crust. It was the palest tan color, and she judged that in a few minutes it would be perfect. That was just enough time to crack four eggs into a fresh bowl and beat in sugar, granulated this time.

She slid the sheet pan out and rested it on the stove top. Into the bowl of eggs and sugar went a bit of salt, a bit of flour, a bit of baking powder, and of course the juice and the zest. The final step was to pour the deep yellow mixture over the crust and return the sheet pan to the oven. She set the timer for twenty minutes, washed the dishes, and checked her email. By the time she returned to the kitchen, the timer was buzzing. She once again slid the sheet pan out and rested it on the stove top. The lemon bars, not yet bars but a rectangular sheet, glowed with a deep lemony translucence. Tomorrow, the rich yellow surface would be dusted with confectioners' sugar, and the whole divided into twenty-four equal parts.

Scarves can grow longer than they need to be, as the soothing motions of yarn passing over needles and needles passing under yarn repeat themselves in a hypnotic rhythm. One more row, the knitter might resolve, but one row becomes two or three or four, and a scarf presents a quandary for the wearer. Wrap it twice around the neck? Loop it over itself an extra time? Let it stream rakishly behind but watch it doesn't get caught in closing doors?

The scarf Pamela was working on for Nell's day-laborer project was nearly finished. This night's work would add a foot or so, and then she was resolved to cast off. That would leave her without a project though. As she clicked along, with Catrina snuggled companionably against her thigh, she pondered. The last thing she'd made for herself had been an Icelandic-style sweater in natural brown wool with a white snowflake pattern. It was a challenging project, and it had turned out well. She'd worn it with great pleasure many times this past winter. But what to make next?

It was Sunday morning. At least ten minutes had passed, and Penny hadn't returned from fetching the newspaper. Pamela had absentmindedly murmured something as Penny headed for the door, then focused on slicing her lemon creation of the previous evening, already dusted with confectioners' sugar, into carefully calibrated bars. Now the bars were arranged on a tray and covered with plastic wrap, ready to be borne across the street in a few hours.

What could be keeping Penny so long? People didn't just disappear on a bright May morning. In the entry, Pamela leaned close to the oval window in her front door and coaxed the lace curtain aside. Penny was not lost after all. She stood on the sidewalk, newspaper already unfolded, with Bettina at her side. They were engaged in intense conversation, Penny's dark curls almost touching Bettina's vivid coif.

Pamela opened the door and stepped out onto the porch in her summer robe. Neither of them noticed her. "Hi!" she called, hesitant to venture much farther in a garment so flimsy.

They both turned. "He's out!" Penny called.

Bettina echoed the words, adding, "Brad Striker's out of jail."

Penny started up the front walk, newspaper rustling. Bettina hurried along behind her. "Here—you can read all about it," Penny said, reaching the porch and extending the paper.

"Nothing *we* didn't already know," Bettina said from halfway up the steps. "But I'm sure people will be buzzing about it in town—and at the barbecue."

"I did the lemon bars," Pamela said. "And the eggs are boiled already."

Bettina studied Pamela for a minute. "You'll wear something a little more special, I hope."

"Well, obviously not this." Pamela fingered the light cotton fabric of the robe.

"I mean more special than what you usually wear." Bettina looked ready for her party in a flirty lavender sundress with a touch of lavender eye shadow accenting her hazel eyes.

"Jeans aren't okay for a barbecue?" Pamela said.

"Richard Larkin will be there," Bettina said.

"*Please!*" Pamela groaned.

"I know he's looking forward to chatting with you about gardening. He mentioned it when he called to ask if he should bring some extra beer."

Pamela sighed. "Let's talk about something else." She shook the newspaper to smooth out the front page. The release of Brad Striker was the lead story, with a headline that read STRIKER FREE BASED ON NEW ALIBI. "Is there a quote from Detective Clayborn?"

"No." Bettina laughed. "What could he say after being so sure the case was wrapped up? And with 'smart police work'?" She backed toward the steps. "I've got to get going—lots more to do at home. But"—she held up a warning finger—"be sure you wear something special."

Back in the kitchen, Pamela poured the tail end of the coffee into her cup and spread the newspaper out on the table. The article about Brad Striker's release would indeed be sensational news to people who knew only what the *Register* had previously reported. In the new version of the story, Candace Flynn had come forward to say Brad Striker was with her all night on the Saturday before Arborfest. His wife had been at her sister's and had believed him when he told her he'd been at home watching the sports channel. So, to give him a solid alibi, she'd lied to the police that she was home too. Then she'd learned about his carryings on with Candace Flynn and retracted her statement.

"Well," Pamela murmured to herself. "Back to square one for Detective Clayborn." She tipped her cup to sip the last drops of coffee, now cold. "But we'll talk to Nancy Billings tomorrow and see what she has to say about the orange and chartreuse hat." She set the cup down on its saucer. "And then," she added, "there's the ghost." She rolled her napkin up and set it next to the cup and saucer. "Not to mention Marcus Verteel." To the tableau she added the knife she'd used to slice the lemon bars. Then she folded the paper for the recycling basket.

Pamela usually got dressed before starting her day's work, even if most days that work was done at her own computer in her own house. Today's work was deviling eggs, but work was work, so she climbed the stairs to her room and traded her robe for jeans and a blouse.

Downstairs again, she soon lost herself in the rhythm of cracking the eggs and slipping them from their shells, slicing them in half, and popping the yolk halves into a small bowl. Part of the fun of making deviled eggs was arranging them in one of her prized possessions, a ceramic platter with the image of a pleased hen in the center and oval hollows around the rim, enough for twenty-four egg halves. She brought the platter out and arranged the empty egg halves in the hollows. When the mashed yolks had been mixed with mayonnaise, powdered mustard, and salt and pepper, and neatly spooned into the holes the yolks had come out of, she began to add capers to each deviled egg for decoration.

She looked up to find Penny standing in the kitchen doorway. She was holding a blouse made of a gauzy fabric with a streaky print like an abstract water color in shades of green and indigo. The neckline was a deep V, and the sleeves were long and full. "Why don't you wear this today?" she said.

"What is it?"

"A blouse, Mom. I found it at a really fancy shop Laine took me to, a hospital charity where rich people from the Upper East Side donate clothes they don't want anymore." She took a few steps toward Pamela. "Feel this fabric—it's so light and soft."

"I have caper juice on my fingers," Pamela said,

tucking her hands behind her back. "I don't want to ruin it."

Penny held the shoulders of the blouse up to Pamela's shoulders and let the soft fabric drape against Pamela's torso. "It looks really nice on you, Mom," she said. "I'll put it in your room."

Chapter Thirteen

The barbecue part of the barbecue was underway by noon. Pamela could smell it the minute she stepped out onto her porch. From across the street wafted the alluring aroma of chicken, basted with piquant sauce, roasting over hot coals. Feeling self-conscious in the fancy blouse, she set off down the steps, bearing the platter of deviled eggs. Penny followed with the tray of lemon bars.

They proceeded across Orchard Street, down Wilfred and Bettina's driveway, and along the little path that led to the grassy backyard, following the drift of smoke from the grill. Bettina was standing on the patio with a couple that Pamela recognized as Bettina's son and daughter-in-law. The son, Wilfred Jr., was a younger and thinner Wilfred with sandy hair, and the daughter-in-law, Maxie, was a sweet-faced charmer dressed in shorts and a tank top. Their children had sought out Woofus, who was sprawled on the grass in the shade of a tree, and now squatted beside him, stroking his fur and talking to him. Wilfred stood at the grill, tending an assortment of chicken breasts, thighs, and legs. At his side was his cousin

John, nearly Wilfred's double with his ruddy cheeks and abundant white hair. A long table was ready with a bedspread-sized cloth and already laid with plates, napkins, and silverware.

Pamela hesitated for a minute at the edge of the patio, mustering her social smile. Penny darted around her and scurried to Bettina's side, where she said hi to Wilfred Jr. and Maxie and then leaned close to Bettina's ear. Bettina smiled and advanced across the patio.

"You look wonderful," she said, stopping a few feet from Pamela and surveying her from head to toe. "The blouse is perfect." She stepped closer and examined the platter of eggs. "And don't these look yummy!" She leaned in toward Pamela's ear and whispered. "I'm talking to Clayborn first thing in the morning. Meet me in the parking lot at nine, and we'll follow up on the hat."

"Hello, hello!" came a voice from the driveway. They turned to see Nell and Harold advancing at a lively pace. "She insisted on walking down the hill," Harold said. "Maybe we can catch a ride back up." He carried a large wooden bowl covered with a dish cloth. "Nell's corn and bean salad," he said. "Shall I put it on the table?"

"Beans and corn together make a complete protein, you know," Nell added. "So, for those who don't care to eat too much meat . . ."

"That wouldn't be me." Harold looked over toward the grill with its sizzling chicken parts. "Where's this homemade sausage? I've been thinking about it all week."

"Greetings!" Wilfred waved the barbecue fork with

which he'd been tending the chicken. "It goes on the grill soon, and I guarantee you won't be disappointed."

"We'll put the food in the kitchen for now," Bettina said, holding out her hands for the wooden bowl. She turned to Pamela. "Do you want to bring the eggs in? And let's get those lemon bars hidden before the bees discover them." She called to Penny, and the three of them headed for the sliding glass door that opened out onto the patio. Bettina's house, a Dutch Colonial, was the oldest on the street, but it had been added onto over the years and featured a large, modern kitchen and family room.

"You know Glenda, I think—Wilfred's cousin's wife." Bettina set the wooden bowl on her pine table and gestured toward a pleasant-looking woman occupied with cutting a string of sausages into separate links and arranging them on a platter.

"Hello, Pamela and Penny from across the street," the pleasant-looking woman said with a smile.

They lined their offerings up next to Nell's salad, a potato salad from Maxie, and a cluster of plump tomatoes waiting to be sliced.

"Wilfred said you were in here." Karen Dowling stepped through the sliding door carrying a plastic bowl with a snap-on lid. "I made the cookies." She offered the bowl to Bettina with a shy smile. "I hope they turned out okay."

"I'm sure they'll be delicious." Bettina popped off the lid. "Lots of chocolate chips—they look very authentic." She set the bowl by the tray with the lemon bars.

"That was quite a story in the *Register* this morning," Karen said, wrinkling her smooth forehead. "I had so hoped it would all be over when they arrested Brad

Striker, and now it turns out it wasn't him after all."
Her pretty mouth twisted as if she was about to cry.
"Everywhere I go in town people are still talking about
the murder and the knitting group and the aardvarks."
She blinked a few times and dabbed at one eye with a
finger.

Bettina put a comforting arm around Karen's thin
shoulders. "I'm sure the police will figure things out
very soon," she said with a wink at Pamela. "Let's go
see what the men are doing—and there's beer in the
cooler." She squeezed Karen's shoulders. "I've got
soda too. I haven't forgotten your exciting news."
Glenda followed them through the sliding glass door
carrying the platter of sausages, so plump their shiny
casings seemed almost ready to burst.

Out in the yard, Dave Dowling, Wilfred Jr., and
Harold had joined Wilfred and his cousin at the grill.
They were holding bottles of beer and watching as
Wilfred moved the chicken pieces this way and that,
as if getting each to the proper state of doneness required the strategic skill of a chess master. An occasional hearty laugh punctuated their conversation.
Smoke from the grill drifted across the patio, bearing
the scent of sizzling chicken and barbecue sauce.

Nell and Maxie were drinking beer too, and sitting
on lawn chairs near where Bettina's grandchildren
were still talking to Woofus. Bettina surveyed the yard,
counting on her fingers. "Fourteen," she said. "Who's
missing?"

"Richard Larkin," Penny said promptly. "And Laine
and Sybil. I wonder what's keeping them."

Bettina had opened the cooler, which was tucked
into a shady spot of patio near the sliding door, and

was lifting out bottles. "Beer?" she said, holding up a dripping green bottle. "Soda? Who wants what?"

"I'll have a beer," Penny said, with a quick look at her mother.

Pamela gave her an amused nod. "You're in college now, I know," she said, and accepted a beer of her own.

Bottles in hand, they strolled toward the pool of shade cast by Bettina's largest maple tree and claimed lawn chairs of their own. Pamela's chair was nearest the driveway and faced the street. In fact, she had a clear view of Richard Larkin's porch.

His front door opened and Laine Larkin stepped out, bearing a bright-red bowl with foil over the top. She was followed by Richard, who was carrying a watermelon, and then Sybil, who pulled the door closed behind her. But they remained on the porch. Laine said something to her father, and he looked down as if to examine what he was wearing. Then he smiled and took a step toward the edge of the porch. Laine didn't move. She said something else and her body stiffened. He smiled again. Sybil added her opinion to whatever was being discussed. She also placed herself between him and the steps that led down to the driveway. She reached for the watermelon. He relinquished it and went back in the house.

Hardly a minute later, Laine was stepping across the grass, the red bowl extended toward Bettina. Sybil was at her side with the watermelon, a huge oblong one with stripes in various shades of green. "I need to put this down," she said.

Wilfred Jr. had been watching their progress. Now he darted across the yard and plucked it from her arms. "Put it in the cooler," Bettina said. "I think there's room."

"My dad's coming," Laine said.

"He's changing his clothes," Sybil added. "Laine made him."

"And this is your salad." Bettina accepted the bowl.

"Tabouli," Laine said.

Nell looked up. She'd been stroking Woofus's shaggy head. "With wheat berries?" she said.

"Yes," Laine smiled, "and fresh mint."

"Where did you get the wheat berries?" Nell asked.

Laine pulled a lawn chair close to Nell. "There's a Middle Eastern grocery in Haversack," she said. Soon they were joined by Maxie, and the three were happily trading notes on healthful cooking.

Meanwhile, Penny and Sybil were heading toward the cooler. Bettina handed Sybil a bottle of beer. Wilfred's cousin left the grill to announce that it was time to put the sausages on, and he and Bettina disappeared into the kitchen. Pamela was about to join them, with an offer to slice tomatoes. She was halfway across the patio when she heard Richard Larkin's voice.

He had a nice voice. She had admitted that from the start. It was deep, but gentle at the same time. She turned. He stepped hesitantly onto the patio from the path that led along the side of the house. He was carrying a six-pack of beer and wearing a pair of jeans so new that they still had horizontal creases where they'd been folded in the shop.

"Am I too late?" he said.

"No, not really. They haven't started grilling the sausages yet." Pamela gestured toward the grill, where the chicken pieces were now arranged around the edges.

He tilted his head in the direction of her gesture.

"Oh, I see. There's a sequence to it. Chicken first, and then sausages." He continued to stare at the grill.

Pamela took a step toward the sliding door. She was about to say that she'd let Bettina know the guest list was now complete, when Richard Larkin spoke again. "Would you like a beer?" He held up the six-pack. He looked very serious for someone making such an offer as that.

"I had one already," Pamela said. "There are plenty . . . in the cooler."

"Oh, of course." He lowered the six-pack back to his side. "The cooler."

"We could put yours in there too."

At that moment, the sliding door opened and Bettina stepped out. She greeted Richard with a hearty "Welcome!" and bustled over to give him a half hug. He smiled for the first time since he had arrived and Pamela noticed again how his smile transformed his face. "Let's get this beer into the cooler—and thank you for the watermelon, by the way." With her arm still around him, Bettina added, "You need to be introduced." And she led him away.

Meanwhile, Glenda was holding the platter of sausages while John plucked them up one by one and arranged them in sizzling rows on the grill. Maxie, Laine, and Nell emerged from the kitchen bearing their salads, complete with serving spoons, and headed toward the long table. Penny followed with two baskets of rolls sliced open to receive sausages. Bettina opened a beer for Richard, then hurried back into the kitchen. Pamela remembered the deviled eggs and hurried after her.

"Hey!" Richard greeted her when she stepped back through the sliding door with the platter of deviled eggs. He had been standing alone near the cooler and gazing across the lawn. Pamela realized the only man at the party who he really knew was Wilfred, and at the moment Wilfred was enjoying himself at the grill, deep in conversation with his cousin.

"I hope you've met some people," Pamela said.

"Oh, yes," he said. "Several. And I already know you and Penny . . . and my daughters, of course." He leaned closer to examine the platter of deviled eggs. "A hen," he said, pointing at the image in the platter's center. "Great image—so 1950s. And deviled eggs. I haven't had one in years." He looked up and his face softened. "Let me guess. Nell made these—she's the one with white hair, isn't she? My grandmother made them all the time. And her house was full of kitschy things like the platter."

"Actually," Pamela said, trying to suppress a smile. "I made them, and I collect deviled-egg platters. This is my favorite one. The hen looks so happy with herself."

Now he looked stern, except for his eyes, which stared directly into hers. "I should have known," he said. "I mean, lots of people can make deviled eggs. They don't have to be grandmothers. And you, of course, don't look like a grandmother at all. You look—" He paused, looking confused. People with smooth olive skin like his didn't blush, Pamela thought, or he would be blushing right now.

Bettina popped up at his elbow, carrying a dish of sliced tomatoes in each hand. "Ready to eat?" she said. "It's time." People were already lined up at the grill with their plates, as Wilfred served pieces of the golden-brown chicken and his cousin tucked sausages between buns.

Potato salad, tabouli with its bright flecks of fresh mint, and Nell's corn and bean salad marched down the middle of the long table. At each end was a bowl of sliced tomatoes. Pamela added her platter of deviled eggs to the arrangement. After a bit of scurrying and rearranging—and mustard and catsup fetched from the kitchen and fresh bottles of beer supplied from the cooler—seventeen people were seated, including two children on pillows. Wilfred and Bettina presided over the feast from opposite ends of the table.

No one seemed inclined to discuss the latest development in the murder case. Perhaps the men had exhausted the topic as they huddled over the grill, and Pamela knew any group Nell was part of would have had the subject changed the second it came up. And at such a long table, no one discussion topic can be general anyway. The occasional phrase drifting from Wilfred's end suggested he and Harold and Dave Dowling were exploring their shared interest in local history. Maxie and Karen Dowling had bonded over Karen's incipient motherhood, and Karen had taken charge of helping Maxie's older boy with his meal. Penny, Laine, and Sybil were sitting in a row laughing as much as they were talking.

Pamela hadn't intended to end up sitting next to Richard Larkin, but somehow here she was. She accepted his courtly offers to hold the salad bowls as she served herself and smiled when he exclaimed that he had never tasted a deviled egg as good as the one he'd sampled from her platter. But once the salads and the eggs had moved along, taking with them the conversational opportunities they offered, Pamela found herself at a loss for words. Bettina was only a few seats away, but she was turned in the other direction having a lively chat with Nell.

Pamela concentrated on eating, applying herself to the task as if the meal demanded her full attention. She allowed herself a quick glance at Richard, who seemed bent on giving the same impression. Even while chewing he kept his eyes focused on his plate. With such a hubbub of conversation all around, Pamela was amazed that the silence between them seemed so awkward. She tested several ice-breaking comments in her mind, settling on "Your daughter's tabouli is delicious."

He turned, looking as startled as if she'd announced a taste for human blood. Terribly shy, Pamela said to herself, awkward in social situations. Though he hadn't seemed so shy when she first met him.

"The tabouli," she said. "Your daughter made it. It's awfully good."

"Yes . . . yes, she is. It is." The look in his eyes was almost desperate. He's searching for something to say, Pamela said to herself. She was about to make a comment about the sausages when Bettina came to the rescue.

She swiveled in their direction and beamed at Richard. "So what do you think of our suburban barbecues, neighbor?" she asked.

"Great, nice, very good food." He nodded enthusiastically.

"And Arborville? Is our little town growing on you? This will be your first summer here." He nodded again and Pamela thought he seemed to relax. Bettina had that effect on people. Bettina chatted on about the weather as Richard nodded, taking occasional bites. "Of course summer means yard work," she added.

"I've hired Joe Taylor," Richard said. "Things have sprouted up everywhere. I'm too busy to tend it all myself, and besides I don't know what's a plant and what's a weed."

"He'll be a big help," Bettina said. "He's been doing some work for Nell." She turned to Nell as if to solicit her testimony, but Nell was now deep in conversation with Glenda. Turning back to Richard, she said, "Wilfred loves to get his hands dirty. Otherwise we'd need help too. I couldn't bear it if we couldn't keep my perennial borders in shape."

He nodded again, and leaned back to include Pamela in the conversation. "Do you have perennial borders?" he said.

Pamela hastily finished chewing a bite of chicken. "Too much shade," she said at last. "Just enough sun for a few tomatoes and some daylilies. I love perennial borders though."

"Miranda Bonham was a wonderful gardener," Bettina said.

"Her perennial borders were fantastic," Pamela said. "I could see them from my kitchen window, and I enjoyed them just as much as if they were my own."

Bettina sighed. "It's a pity she had to move, after all that work."

"I suppose it is," Richard said thoughtfully. "But I understood that she and her husband wanted to live someplace warm."

"They did. And of course we're delighted to have you for a neighbor now." Bettina set down her fork and squeezed his arm. "Wilfred so enjoys talking to you about his dollhouse projects."

The children had already left the table and were hopping around on the lawn. But the salads, eggs, and tomatoes made their way around again, and Wilfred returned to the grill, calling out that anyone who wanted more chicken or another sausage was welcome to claim it. Richard's chat with Bettina seemed to have given him the courage to launch a conversation with Pamela. Soon they were talking quite comfortably about their jobs, and the volunteer work he did every summer in Maine.

Chapter Fourteen

Half an hour passed. Finally all forks reposed on empty or almost empty plates. "Dessert still to come," Bettina sang out, as she and Maxie and Dave and Karen Dowling began clearing the table.

"I can help," Richard announced suddenly. He jumped up and seized his and Pamela's plates. Pamela watched him lope across the patio, taller than any other man there and wearing the stiff new jeans. When he reemerged, he was carrying a serious-looking knife, its gleaming silver blade over a foot long. Bettina bustled after him. She pointed to a small table that had served to hold barbecue sauce, and the chicken and sausages awaiting their turn on the grill. He handed Bettina the knife, stooped over the cooler, and removed the lid. When he rose again, he was bearing the watermelon, wet from its sojourn in melting ice. Bettina, looking for all the world like a nurse assisting at a surgical procedure, handed over the knife and watched with fascination as he made the first incision.

Pamela was watching too, admiring the precision

with which Richard sliced the watermelon into two
equal halves and then four equal quarters. But when
Karen appeared with her bowl of chocolate chip cookies,
she remembered the lemon bars. As she stepped
back out onto the patio with them, Richard was offering child-sized slices of watermelon to Bettina's
grandsons.

"You carved up that watermelon like an expert,"
Pamela said when they were again seated at the long
table with slices of watermelon before them. The cookies and lemon bars were making their way around.

"Carving a watermelon is rather like carpentry,"
he said. "Measure twice and cut once—the same rule
applies."

"Do you do a lot of carpentry?" She'd pictured him
spending his workdays at a desk in a Manhattan office
with chic furnishings and a stunning view. She stole a
glance at his hands. They were large and well shaped,
but they didn't look like a worker's hands.

"Sometimes it's part of the work in Maine," he said.
"Helping people use recycled materials to fix up their
houses." He concentrated on his slice of watermelon
until it was reduced to a pale pink crescent shading to
white, with a green peel. The lemon bars arrived at
their end of the table and Bettina made sure to point
out to Richard that Pamela had made them. He barely
had a chance to take a bite and offer the requisite
compliment before Wilfred pulled up a chair between
him and Bettina. "Pamela has outdone herself," he
said to nobody in particular, reaching for a lemon bar.
"This is my third." Then he leaned toward Richard
and said, "I've made a lot of progress on my model of
the Mittendorf House. Come on down to the basement
and take a look."

Wilfred led him off, lemon bar in hand. They walked across the patio, Richard bending solicitously toward Wilfred's white-thatched head. "So nice looking," Bettina said. "You and he had quite the conversation."

Pamela stood up. "Why don't I help you clear away?" They were the only people left at the table. The men, minus Wilfred and Richard, were standing around the cooler, fresh bottles of beer in hand. Penny and Richard's daughters had retired to the lawn chairs under the big tree. Karen Dowling and Maxie were watching the two boys caper in the grass. The other women were in the kitchen. Pamela and Bettina joined them, washing dishes that would go home with their owners, packaging up leftovers, and filling the dishwasher with plates and silver. Pamela's deviled-egg platter sat on the pine table, one deviled egg remaining.

The sliding door opened and Karen and Dave Dowling peeked in. "We're on our way," he said.

"Wonderful party," Karen chimed in. "Thank you so much."

"And thank *you* for the cookies," Bettina said. "They were certainly a success. Your bowl is empty." She hugged Karen and handed over the plastic bowl with the snap-on lid. "I guess we're at your house Tuesday night," she added.

"It might be chocolate chip cookies again," Karen said, blushing slightly. "They're the only dessert I know how to make."

A few at a time, the other guests bade their farewells, picked up their bowls, trays, or platters, and went on their way. Wilfred's cousin John offered Nell and Harold a ride up the hill, collected his wife, and made a detour to the basement to tell Wilfred good-bye. Bettina's son, daughter-in-law, and grandsons got special hugs from Bettina and called good-bye to Wilfred down the basement stairs. Penny stuck her head in to say she and Laine and Sybil were heading back across the street and to tell Richard to bring the tabouli bowl home.

"What are those men up to?" Bettina said when she and Pamela were alone in the kitchen. They chatted for a few minutes about the barbecue, pausing when they heard feet coming up the basement stairs.

"Rick gave me some good ideas about how to do the windows," Wilfred said as he stepped into the kitchen, Richard following behind.

"Nice job," Richard said. "I'm impressed. You got a very convincing sandstone effect with that clay."

The deviled-egg platter with the one remaining deviled egg still sat on the pine table. Wilfred stopped a few feet away. "I see you eyeing that egg," Bettina said.

"It's yours." Pamela moved the platter a bit closer to the table's edge.

"Unless . . ." Wilfred looked up at Richard.

"No, really." Richard laughed and waved his hands as if to ward off the egg.

"Well . . . waste not, want not," Wilfred said, and popped the egg into his mouth.

"Tomorrow morning then," Bettina said to Pamela. "In the library parking lot." They stood at the end of the driveway, accompanied by Richard. Pamela carried her tray and her platter, and Richard carried the bright-red tabouli bowl.

"It's very nice of you to talk to Wilfred about the dollhouses," Pamela said after Bettina had retreated toward her backyard and they had set out across the street.

"I'm trying to fit in. Besides, he's an interesting guy," Richard said. "Reminds me of the father I always wished I had."

"You didn't—?" Pamela wasn't sure how to finish the question.

"Oh, I had a dad, a decent dad, but he was always busy with work." They'd reached the sidewalk in front of Pamela's house. Richard looked toward his own house, then down at the sidewalk, then back at her. "Could I ask you something?" She tilted her head to meet his eyes. They had that desperate look they sometimes got.

"Yes?" She wasn't sure whether it was a good idea to seem too eager.

"What's a perennial border?"

"Oh!" The word burst out accompanied by a laugh. He took a step back and his eyes shifted from desperate to hurt. "I didn't mean to laugh," she said. "Nobody would know unless they gardened, and even then, not necessarily. I thought you were going to ask me something . . ." Her voice trailed off. What had she thought he was going to ask her? "I'll show you," she said. "Come with me."

She led him onto his lawn and along the side of his hedge past his recycling containers and his side door. When they reached his backyard, she advanced toward the unruly swathe of vegetation stretching along the wooden fence that marked the boundary between his lot and the lot behind.

"These are iris," she said, pointing to a plant with long blade-shaped leaves and stiff stalks topped by the shriveled remains of flowers. "And these are peonies."

The few remaining blooms, blowsy globes faded to the barest tint of pink, drooped among the deep green foliage. Below, the ground was strewn with petals already turning brown. "And these are cone flowers, and salvia, and goldenrod"—she paced along the edge of the flower bed—"and black-eyed Susans, and yarrow."

She paused. "And this is a weed." She pointed to a sturdy plant that was already taller than the peony bushes. "And there are more weeds down there." She waved her hand. "And also that tall grass is crabgrass, and it will take over if you don't pull it out." To illustrate, she leaned over, gathered a handful of the tall, stiff blades, and pulled. Up came a satisfying clump, trailing roots and small knobs of dirt.

"The point of a perennial garden," she said, "is that the plants come back year after year, and people plant them so the colors and sizes and shapes make a nice design. But you have to tend it, or it just gets wild—like this." She paused, feeling a bit breathless, and looked back toward Richard, who was still standing where she'd left him when she began to pace. She was still holding the clump of crabgrass. He was studying her as if she herself was a botanical specimen.

"So"—she shrugged, suddenly feeling self-conscious—"that's pretty much it."

"I guess it is." He stepped across the grass and reached out for the crabgrass. She put it into his hand. "I'll do something with this," he said. He continued studying her. "Maybe you'll come and look at it again . . . when I get it fixed up. We could sit out here." Now he glanced away, toward two Adirondack chairs sitting in the middle of the grass. "The Bonhams left their lawn furniture."

"I can see the border from my kitchen window," Pamela said, and then wished she hadn't.

* * *

Back at home she changed out of the fancy blouse, noticing as she caught a glimpse of herself in her bedroom mirror, that her eyes seemed darker and somehow mysterious. Maybe it had something to do with the deep colors in the blouse. Downstairs, she looked out the kitchen window. Richard Larkin was on his knees pulling crabgrass out of the perennial border.

Chapter Fifteen

"Well, he's really up a creek without a paddle!" Because she was talking about Detective Clayborn, Bettina waited until she was a goodly distance from the police station to make that announcement. It was Monday morning and Pamela had been waiting for her in the parking lot shared by the police department and the library. "He doesn't have any idea what to do next." Bettina shook her head pityingly. "Of course, he didn't tell me that, but I could see he wasn't himself."

"They don't have any other suspects?" Pamela said. "You said he didn't get excited when you told him about Marcus Verteel."

"He couldn't see how insulting each other in the pages of a journal devoted to eighteenth-century history could escalate into one guy clunking the other with a rock—or even how two guys writing a book on the same subject could be a problem. And besides, how would the aardvark come into it? This morning I suggested there might be a romantic angle, as in romance gone awry," Bettina said. "But I didn't tell him about the hat," she added quickly. "He said no one they had interviewed after the murder said anything about Jefferson being involved with a woman."

Pamela reached into the canvas bag she carried and pulled up the orange and chartreuse hat. "This is our own scoop then." She tucked the hat back in her bag and they strolled toward the library.

"Did anything interesting happen after Richard walked you home last night?" Bettina asked.

"I showed him what a perennial border is," Pamela said.

"He certainly liked your eggs." Pamela scowled at her friend, who was suppressing a smile. "You looked nice in that outfit."

Pamela had reverted to her uniform of jeans and a casual blouse. Bettina was wearing light-blue pants that ended right below her knees, a matching sleeveless top, and wedge-heeled espadrilles with ties that wrapped around her ankles. They strolled past the azaleas, the pretty wooden bench, and the rock garden with the rock-sized gap in the border.

The Arborville Public Library was quiet on a Monday morning. A few young mothers browsed the children's section with toddlers in tow. In the chairs near the big windows that looked out onto the street, a gray-haired man paged through a newspaper. The young woman Pamela had spoken to on Saturday and recognized as one of Penny's classmates from Arborville High was on duty again at the circulation counter.

Pamela greeted the young woman with a whispered "Hello," though she knew libraries weren't the bastions of silence they had been when she was a child. "I was here Saturday," she added, "looking for Nancy Billings. Is she in today?"

The young woman gave her a curious look, then nodded toward a row of shelves where a mousy woman with faded auburn hair was reshelving books from a wheeled cart.

"Her hair *is* kind of red, but it's not wild or flyaway," the young woman noted, somewhat unnecessarily.

Pamela tugged the orange and chartreuse hat from her bag and shaped her lips into her social smile. The errand, she reminded herself, was to seem simply an effort to track down an interesting knitting pattern. The mousy woman—Nancy Billings—was studying the spine of a book as they approached. She stooped to slip it into place on a lower shelf and caught sight of Pamela and Bettina as she rose. Her eyes didn't linger on their faces, however. They darted immediately to the hat. Pamela held it in both hands, the ears flopping over her knuckles and the tail dangling nearly to her knees.

"Oh, no!" Nancy Billings held up her hands in mock alarm. "I plead guilty." She smiled, a smile that revealed pretty teeth and lit up her plain face. She reached toward the hat. "I knew it wouldn't stay gone," she said.

Pamela hadn't expected this reaction, though she wasn't sure what reaction she had expected. How to request a knitting pattern from someone who seemed determined to disown the creation? But Bettina came to the rescue.

"We love the hat," she said. Nancy's face registered amazement, then curiosity. "So imaginative . . ." Bettina paused.

Pamela took over. "Though maybe a different color scheme would be more wearable for most people. I found it at St. Willibrod's rummage sale, and the woman at the yarn crafts table said you'd donated it. We're part of the Arborville knitting club. I was wondering if we could get the pattern for the hat."

"Oh, heavens!" Nancy showed her pretty teeth again. "I didn't make it. I'm quite hopeless when it comes to crafts. It was a gift from my cousin, Nightingale, to my daughter. Sara's in high school and would never wear such an odd thing, so . . . the rummage sale."

"Could we get the pattern from . . . Nightingale?" Bettina asked.

Nancy shrugged. "I don't see her that often. She's a total free spirit, if you know what I mean. Nightingale isn't her real name—she just calls herself that, now. She called herself something different before, back when she was a Wiccan. Her real name is Alison Denny."

Pamela took over. "Does she live in Arborville?"

"No." Nancy laughed. "Haversack. She'd never be able to afford Arborville. She doesn't work, and I don't know what she uses for money. And forget email or even the phone to track her down. Half the time she doesn't turn the phone on, and the other half she hasn't paid the bill."

"I know our club members would love to have the pattern for the hat," Bettina said.

"Well, like you say, maybe a different color scheme . . ." Nancy didn't seem convinced. She reached out to finger the tail.

"And for a younger recipient," Bettina supplied.

"I can give you her address if you're so determined," Nancy said. Bettina pulled a notepad and pen from her purse, and Nancy dictated a number and street. "Apartment 3B," she added, "but she won't respond if you write. No sense of responsibility whatsoever."

"You didn't ask Nancy if her cousin has red hair," Bettina said as she led the way to her car.

"Neither did you," Pamela said. "I couldn't figure

out how to work it in, since as far as she knew we were just trying to track down the pattern for the hat. If her cousin could give us the pattern, why would it matter what color her hair was?"

"It's probably her though, don't you think? The woman that nosy neighbor saw coming and going." Bettina's car was on the far side of the lot, near the kiddy playground that formed part of the town park. The playground was already busy, with nannies chatting on benches as children shrieked on the slides and giggled on the merry-go-round.

"Yes," Pamela said. "It's probably her. So . . . off to Haversack?"

"Off to Haversack." Bettina unlocked the passenger side of her faithful Toyota and Pamela climbed in. As Bettina settled into place behind the steering wheel, she remarked, "I'm not sure I've ever met a free spirit."

Haversack was the county seat and locus of the courthouse and the jail. The Haversack River separated it from its affluent suburban neighbors to the east. Nightingale's apartment building proved to be a sturdy brick structure with a flat roof and a fire escape, like something one would see in a black and white photo from the turn of the last century. Its neighbors along the busy commercial street where it was located included a car wash and an auto body shop. A billboard on the corner announced the services of a personal injury lawyer with a 1-800 number.

The narrow card next to the bell for apartment 3B was illegible, having long since succumbed to the elements. Pamela backed up to double-check the street address carved into the stone lintel over the doorway and, satisfied that she and Bettina were in the right place, gave the button a firm push. They waited, blinking in the bright sunlight reflecting off the sidewalk and the passing cars. After a few minutes, Pamela gave the bell another push. There was still no response. She and Bettina looked at each other. "Off somewhere being a free spirit," Bettina murmured.

As they stood there, the door opened partway and a woman started to push through, tugging a small upright cart laden with what looked like laundry.

"You've got *your* hands full," Bettina exclaimed, leaning an elbow against the door to open it farther.

"Why, thank you," the woman said. Her homely face and shapeless body were offset by her outfit, brightly-patterned leggings and a form-fitting tank top. She stepped out onto the concrete walk that ended at the building's entrance, and the heavy glass door closed behind her. "I haven't met you before," she said with a smile that revealed a missing tooth. "Did you just move in?"

"We're looking for somebody," Bettina said. "Nightingale. Do you know her?"

Shaking her head slowly, the woman said, "Not to talk to. She's kind of weird, used to be a witch somebody told me. Not a bad person though, at least not anymore."

"She doesn't answer her bell," Pamela said.

The woman continued shaking her head. "Now that you mention it, I haven't seen her for days. Or heard her. We're on the same floor and she's got this guitar. Live and let live is what I say, but not after eleven p.m."

"Could we leave a note?" Pamela said. "In her mailbox maybe? Are the mailboxes in there?" She nodded toward the small foyer visible through the heavy glass of the door.

"No way to get into the boxes unless you're the

mailman," the woman said. "He has a key. But"—she reached into a nondescript handbag that dangled from one handle of the cart and came up with a set of keys—"you could slip a note under her door. I've got laundry to do, but I'll let you in. You two look honest."

Bettina pushed the door open as the woman twisted the key in the lock. The woman aimed her cart toward the sidewalk and started off, but then turned.

"You could ask in the park," she said. "She takes sandwiches for the guys who hang out there, plays her guitar. Like I said, she's not a bad person."

A steep flight of stairs confronted Pamela and Bettina once they stepped into the small, dark foyer. "No elevator, I guess," Bettina said. "I wonder how that woman made it down with her laundry cart."

"I suppose people get used to it," Pamela said. "All apartment buildings were walkups once." She regarded the stairs. "Apartment 3B. Let's start climbing."

Both were panting by the time they reached the third floor. A hallway with grimy and worn carpeting stretched from the front to the back of the building, with a small window at each end. Four doors opened off each side of the hallway. The door they were seeking was halfway down on the right.

Pamela knocked. Bettina gave her a quizzical look.

"Maybe she just doesn't like to buzz people into the building unless she's expecting someone," Pamela said. "We might as well check if she's in there before we push a note under the door."

"But that woman with the laundry said she hadn't seen—or heard—her for days."

Pamela nodded and knocked again. She put her ear to the door. Now Bettina looked worried. "Do you hear anything?" she asked with a frown that carved a tiny wrinkle between her carefully shaped brows.

"Not really," Pamela said, biting her lip and looking toward the ceiling as if in search of an idea. "I wonder if there's some way we could get into the apartment." She reached for the doorknob and gave it a sharp twist.

Bettina uttered a muted squeal, but the door remained closed.

"Okay," Pamela said. "Let's write that note. Then we'll visit Nightingale's friends in the park. The people she brings sandwiches to."

"Florence!" Bettina said suddenly. "Florence Nightingale."

"That could be it," Pamela said. "She fancies herself a ministering angel."

"Could she also be a killer then?" The wrinkle between Bettina's brows deepened. She pulled her notepad and pen from her purse. Pamela dictated as Bettina wrote. "Dear Nightingale . . ." She paused. "Wait a minute—we can't tell her the hat she made for her niece ended up at the St. Willibrod's rummage sale."

Bettina looked up from her task. "We'll say we're friends of Nancy Billings, and she showed it to us because she knows we're knitters."

"Yes, that's it," Pamela said. "Put that, and say we'd love to share the pattern with our knitting club, and then put our names and phone numbers." Bettina finished the note, tore the sheet of paper from her notepad, folded it in half, and pushed it under the door. "We'll wait a couple of days, and if we don't hear from her we'll come back. I'm not sure I'd respond if somebody I'd never heard of pushed a note under my door."

"What park do you think that woman meant?" Bettina asked as they made their way back down the stairs.

"Probably the one we drove past when we crossed

the river," Pamela said. "The stretch of grass that turns into a pond every time the Haversack floods."

The man was sunning himself on a bench with his eyes closed and a beer can in his hand. The river was low, the water a murky green. The park extended all the way to the riverbank, where scraggly grass gave way to a line of jagged rocks streaked with moss. On the opposite bank, the well-groomed grounds of Wendelstaff College sloped down to the water's edge.

Pamela hesitated a few yards from the bench with the dozing man. It was getting on toward lunchtime, but no one else was in the park, suggesting that perhaps sandwiches hadn't been forthcoming lately, and the park's regulars had changed their routines. "He looks so comfortable. I hate to disturb him," Pamela whispered to Bettina.

"Then we won't," Bettina said. The man's bench was one in a row that faced the river. Bettina made her way over the grass, Pamela following, and lowered herself onto a neighboring bench. Pamela joined her. "Pretty, isn't it?" Bettina nodded toward the Wendelstaff campus.

"It makes me think of Marcus Verteel," Pamela said. "If we actually track Nightingale down and decide she didn't have anything to do with killing Randall Jefferson, he's the only suspect we've got left."

"Well, there *is* the ghost." Bettina half laughed as she said it.

"I don't know how we'd follow up on that though." They sat in silence, gazing across the water, until a man's voice spoke.

"Good morning, ladies." The dozing man was awake.

"Good morning, sir," Bettina replied in her most sociable tones. "How are you today?"

"Well, just fine I'd say." His voice suggested the can of beer in his hand wasn't his first of the day, but he seemed genial enough. "I ain't seen you ladies down here before." He looked to be in his fifties and was dressed in jeans and a T-shirt.

"We're looking for somebody." Bettina scooted along the bench till she reached the end and turned to face the man. "A red-haired woman who comes down here sometimes with a guitar."

His weathered face creased into a smile. "That would be Nightingale." The smile vanished. "She ain't in trouble?"

"Oh, no!" Bettina shook her head. "She's a friend of a friend. We were in the neighborhood and thought we'd stop by to say hello. We heard she's a pretty good guitar player."

"She is that." He smiled again. "But she ain't been around . . ." He frowned and looked off toward the river. "Ain't been around three, four days . . . no, make that five . . . or six. Seven maybe."

Bettina turned back toward Pamela and raised her eyebrows, then turned back toward the man. "Did she say anything about a trip? A plan to go somewhere?"

One shoulder rose, and he pursed his lips. "Not to me."

Pamela slid down the bench until she was side by side with Bettina. She leaned around her friend to face the man. "And you haven't seen her for a week?"

The man raised his empty hand and counted off slowly, wiggling one finger at a time. "Monday . . . Tuesday . . . Wednesday . . ." He shook his head. "Not all week." He raised the beer can and, seeming to realize it was empty, lowered it again. "Not all week," he said again.

"How about last Sunday," Pamela said. "Not yesterday but the Sunday before."

He pursed his lips again. "Couldn't say for sure. That was a long time ago."

"It was," Pamela said, half to herself. She leaned back against the bench.

"Well . . ." Bettina looked into Pamela's eyes and smiled a hopeless smile.

"You're right," Pamela said in a quiet voice. "This is as far as we'll get." They stood up. The man watched them.

"If she comes back, I'll tell her you were here," he said.

"She doesn't know us," Bettina said. "We're friends of a friend."

The man jiggled the empty beer can. "You ain't got any spare change, do you?"

Pamela reached in her purse and came up with a ten-dollar bill. "Have a sandwich too, please," she said as she slipped it into the man's grimy hand.

As they walked across the grass toward where the park's few parking spaces had been marked out on a patch of faded asphalt, Pamela suddenly chuckled. "Well," she said, "you managed to work in the red hair."

"I did," Bettina said with a contented smile. "Now we know it's definitely her."

"But we don't know where she is."

"No, we don't know where she is."

"But we know she's disappeared," Pamela said. "That could be a clue in itself."

"You're right!" Bettina picked up her pace. "Let's talk about it over lunch."

"A tuna melt and a vanilla milkshake," Pamela said, handing the oversized menu back to the server.

"And I'll have the same," Bettina added, holding out her menu as well.

They were in a booth at Hyler's Luncheonette on Arborville Avenue, facing each other across a worn wooden table and sitting on benches upholstered in burgundy Naugahyde. The booth was in a remote corner, near the swinging doors that led to the kitchen, and they'd chosen it in hopes of avoiding conversations with their fellow townspeople. Certainly the dramatic arrest and then release of Brad Striker had reawakened interest in the "Killer Aardvark" murder case—if, indeed, interest had ever slept.

"Disappearing could mean Nightingale did it," Pamela said. "Our friend in the park didn't have too clear a sense of time, but it sounded like she hadn't been to the park at least since the Sunday of Arborfest, and maybe not even that day."

Bettina nodded. "So they quarrel Saturday night in the parking lot. She clunks him with the rock and hides him in the booth. And on Sunday while everybody's at the parade, she puts the aardvark on his chest." Bettina nodded again, but Pamela frowned.

"Why bother with the aardvark? Why not just take off as soon as she realizes she's killed him?"

"She's going to need money for a getaway," Bettina said. "She goes up to his house and grabs a few portable goodies that can be sold—or pawned. I'm sure Haversack has pawnshops."

"How would she get in his house?" Pamela said.

"Maybe she has a key—given their special relationship, *whatever* it was." Bettina looked up. "Ah," she said, "the milkshakes."

The milkshakes arrived in frosty glasses, tall and slim, etched with trails left by ice-cream drips and crowned with a froth of creamy bubbles. Pamela peeled a straw, slipped it through the bubbles, and took a long sip of the cool, sweet liquid with its slight hint of vanilla.

"Why bother with the aardvark?" she said again, gazing at Bettina, who was engrossed in sampling her own milkshake.

"Um. That is delicious!" Bettina held onto her straw, lifted her head, and gazed back. "Maybe she hates organized sports, being a free spirit and all. She kills him because of the unrequited-love angle, but then gets the idea to implicate Brad Striker. And she knows about Jefferson's disapproval of the sports program, of course, because—after all—she knows him quite well."

"Why did she take *two* aardvarks?" Pamela took another sip of her milkshake then slid it off to the side to wait until her tuna melt arrived.

Bettina shrugged. "Confuse people? Keep them guessing?"

Pamela shuddered. "Or keep them wondering who's going to die next?"

Chapter Sixteen

At that moment, the sandwiches arrived, on cream-colored oval plates with slender pickle spears tucked alongside. Gobbets of tuna salad and golden streaks of melted cheddar were barely contained by bread that had been grilled to buttery and toasty perfection. Forks were required, and for a few minutes neither Pamela nor Bettina spoke.

After half of her sandwich had been dispatched, Pamela ate a pickle spear. "I keep returning to the Florence Nightingale idea," she said, wiping her fingers on a napkin.

"Um?" Bettina continued chewing but set her fork down.

"Taking sandwiches to the men in the park. She seems like a charitable person, not a murderer. Maybe there was something charitable about her relationship with Randall Jefferson."

Bettina swallowed. "He didn't need money. Or sandwiches."

"Maybe he was lonely," Pamela said. "Unable to make friends because he was so focused on his books." She picked up her fork and aimed it at the second half of the sandwich.

"But then why would she disappear?" Bettina's voice rose in pitch, and she added, "And why wouldn't she go to the funeral?"

Pamela set her fork down suddenly, and it clinked against the heavy plate. "Maybe she's dead too!" she exclaimed. "Someone was after them both."

Bettina's eyes grew wide. "The second aardvark!"

Pamela nodded. "The second aardvark."

The distance between Hyler's Luncheonette and Orchard Street was only a few blocks, but Bettina's car awaited them in the parking lot behind the hardware store. Pamela didn't speak until they turned off Arborville Avenue and were nearing Bettina's house. Then she said, "I don't think we should tell Nancy Billings that her cousin has disappeared."

"No," Bettina said. "We shouldn't. At least not yet."

Bettina pulled into her driveway and parked, and Pamela climbed out of the car. Looking across the street, she could see that her mail had arrived. The ends of a few envelopes protruded from under the hinged cover of her mailbox. And apparently reluctant to jam the day's batch of catalogs into a mailbox designed for an earlier era, the mail carrier had tossed them onto the porch. Next to the untidy stack of catalogs was a package the size of a shoebox.

Back on her own side of the street, Pamela climbed the steps to her porch. Slinging her canvas bag and purse over her shoulder, she gathered the envelopes and stooped to collect the rest of the mail, reaching out to corral the catalogs first. But the package distracted her from that task. It, in fact, *was* a shoebox, with no additional wrapping and no address.

Later it occurred to her that, given the current state of things in Arborville, a warier person would, at that moment, have retreated indoors and called the police. But, despite having come upon a dead body in her knitting group's Arborfest booth only a week earlier, Pamela wasn't a wary person. She woke up every morning expecting the day to unfold predictably, just the way a knitting project moved predictably toward completion, with only an occasional dropped stitch that could easily be picked up again. Besides, the shoebox bore the logo of an upscale brand that she recognized from advertisements for the department store that anchored the local mall.

So, not being a wary person, and not imagining that someone with a taste for such an elegant brand of shoes could have evil in mind, she scooped the shoebox up. She carried it and the envelopes to the kitchen table, shedding her purse and the canvas bag containing the hat on her way through the entry.

Could the box even contain shoes? A teasing gift from Bettina, delivered by Wilfred while they were out, intended to further perk up her wardrobe? She lifted the lid to discover that the contents—whatever they were—had been swathed in tissue paper. She lifted a flap of the paper, caught her breath, and stepped back from the table.

The experience wasn't quite as dramatic as the moment when she pulled the canvas panel loose at Arborfest and discovered the body of Randall Jefferson. But just like then, the surface under her feet no longer felt solid, the familiar glazed tiles of her kitchen floor swaying as she fought to keep her balance. She sank into the chair nearest her, still holding the shoebox lid as if it had been grafted to her fingers.

Lying in the box, cushioned on a bed of crumpled tissue paper, was a miniature version of Randall Jefferson, complete with natty jacket and bow tie. But unlike Randall Jefferson in real life, or even in death, the figure bristled with pins, ordinary sewing pins except for an especially large pin, like an old-fashioned hat pin, in its forehead.

Bettina was there in a flash, Wilfred following close behind, the apron he wore when he did his cooking projects tied over his bib overalls. "Not a threat," Bettina declared in a common-sense tone that soothed Pamela immensely. "At least not directed at you. Otherwise, it would *be* you." She reached into the box and raised the figure aloft. Wilfred actually laughed.

"No ill of the dead and all," he observed, "but I can think of more than one person who'd have been happy to stick him full of pins while he was still alive."

"It was sitting on the porch with all my other mail," Pamela said. "But it wasn't really mail. It was just in this shoebox, without an address or anything." She displayed the lid of the box, which bore no markings except the swirling curlicues of the upscale brand's logo.

"No aardvark." Bettina steered a finger among the pins to point at the figure's chest. "So I don't think it's somebody still fixated on the 'Killer Aardvark' theme."

"Why put it on my porch though?"

Bettina shrugged. "It's a clue? Somebody knows we've been poking around and wants to help us? First the killer makes this . . . *doll* . . . of Jefferson and sticks it full of pins, and then the killer goes after Jefferson in person."

Pamela's face had brightened as Bettina spoke, but now she frowned. "Having the doll isn't helpful if we don't know who made it."

"Maybe we *do* know." Bettina set the doll on the kitchen table and began pulling the tissue out of the box. Wilfred grabbed each piece, smoothed it out, and examined both sides.

"Nothing," all three said in unison after a small pile of uncrumpled tissue had accumulated next to the doll.

"How about the box?" Pamela said. She peered inside, then turned it in her hands to examine the sides and bottom.

Bettina reached for the lid. "Nothing inside the lid either," she reported, setting it atop the box. They all looked at each other.

"I'll take it to Clayborn," Bettina said. "That will be best."

"And besides," Wilfred said with a chuckle, "then he'll owe her a favor."

Upstairs, Pamela sat down at her computer and removed Catrina from the keyboard. An email message from her boss at *Fiber Craft* awaited, with instructions to evaluate ten more submissions (attached) and advise for or against publication. She set to work, hoping to be distracted from this strange new development in the Randall Jefferson murder case. But she found it hard to concentrate. Whoever had left the Jefferson doll on her front porch obviously knew where she lived and had something on his or her mind.

She pushed her chair back from her desk and gazed toward the window. At least the day was bright. It was hard to feel too threatened on a beautiful May afternoon, and Wilfred and Bettina were just across the street. She returned to the article she'd been reading, made a determined effort to focus, and labored steadily until a craving for coffee led her downstairs.

With a cup of coffee reheated from breakfast in hand, she considered taking her break on the front porch. Through the lace that curtained the oval window, she could see green lawns, flowering shrubs, and tree branches swaying in the summer breeze—and no mysterious callers lurking nearby. But nevertheless she retreated instead to the safety of the kitchen table, where she pondered the article she'd just finished reading. Its author had traveled by bus to a Ghanaian city where Kente cloth was still made on traditional looms and had learned the techniques herself. How adventurous some people were!

Back in her office, Pamela once again removed Catrina from her computer keyboard and wrote an enthusiastic recommendation that the Kente cloth article be published. She was deeply immersed in the world of contemporary lace-making when Catrina leapt from the windowsill where she'd been napping and cocked her ears toward the hall. The front door opened and Penny's voice sang out, "I'm home—but I'm going out again!"

Pamela checked the clock. Sun still glowed through the curtains at her office windows, but somehow it had gotten to be six p.m. She closed the file she'd been reading, arched her back and stretched, and made her way to the stairs. Penny stood in the entry, going through the mail.

"Does anyone your age get snail mail anymore?" Pamela asked with a laugh as she descended.

"Grandma sends me things," Penny said. She was wearing the yellow dress with the parade of roosters at the hem. "Lorie and I are meeting one of her friends from her college. We're going to the mall." She set the mail back on the mail table. "Anything new?"

Something was new. Pamela was debating whether to tell Penny about the shoebox with the mysterious contents when a tapping called her attention to the door. Through the lace that curtained the oval window she could see a short figure dressed in light blue, with a bobbing head topped by vivid red hair. Penny twisted the knob, the door popped open, and Bettina stepped in.

"I've brought you some leftovers from the barbecue," she said, setting a large plastic container on the mail table. She studied her friend for a few seconds. "Well . . ." She smiled. "You look like you've recovered." She laid a gentle hand on Pamela's shoulder.

"Recovered from what?" Penny glanced from Bettina to Pamela and back to Bettina. The smile with which she'd greeted Bettina was replaced by a look of alarm. She focused her eyes on her mother. "*Mo-om*," she said, her voice rising. "What happened that you'd have to recover from?"

"Nothing, nothing!" Bettina reached her other hand toward Penny, but Penny stepped back.

"You're up to something. Both of you. And it has to do with that murder," Penny said. "Am I the only person around here with any sense?"

"It's okay," Bettina said. "I gave it to the police."

"Gave *what* to the police?" Penny sounded frantic. "*Mo-om!* I don't want to have to worry about you."

"Let's all go in here." Pamela took her daughter by the hand and started for the kitchen. Bettina followed, dodging Catrina, who had been waiting near the kitchen door.

When they were all seated at the table, Pamela

described coming home and finding the shoebox on the porch and the miniature version of Randall Jefferson inside, stuck full of pins.

"Kids make them when they hate a teacher," Penny said, nodding.

Bettina agreed. "That's what Clayborn said."

"So, does he think it's a clue?" Pamela asked.

"He's looking into it." Bettina's expression was noncommittal. "At least that's what he said. Maybe he'll have it checked for DNA, and compare the DNA with DNA from the rock." She went on, "But I don't know if it *is* much of a clue. Let's say somebody made the doll because they hated Jefferson, and then they killed Jefferson. Wouldn't it be stupid to then advertise that they hated Jefferson?"

"Mean girls," Penny said suddenly. Pamela and Bettina stared at her. "Arborville High is full of mean girls. The person who made the doll is most likely *not* the person who left it on the porch. What a great way to get your rival mean girl in trouble—let the world, or at least the Arborville knitting club, think that she might be the murderer."

"But then, wouldn't there have been a note?" Pamela said. "Something like, 'This doll was made by . . . whoever . . . because Mr. Jefferson gave her an F in American History, and she detested him.'"

"Maybe there *was* a note," Penny said. "Today was quite breezy. Maybe the breeze blew the note away."

Suddenly all three of them were on their feet and out the door. But a search of the yard turned up no doll-related messages.

Penny hurried upstairs to change into jeans for her trip to the mall, and Bettina set off across the street. "Enjoy your barbecue leftovers," she called. "No cooking for me tonight either." Back in the kitchen, Pamela scooped a few tablespoons of cat food into one of Catrina's special bowls. She watched as Catrina circled the bowl, tail erect, as if stalking a creature envisioned as a potential meal and contemplating the best angle from which to attack. Then, as Catrina settled down to eat, Pamela opened the plastic container Bettina had brought.

After a dinner of leftover barbecued chicken and three kinds of salad, Pamela finished her work for the magazine then retreated to the sofa. She found a British cooking program on the television and picked up the nearly finished scarf she was making for Nell to give to the day laborers. Soon Catrina was perched nearby, forelegs tucked beneath her chest and half-closed eyes mere yellow slivers. The steady motion of the needles and the soothing British voices lulled Pamela into a similar state.

She awoke suddenly to find that she'd dropped her needles, as well as several stitches. She shook herself awake, imagined the satisfaction with which she'd hand the finished scarf over to Nell the next evening, and got back to work.

Catrina had been bewitched. With her jet-black fur and yellow eyes, she'd always looked like a suitable accomplice to a practitioner of the dark arts. But since her adoption as a pitiful stray the previous fall, she'd seemed the most domestic of creatures. Now, however, she was rolling on the kitchen floor in a frenzy, uttering wails like nothing that had ever come out of her mouth before.

Pamela watched her in alarm, coffee untouched

and newspaper still encased in its plastic sleeve. The
cat had spent the night in Penny's bed, greeted Pamela
when she stepped into the hall on her way to the bathroom, and followed her down the stairs at a sedate
pace. She'd nibbled a few bites of cat food then looked
up as if hearing an urgent call. Suddenly, she'd scooted
across the room and tossed herself onto her back.

Penny had already dressed and left to catch her bus,
and anyway she knew no more about cats than Pamela
did. Bettina had Woofus, but dogs were not cats, so
Bettina would be no help. A vet would have to be consulted. Pamela opened a cupboard to retrieve the little
directory of local businesses that appeared on the
driveway every fall. She had no sooner opened to
the *V* pages than it seemed the spell had been lifted.
Catrina flopped onto her belly, locked eyes with
Pamela as if to say "forget you saw this," and returned
to her meal. Relieved, Pamela closed the little book
and returned to her own breakfast and the newspaper.

She'd finished the scarf the previous night, cast off,
and woven the tails at the beginning and end back
through the knitted fabric with a yarn needle. Now the
scarf sat on the mail table, waiting to be delivered to
Nell when the group met that evening at Karen Dowling's house. The newspaper contained no update on
the Randall Jefferson case, and the Jefferson doll had
been handed over to Detective Clayborn. She'd
checked her email before she came downstairs and
found a message from her boss thanking her for the
quick turnaround on the submissions she'd evaluated.
But one question loomed.

What would she knit tonight? She refreshed her
coffee. She had no project. After the Icelandic-style
sweater for herself last fall, she'd made a sweater for
Penny for Christmas. Then the aardvark project had

come along, and she'd worked on aardvarks all spring. And for the past week she'd labored on the scarf—not challenging, by any means, but a worthy cause like all of Nell's do-good projects.

The sound of footsteps signaled that someone was on the porch, and the squeak of the mailbox cover identified that someone as the mail carrier. Pamela stepped over Catrina and made her way to the front door. No catalogs littered the porch today, but—she caught her breath—another curious package had appeared. A few envelopes protruded from the flap of the mailbox cover, but the package clearly hadn't been part of the mail delivery. There was no postage, and the only address was the word PAMELA, written in a bold hand on brown paper that had been carefully folded and taped around the object, whatever it was.

Pamela glanced quickly toward Bettina's house. But, no—she could handle this on her own. Besides, the package was small, and flat, the size and shape of a not-too-large pizza. It was nothing like the package that had contained the Jefferson doll. She picked it up—it was not light, but not heavy either—and retired to one of her porch chairs to peel off the wrapping paper. Then she laughed. In her hands she held a deviled-egg platter, glossy green ceramic, with a dramatically colored rooster in the center, complete with a bright-red comb. She turned the platter over. Taped to the bottom was a note, in the same bold hand: "*I walked past a shop yesterday that had this in the window. I thought you might like it for your collection.*" It was signed "*Rick Larkin.*"

Pamela glanced toward Bettina's house again. No, she'd keep this to herself. Bettina was already hopeless enough on the subject of Richard Larkin. Upstairs, dressing, Pamela discovered that she was humming to

herself. Perhaps she deserved a little treat, a trip to the
yarn store in Timberley. That was where she'd bought
the special wool for the Icelandic sweater, natural brown
and natural cream, from brown and cream Icelandic
sheep. She'd make something else for herself, perhaps
even something fashionable, like the striking sweater
Holly was knitting with the giant needles and yarn.

It was pleasant to be anonymous, to dawdle along
the sidewalk and pause at a shop window with no fear
of being accosted with a question or theory about the
Randall Jefferson murder case. Timberley was a few
towns to the north, larger than Arborville and with
grander houses on grander lots. Its commercial district
offered many diversions lacking in Arborville, including
a clothing boutique featuring designer labels, a shop
that sold only cheese, a florist, and—the object of
today's visit—a yarn store.

It almost seemed that the walls were made of yarn.
Shelves reached nearly to the ceiling, piled with skeins
in every color and texture, each luring eyes and hands
to marvel and touch. Every shade from deepest
purple, in a soft mohair, to a delicate pink the color of
early spring blossoms, was represented.

"Hello," said a stylish blonde woman from behind a
counter. "Please let me know if you're looking for
something special. Otherwise—enjoy yourself!"

"I want to make something for myself," Pamela
blurted out. "With fancy yarn."

"Shall we start with the yarn or the pattern?" the
woman asked.

"I don't know," Pamela said. Being in the shop was

like deciding which crayon in a new, giant, box to use first.

"How about a ruby red?" From a shelf behind her the woman reached a skein and laid it on the counter. "Such a glamorous color, and with your skin and hair . . ." She slid a mirror along the counter and offered Pamela the skein of yarn. Pamela lifted the yarn to her cheek—it was incredibly soft—and leaned toward the mirror. "See," the woman said. Pamela studied herself.

With her brown hair and brown eyes, she had always felt anything but glamorous. Pleasant-looking certainly, but not a person to draw stares from across a room. The deep red of the yarn, however, made her skin glow.

"We import it from France," the woman said. "Free-range sheep, and the dyes are all natural, made from organic ingredients."

"I'll take it." Pamela lowered the yarn to the counter.

"And now the pattern."

"Yes," Pamela said, "the pattern . . . for something . . . something ravishing."

"Let's look in here." The woman stepped out from behind the counter and selected a pattern book from a rack. The cover showed an ultra-chic model posing in a slouchy black and white striped sweater with a ribbed turtleneck in solid black. She paged through the book and paused to exhibit a page. "Something like this, perhaps?"

The garment being modeled was also ruby red, and the model had Pamela's pale skin and dark hair and eyes. It was a sweater, but like many fashionable garments, seemed designed to subvert the very purpose for which it was intended. Of what use would a wool sweater with long sleeves and a high neck be if it left one's shoulders bare?

"Her shoulders look cold," Pamela said.

"The look is very on trend," the woman said. "A charming look for après-ski . . . or holiday parties— winter will be here again before we know it. You can see, it's more a tunic than a sweater. I'd wear it with black leggings. Or even high black boots. That would be stunning." She backed up and studied Pamela from a few yards away. "With your figure you could definitely pull it off."

Ten minutes later Pamela was on her way back to Arborville. A shopping bag bulging with ruby-red yarn sat in the passenger seat. Beside it was a knitting pattern book whose cover featured an ultra-chic model posing in a slouchy black and white striped sweater.

Chapter Seventeen

"You found a new egg platter?" Penny's voice carried in from the entry.

Pamela had been studying what remained of the barbecue leftovers, wondering whether there was enough to feed two people. There would be, she had decided, if she sliced the rest of the chicken and made sandwiches. There was plenty of the corn and bean salad left to go alongside, and she had a tomato in the bowl on the counter.

Penny appeared in the doorway, holding the platter in such a way as to display the gaudy rooster at its center.

"It was a gift," Pamela said.

"From Bettina?"

"No." Pamela transferred a chicken breast to the cutting board, picked up her favorite knife, and bent to the task of carving off sandwich-worthy slices. She hoped her obvious busyness would discourage further conversation. Just to make sure, she said, "I have knitting club tonight, so I want to get us fed as soon as possible."

"The rooster looks very self-confident," Penny said, setting the platter on the kitchen table. "Are you going to make something for yourself with that red yarn in the bag in the entry?"

"Yes," Pamela said, tackling a second chicken breast.

Penny went up to change and reappeared as Pamela was arranging napkins, silverware, and two plates on the kitchen table. She tucked the platter away in the cupboard where she kept the rest of her collection, making a mental note to write a quick thank-you to Richard Larkin the next day. She made sandwiches, spooned the remains of the corn and bean salad into a smaller bowl, and sliced the tomato. Catrina, seemingly herself again after her dramatic performance that morning, greeted the arrival of her dinner with becoming gratitude and nibbled delicately at what the can described as chicken-fish combo.

Pamela and Penny chatted about Penny's day at work, and Pamela described Catrina's curious spell and her own visit to the yarn shop. "I needed a new project," she explained. "I spent months on those aardvarks, and I thought it was time to make something for myself."

"The red is very dramatic," Penny said. "What are you going to make?"

"A sweater," Pamela said. "Or more like a tunic, really." The image from the pattern book came unbidden into her mind—the long sleeves with the little flare at the wrists, the high neck that called attention to the model's elegant cheekbones, and the cutaway shoulders that seemed more tantalizing than a plunging décolletage. She could think about the shoulders when she got to that part, she decided. She knew enough about knitting to improvise a version of the garment that wouldn't leave her shoulders bare.

Pamela glanced at the clock. It was six-thirty, and Bettina would be ringing the bell at a quarter to seven.

She hurried upstairs to comb her hair and put on a bit of lipstick, then back downstairs to slip the new pattern book, a skein of the new yarn, and a pair of size ten needles into her knitting bag. She perched on the chair next to the mail table, waiting to hear Bettina's feet on the porch. Then from the kitchen came an unearthly sound, like a voice imitating an ambulance siren.

Penny was upstairs, so the sound hadn't come from her—and anyway, what in the safe environs of her mother's kitchen would provoke such a dramatic response? Pamela jumped up from the chair, upsetting the knitting bag on the floor at her feet. She tiptoed to the kitchen door and peered hesitantly around the door frame. Catrina was crouching on the kitchen windowsill, back arched and tail erect. Her face was pressed against the screen.

"Kitty cat," Pamela said gently as she stepped into the room. She held out her hand, palm up. "What's wrong, kitty cat?"

Catrina turned from the window to regard Pamela. Her eyes looked yellower than they had ever looked before. Her mouth opened, showing her tiny pointed fangs, and her eyes narrowed. The unearthly sound echoed through the kitchen. She turned back toward the screen.

Penny rushed in from the entry. "What's going on down here?" she asked, her eyes scanning the room and resting on Catrina. "What's wrong with her, Mom?"

"It looks like she wants to be outside. She was so young when I adopted her . . . this is her first spring. She hears birds. There must be interesting smells . . ."

"I hope she's okay." Penny took a step toward the counter. Catrina relaxed her pose. She lowered her tail and glanced at Pamela and Penny, looking slightly embarrassed. She leapt delicately into the sink and from there to the counter and then the floor.

Pamela returned to the entry and had no sooner righted her knitting bag and perched back on her chair when footsteps on the porch announced the arrival of Bettina. Bettina had news, and she launched upon her tale even before the door was fully open.

"I just ran into Richard Larkin," she announced, "on his way home. Such a thoughtful man. He did some research for Wilfred, to help with the Mittendorf House, and he's going to drop it off this evening while I'm at knitting club. He said he had a wonderful time at the barbecue . . . and"—she stepped inside and squeezed Pamela's arm—"I know all about the egg platter. I hope you're going to thank him."

"Of course," Pamela said, somewhat stiffly. "Shall we go?"

"We're going to have rain," Bettina said as they walked to the car. Indeed, the bright day had become cloudy since Pamela left her desk. As if on cue, thunder rumbled in the distance.

Despite its sagging porch and faded paint, the Dowlings' house had a welcoming air. The lawn was lush, its color deepened by the darkening sky, and clusters of tulips bloomed under the trees along the curb and among the shrubs that edged the porch. A wreath of twisted vines adorned with silk flowers in shades of coral and peach decorated the front door. Karen greeted them and led them inside.

Karen and Dave's living room was furnished with a mix of what looked like hand-me-downs and IKEA. A streamlined sofa in a pretty shade of blue faced a coffee table that seemed to have spent time stored in a garage, or even outside. At one end of the sofa stood a brass floor lamp much the worse for wear. At the other, a table lamp with a white plastic base sat atop a small table with a glossy coat of dark green paint. Dramatic black and white photos decorated the sand-colored walls. A few straight-backed wooden chairs and a folding chair completed the seating arrangement, and further lighting had been improvised, perhaps just for the evening, with a gooseneck lamp perched on the mantel.

Holly and Nell sat side by side on the sofa, Holly displaying her dimple in response to one of Nell's gentle smiles. Roland had claimed the folding chair and was already at work on his new project, the pink angora dog sweater.

"Please sit down," Karen said to Pamela and Bettina. "There's room for one more on the sofa and—" She gestured uncertainly toward the wooden chairs.

Holly jumped up. "You can both sit here," she said. "I'll take a wooden chair."

"You're sure?" Bettina asked.

"Positive." Holly collected her knitting bag and pulled a wooden chair into the pool of light cast by the gooseneck lamp. Pamela settled next to Nell and handed over the scarf.

"Thank you so much," Nell said, stroking it.

"How speedy you are!" Holly beamed at Pamela. "Scarves for the day laborers. Such an amazing thing to do." She turned her lively gaze toward Roland. "And how have you been this past week?" she said.

"Quite well," he replied without looking up from his knitting.

Undaunted, she continued. "I love that shade of pink. I can't wait to meet your doggie. What color is she?"

Meanwhile, Bettina took her place on the sofa and

pulled out her cat project. Pamela consulted her pattern book to see how many stitches she needed to cast on for the first section of the fashionable tunic sweater. She reached into her knitting bag for the skein of ruby-red yarn, wondering how long it would take before someone noticed the dramatic color and asked about her plans for it.

"You have tulips." Bettina leaned toward Karen, who had pulled the other wooden chair close to the white plastic lamp at Bettina's end of the sofa. A tiny white rectangle with ribbing at the end dangled from one of Karen's knitting needles, and a strand of delicate white yarn led from it to the skein in her lap.

"They came up," Karen said. "I wasn't sure. I never did them before—I'm not used to having a yard."

"It's a beautiful time of year," Nell said. "Everything is so alive."

"Even Catrina seems to be affected," Pamela said with a laugh. "Now that I have the windows open, she's realized that the big cold world I rescued her from isn't so cold anymore." She paused to form a slip knot and tug it tight around one of her needles. "She's been making the oddest noises, yowling like no sound she's ever made before, and climbing up on the sill to stare out the kitchen window. This morning she was rolling on the floor like she was possessed."

"Oh, my dear," Nell said, resting a hand on Pamela's shoulder. "She's in heat."

Pamela felt her eyes open wide. "What?"

"Didn't you have her fixed?"

Everyone was staring at her, even Roland. Karen was blushing slightly.

"I . . . no . . . she was so little. She'd been through so much." Pamela stuttered. "I . . . I thought she'd be an indoor cat." The complicated under and over of the casting-on process faltered and her knitting needle slipped from her hand. A strand of the ruby-red yarn remained draped over her thumb. "I . . . I just didn't think," she finished lamely.

Roland sighed and shook his head. "Too many animals in the world, and of course the county just encourages people to be irresponsible with that overfunded animal shelter in Haversack."

"A decent society takes care of those that can't take care of themselves," Nell said. "Even animals."

"With my tax dollars." Roland frowned, surveyed the length of pink angora knitting that hung from one of his needles, and flipped it around to start a new row.

For a while, there was no conversation. Even the irrepressible Holly was silent, working steadily away with her giant yarn, occasionally furrowing her brow and consulting her pattern. A bulky off-white panel dangled from the gigantic needles, its stitches so large they could be counted from across the room.

Pamela had wondered if anyone would bring up the murder case. The people who'd been at the barbecue had already had a chance to discuss the latest developments, and Roland's introduction of the "Killer Aardvark" theme at the knitting club's last meeting had upset Bettina and Nell so much that perhaps he'd resolved to hold his tongue. In any event, when a topic was introduced, it was the relatively benign issue of the Arborville community garden. Additional territory had been annexed by the community-garden committee, and a lottery was being held to distribute the new plots.

"Such a boon for Arborville's apartment-dwellers," Nell said. "Food you grow yourself is so much more economical, not to mention nutritious."

"But they should have held the lottery earlier," Bettina said. "They've been talking about the new plots forever. I did an article for the *Advocate* in January. Anybody who wanted to grow their own food should have had plants in the ground a month ago."

"Mother's Day," Nell said. "That's when tomatoes go in." She paused her busy fingers and shook out the woolly olive-green heap on her lap. A scarf unfurled, nearly finished. "It's easy to remember if you're a mother." She leaned forward to catch Karen's eye. Karen blushed and ducked her head.

Across the room, Holly stood up. "I don't know about the rest of you," she said, "but my fingers are getting tired." She clenched and unclenched her fists, and her fingernails, polished the same dramatic purple as the streaks in her hair, glittered. From outside came the sound of rain.

"How's the jacket coming?" Pamela asked. So far, her own project consisted of a strip twenty inches wide and an inch long.

"Great," Holly said, snatching up the knitting she had tossed on top of her knitting bag. "This is the front." She held the panel against her chest. "Half of it anyway. On the other half I have to make giant buttonholes."

Karen was on her feet now too. "We could have the refreshments," she said hesitantly. "It's just cookies though."

Bettina pushed her knitting aside and bounced to her feet. "You don't have to apologize for your chocolate chip cookies," she said. "I could eat them every day." She put an arm around Karen and took a few steps. "Let's get some coffee going." She turned to look at Nell. "And tea, of course."

"I'll help with the cups," Nell said, and followed them from the room.

Roland remained in his chair, knitting industriously. "Don't your fingers get tired?" Holly said, leaning over him.

He looked up, puzzled. At last he said, "Mind over matter," and returned to his task.

Holly shrugged and crossed to where Pamela was still sitting on the sofa. "That's an amazing color," she said, offering one of the radiant smiles that revealed her perfect teeth. "Are you making another scarf for the day laborers?"

"No." Pamela held up what she'd done so far. "It's to be a sweater. Sort of a sweater, more like a tunic. It's—" She fumbled in her knitting bag, brought up the pattern book, and displayed the page with the high-cheekboned model. "It's this."

"OMG!" Holly clapped her hands and the nail polish glittered. Her smile became even wider. "That is *amazing*! And this yarn—" She fingered the strand that led from the needles to the skein in Pamela's lap. "It's amazing. Where did you ever find it?"

"Timberley," Pamela said. "There's an—" She started to say "amazing" and checked herself. "There's a really nice yarn shop." She paused and studied the image in the pattern book. "But I have to say the woman there sort of talked me into this pattern, and this yarn. I don't usually wear things that are so . . . daring."

"Why not?" Holly raised her brows. "You could *be* this model. You've got the same hair and eyes, and you're so tall and thin."

"Well, I . . . Arborville is . . . not very . . ." Pamela wasn't sure where she was going with the thought and was relieved when Bettina came bustling in and deposited a tray piled with chocolate chip cookies on the coffee table. "Coffee coming right up," she announced.

"I'll help," Holly said, and bounced away.

Six steaming mugs soon joined the tray of cookies, along with milk and sugar, and a small pile of paper napkins.

Roland bit into a cookie and pronounced it excellent. Bettina said again that she could eat Karen's chocolate chip cookies every day. Nell observed that delicious as they were, cookies—any cookies—should be an occasional treat. Holly asked Karen if she'd teach her how to make the cookies.

Mugs were emptied and refills refused, but cookies remained on the tray—perhaps an effect of people taking Nell's observation to heart. Soon knitters bent again to their works in progress and quiet conversations ebbed and flowed. Bettina and Karen talked about preparations for the expected baby. All home-improvement efforts henceforth were to be focused on the nursery-to-be. Holly had given up on Roland, pulled her chair nearer to Nell's end of the sofa, and was nodding delightedly as Nell described life in Manhattan in the early days of her marriage.

"People could afford to live there then," Nell said. "Young ordinary people."

"Then you moved here," Holly said.

"We had a baby." Nell smiled her gentle smile. "And after we moved here we had two more."

"I'd love to meet your children," Holly said. "I'll bet they're amazing."

Seated between Bettina and Nell, Pamela found herself nearly lulled into a trance by the steady motion of her fingers as the band of ruby red hanging from her needles grew, one row at a time. Even Roland's announcement that nine o'clock had arrived and it was time, at least for him, to pack up didn't interrupt her rhythm. But next to her, Bettina dropped both knitting needles into her lap, held up a small yellow square, and pronounced another cat leg finished.

"I'm ready to pack up too," Nell said, tucking the long swathe of olive green into her bag.

Bettina leaned across Pamela and touched Nell on the arm. "Did you walk down the hill?" she asked.

"Of course," Nell said. "It's a shame to get in the car for only a few blocks. And I have my umbrella, of course."

"It sounds pretty soggy out there," Bettina said. "And I didn't walk. Let me give you a ride back up."

"Well, okay," Nell said. "I'll accept a ride."

Outside, a gust of damp air met them as they descended the porch steps. The night smelled like wet soil, and streams of water rushed along the curbs in waves that reflected the light from the streetlamps.

"Squishy," Bettina said. "I wish I hadn't worn sandals." She raised her umbrella and linked an arm through Nell's. Pamela followed with her own umbrella, struggling to keep the wind from grabbing it out of her hands. She had barely taken three steps before her feet were soaked and slippery, and threatening to slide right out of her sandals. Huge raindrops thumped on her umbrella.

"I'll take the back seat," she said, opening the passenger-side door for Nell. Once Nell was seated, Pamela climbed gratefully into the car, her jeans wet from the knees down.

They'd barely gone two blocks when, as Bettina stopped for a cross street, Nell bent toward the windshield and said, "What is that? Up ahead?" She pointed toward the left.

Pamela leaned forward, her head between Bettina and Nell, and strained to look where Nell was pointing. A figure half-hidden by a huge umbrella was making its way toward them, or at least down the hill. Its slender legs were clad in trousers but no other details were visible.

"It's a wet night for anybody to be out," Bettina said. "Whoever it is can't be just taking a stroll."

Could it be the ghost? The thought came unbidden and Pamela felt a chill. The ghost the gossipy dog-walking woman claimed to have seen? They were near Randall Jefferson's house now, and what corporeal being would be out on a night like this?

A particularly strong gust of wind buffeted the car. It caught the stroller's umbrella in an updraft and suddenly a torso, and then a face, were revealed.

"For heaven's sake!" Bettina swerved across the street and pulled up at the opposite curb. She rolled down her window and a sprinkling of rain blew in. "Where on earth are you going?" she called to the figure on the sidewalk.

"Bettina?" Harold Bascomb answered. He approached the car, ignoring the torrent of water that gushed over his feet as he stepped off the curb. He leaned close to the open window, scrunched up his face, and said, "Nell, is that you?"

"Yes, it is," Nell said, sounding perturbed. "What are you doing out in the rain, Harold?"

"I was coming down to pick you up," he said meekly. "I didn't think you had an umbrella."

"I always take an umbrella when rain is threatening," Nell answered, no less perturbed. "Don't you know by now that I'm a sensible person?"

"I do know that," he said. "But I was worried about you. I—"

Bettina interrupted. "Get in the car before you get washed away. There's room in the back seat."

Pamela reached for the door handle and swung the door open. Harold collapsed his umbrella and climbed in next to Pamela. They rode the few blocks up the hill in soggy companionability.

As Bettina pulled up in front of the Bascombs' house, Harold leaned close to whisper in Pamela's ear. "Wait here while I take Nell into the house. I have something to tell you." He got out, put up his umbrella, and hurried around to offer a hand to Nell.

"I'm quite fine, Harold," she said, easing her feet to the ground and springing up to her full height. She ducked her head back into the car to thank Bettina.

As Nell and Harold began to climb the shrubbery-edged steps that led to their front door, Pamela touched Bettina on the shoulder and said, "Harold wants us to wait a minute." They watched the couple mount the steps. On the porch, Harold unlocked the door and pushed it inward. Then he gestured toward the garage, pushed the door open farther, and gave Nell a gentle nudge that propelled her through it. He started back down the steps.

"I told her I wasn't sure I locked the garage door," he said, opening the passenger-side door and leaning into the car. "She can be hard to fool, so I've got to hurry back in. But I wanted to tell you—something's been going on at Randall Jefferson's house. Two mornings in a row there've been boxes piled in the driveway, and yesterday I saw a black SUV pull up. It seems awfully soon for his estate to have been settled and heirs to be claiming things. I called the police, but they said without a license number they couldn't do much."

The Bascombs' porch light came on and the front door opened. "I'd better run," Harold whispered, and bounded toward the steps.

"Shall we pay another visit to Jefferson's house tomorrow?" Bettina asked as she pulled away from the curb.

"I'm game," Pamela answered from the back seat.

The rain was slacking off. By the time Bettina pulled up in front of Pamela's house, she'd turned her windshield wipers off. "Nine a.m.?" she said as Pamela collected her knitting bag and prepared to climb out of the car.

"I'll come over," Pamela said.

Bettina turned to face Pamela. "You'll make sure to keep that kitty inside, won't you? And when she's herself again you'll take her to be fixed."

"Of course," Pamela said, reaching for the door handle.

"A big tomcat's been hanging around," Bettina said. "I saw him creeping out of Richard Larkin's yard while I was ringing your doorbell this evening."

"Bettina!" Pamela scowled at her friend. "That is not funny at all."

"I'm serious," Bettina said with a laugh. "There really is a tomcat in the neighborhood. So you'd better keep close tabs on that kitty."

Catrina met Pamela with a wail that sounded like a baby crying. She pranced around Pamela's feet, weaving this way and that, her fur soft against Pamela's bare ankles. "She's been rubbing herself on everything," Penny said from the sofa.

"Bettina says there's a tomcat around," Pamela said. "I suppose Catrina senses that and she . . . they . . . just like people . . . want to . . ." She paused, wondering where she had meant to take the thought.

"I know what you mean, Mom." Penny looked vaguely embarrassed. "How was your meeting?"

"Fine," Pamela said. "Harold Bascomb is a remarkable man."

Chapter Eighteen

This note-writing occasion called for stationery other than a sheet torn from one of the free notepads that arrived almost daily from various charities. In the living room, Pamela opened a drawer in her old oak desk and picked out a card with a bouquet of peonies on the front. At the kitchen table, she sipped her coffee and pondered for a moment. As she pondered, Catrina strolled through from the back hallway. Pamela reached for her pen and wrote:

> *Dear Richard,*
>   *Thank you very much for the addition to my*
> *collection of deviled-egg platters. It was thoughtful of*
> *you to think of me.*
>
> > *Yours sincerely,*
> > *Pamela Paterson*

"Thoughtful of you to think of me" was quite redundant, she realized, scanning the finished message. Had she come upon something like it in an article she was editing, she would have pounced. But instead of starting over with a fresh card, she tucked the finished note into an envelope, wrote "Richard Larkin" on the front, and set the envelope on the mail table. In a few minutes she'd leave to meet Bettina for the adventure they'd planned, and she'd drop the note in Richard's mailbox on the way. But first she finished the last few swallows of coffee and rinsed the carafe and her cup at the sink.

She stepped onto the porch. The day was bright and clear, and the greenery all the greener for being washed by the heavy rain. But the wind had strewn lawns with twigs and even sizeable branches. She'd take a break from the magazine work later and spend an hour in the yard with a rake. She glanced toward Richard's house. It was late enough, certainly, that he'd have left for work, and she wouldn't come face-to-face with him as she hand delivered her thank-you note.

That errand done, she hurried across the street. Bettina was standing in the driveway, car doors already open.

"You don't want to just walk?" Pamela said. "It's a beautiful day."

"I'm not walking up that hill in these." Bettina lifted a foot to display a sandal with a delicate heel and narrow crisscrossing straps. The sandals complemented the rest of the outfit, a full skirt and a peasanty blouse with embroidered trim. "I could barely sleep," she said. "Aren't you excited?"

"I *am* curious," Pamela said. "If the car Harold saw is there now, that could be a very useful clue. And if the door to the house is open, I'm sure Detective Clayborn would appreciate a call." She slipped into the passenger seat. "Especially if we see somebody carrying out boxes."

"Why involve Clayborn?" Bettina said. "Maybe we just introduce ourselves as neighbors, always up for a chat." She settled herself behind the steering wheel and turned to Pamela. "What were you doing on Richard Larkin's porch?" she asked.

"Dropping off a thank-you note," Pamela said.

"Good," Bettina said with a satisfied nod. "I'm glad you took my advice."

"I always write thank-you notes," Pamela said with a sideways glance at her friend.

Jefferson's imposing house, with its half-timber details and steep roof, loomed ahead on its shrubbery-covered hillside. Bettina paused at the cross street and then continued up the hill, slowing to a crawl.

"No boxes in the driveway," she observed.

"And no SUVs at the curb," Pamela added. "But it might be interesting to see how things look inside. If somebody's been carrying boxes out, what have they been taking?"

Bettina nodded. "Jefferson had an awful lot of nice stuff. But if the killer's only motive was to get his stuff, why not just break in, like a burglar?" They had cruised past Jefferson's house. Bettina put the car in reverse and began to back up.

Pamela squirmed around in her seat to make sure Bettina wasn't about to back into anything. "You couldn't carry away boxes and boxes of stuff in a break-in."

"But somebody who knew about all his stuff—"

Pamela cut in. "Like the red-haired woman . . ."

"And now she's raiding the house." Bettina swung the steering wheel to the left and eased closer to the curb. "Maybe she's even sleeping here. Sneaking around with candles so nobody will see lights."

"But she couldn't move in or get started with the

raiding until the police were through." Pamela turned to face her friend.

Bettina twisted her key in the ignition. The car's engine growled and then was silent. "So she lies low for a few days. Then she gets busy."

An exciting thought came to Pamela, and she greeted it with a sharp intake of breath. "I know how we can figure out if it's her!"

"I'll bite." Bettina turned toward Pamela and waited, her eyes wide.

"See if the hat's still under the pillow." Pamela smiled a satisfied smile. "If I was her, I'd have grabbed the hat right away. Even if the police didn't find it, I wouldn't want anything lying around that could ever be followed up—by anybody—as a clue of any kind."

Bettina set the emergency brake. Pamela opened the car door and swung her feet onto the grass. "Let's go," she said.

They found themselves tiptoeing as they made their way along the dim, wood-paneled hall. When they reached the doorway that opened into the living room, Pamela entered first. She scanned the room and heard herself whisper, "Uh-oh." Brocade swags still accented the windows, velvety sofas and chairs still occupied their places on the richly patterned carpet, and elegant lamps still perched on graceful wooden pieces. But the walls were bare. Gone were the gold-framed paintings of landscapes, fruits, flowers, and beautiful women.

Bettina joined her and added her whispered, "Uh-oh."

A peek into the dining room across the hall revealed walls stripped of paintings and a sideboard relieved of crystal decanters. "Well," Bettina said, no longer whispering. "We've answered one question. The boxes on the driveway *were* full of Randall Jefferson's goodies."

"And to answer the question of who might be taking them—on to the second floor and the bedroom."

They continued along the hall and up the wood-paneled stairs with their sweeping banisters. On the landing at the top, they hesitated. "His bedroom was this door on the left," Pamela said, turning the knob.

This room looked just as it had looked on their first visit, with its grand bed, its reading chair, and its dresser, except—

"The cufflinks are gone," Bettina pointed out with a laugh. "Gold, probably, and easy to carry off."

"But let's check what we came for." Pamela advanced toward the bed. *Legacy of the Revolution* still rested on the night table to the right, as if waiting for its reader to return. And the quilted spread, even where it curved up over the pillows, looked undisturbed. Pamela edged along the left side of the bed and flipped the spread back. As Bettina watched, she lifted the pillow. And there, just as they had left them, were the skein of yarn, the neon-orange and chartreuse creation, and, dangling from one knitting needle, the beginnings of a tail—an incomplete version of the curious hat Pamela had found at St. Willibrod's.

They looked at each other and shrugged.

"Want to take another look in his study?" Bettina asked.

"Might as well." Pamela shrugged again. They headed toward the door, Pamela carrying the hat, yarn, and knitting needles.

Randall Jefferson's study seemed undisturbed. The floor-to-ceiling bookshelves were still tightly packed with books whose sturdy spines hinted at the weighty content within. The huge wooden desk still dominated the room and was still bare, except for an expensive-looking pen and some paper clips in a crystal bowl. Apparently the police were still holding onto Jefferson's computer.

"Bettina?" Pamela turned to see Bettina, head tilted back, staring at the ceiling.

"Shh!" Bettina raised a warning finger and whispered, "Someone's up there."

Pamela closed her eyes, held her breath, and listened. From overhead came the scuffling sound of something being dragged across the floor, then more scuffling, and more and more, as if several large objects were being repositioned. The scuffling stopped, but it was replaced by a series of thuds. The thuds grew steadily louder, resolving into footsteps.

"He's coming down the stairs from the attic!" Bettina whispered, hugging herself, her face tight with fear. "What do we do?"

"Behind the desk," Pamela whispered back. She motioned for Bettina to join her. Together they crouched close to the bookshelf, the massive desk between them and the door to the landing.

Out on the landing, the attic door opened and the footsteps came closer, but muffled by the carpet. Pamela and Bettina looked at each other. Pamela was aware that she was holding her breath. The footsteps paused and they heard a heavy thump, as if something ponderous had been deposited right outside the study door.

Pamela felt a clammy hand grab hers and squeeze. She squeezed back. From beyond the door, a male voice said, "Damn!" It paused and added, "Onward!"

Was it too soon to feel relief? Bettina relaxed the pressure on Pamela's hand, and Pamela felt herself go limp, though her hairline still prickled with a film of sweat.

The footsteps were loud again for a moment, but then began to fade. Soon it was clear that the owner of the feet was heading down the grand staircase that connected the landing to the entry hall and thence—*hopefully,* Pamela prayed—to the door. She eased herself out of the uncomfortable crouch and rocked back so she was sitting on the floor.

"Wow," Bettina said, latching onto the edge of the desk and pulling herself to her feet. "That was an experience."

But they waited in vain for the solid clunk of a heavy wooden door being pulled shut.

"I do think he's leaving," Bettina whispered. "But maybe by the back door. Harold saw the boxes on the driveway."

"Let's see what's happening." Pamela bounded up and hurried to the window that looked out on the street that ran past the side of Jefferson's house. "I can't see the driveway from here," she said. "Let's check from another room."

Walking on tiptoe in case they weren't alone, they made their way along the edge of the landing to the room behind the study, one of the rooms still furnished as if for children. There, from the back window, they had a clear view of the driveway. A box sat on the pavers near the back door, but there was no sign of the person who had deposited it.

"He loaded up a bunch of boxes," Bettina said, "and now he's carrying them out one by one."

Sure enough, in a few minutes they heard feet on the grand stairway. The footsteps became muffled as they reached the stretch of carpet on the landing, the door to the attic stairs opened and closed, and soon the feet were thudding about on the floor above.

Pamela and Bettina watched and waited. The pattern they'd heard the first time was repeated, complete with the exasperated "Damn!" but minus the "Onward!" Soon they saw a man emerge from the back door, bearing a gigantic cardboard box which he deposited next to the other box.

"It's the ghost!" Pamela exclaimed.

"He looks just like Randall Jefferson," Bettina said.

"It's the man the gossipy dog-walking woman saw, the man she thought was Randall Jefferson returned from the dead." Pamela studied the figure now heading back toward the door.

Instead of a linen sports jacket like Jefferson's usual summer choice, this man wore a pale suit that, seen up close, might have been seersucker. But he'd accented it with a spiffy bow tie, and his smooth gray hair had been recently barbered.

"I don't see a car." Bettina crossed to the window that looked out the side of the house. "Nothing out here either."

"Maybe he parked farther up the hill, or on a cross street. I doubt he wants to call attention to what he's up to. Or he's got an accomplice who'll pull up as soon as he's summoned." Pamela raised a finger and modulated her voice to a whisper. "Shh," she said. "He's on his way to the attic again."

Sure enough, footsteps were growing louder, and closer.

"We've got to find out where he's going with all that stuff," Bettina whispered back.

Pamela nodded, feeling her heart speed up. "As soon as we hear the attic door slam we'll hurry down to your car. We parked in a good spot to watch the driveway, and when he takes off, we'll wait a few seconds and take off too."

Holding their breath, they made their way stealthily across the landing and down the grand stairway. In a few minutes they were back in Bettina's car, Pamela still clutching the hat, the skein of yarn, and the knitting needles. She set them on the back seat.

Apparently, filling three large boxes and carrying them down two flights of stairs had exhausted the mysterious man's energies for that day. Even before he reappeared, a black Mercedes SUV came cruising slowly down the hill, veered to the right, and backed into Jefferson's driveway.

"New York plates," Bettina observed. "We might be gone for a while."

"Maybe we'd better drive up the hill and wait," Pamela said. "It will seem too obvious if we sit here till they leave and then start right after them."

From their new vantage point a block away, they watched the driver of the SUV get out, but he was too far away for them to notice more than that he looked young and thin. The huge SUV hid the back door of the house, as well as the boxes already piled on the driveway, but soon the car was in motion again, two figures visible in the front seat.

The SUV proceeded down the hill to Arborville Avenue and turned right, Bettina and Pamela following. The little procession passed the Co-Op Grocery, then turned right again and headed back up the hill for half a mile. "On his way to the bridge," Bettina said. "Hopefully there won't be much traffic this time of day."

The lush greenery of Arborville receded behind them as they jogged left for the bridge ramp and joined the cars speeding along one of the concrete arteries that led toward the vast toll plaza and the George Washington Bridge beyond. Two lanes joined ten, and a rush of traffic converged on the long row of booths. A speedy little sports car cut in front of Bettina, and the black SUV sprinted across two lanes and made for a booth with a flashing E-ZPass sign.

"Don't worry," Pamela said. "I'll keep my eye on him. Just stay in this lane and we'll catch up with him on the bridge."

Once through the toll booth, they entered the dim lower level of the bridge, the river and the western rim of Manhattan visible off to the right through the criss-crossed steel of the bridge struts. The river was flat and bright on this May morning, the Manhattan skyline jagged against the clear May sky.

"Middle lane," Pamela said. "Three cars ahead. Get in the middle too, so we can go either way when we get to the split for the Cross Bronx and the West Side Highway."

They rode in silence for a few minutes. Pamela tried to take a breath and realized she hadn't exhaled lately. She closed her eyes and forced her lungs to empty and fill, sighed deeply, and breathed in again. In her chest, her heart was ticking like a busy clock.

Up ahead, the black SUV veered right. "He's going for the West Side Highway," Pamela said. "Get ready." Bettina swung the steering wheel to the right and took the lane that curved off the bridge and down to parallel the Hudson.

Along the river they caught up with him again, as they cruised past runners bouncing down the path that bisected the flat grassy strip between highway and water.

Bettina allowed a van and a motorcycle to cut in front of her, but she kept her speed steady. "We'll have plenty of warning," she said. "The exits aren't that frequent—just make sure to keep your eye on him." They drove in silence for a few minutes, then Bettina spoke again. "I guess he's not heading for the boat basin," she said as they passed the exit for 72nd Street. Off to the right bobbed a cluster of boats, their sails white against the deep blue water. "And not Midtown either," she added a few minutes later, as traffic clogged at the exit for 42nd Street but the black SUV made no attempt to move left.

Now they were speeding along the edge of Chelsea, old brick buildings in random heights alternating with sleek new construction and the High Line arching above. The roadway was divided here, the median strip a tangled jungle of carpet roses that thrived despite the exhaust fumes.

The SUV ignored several chances to exit, but just past 16th, Pamela leaned forward. "He's edging left," she said, her voice urgent. "Get ready—I think he's going to take 14th Street."

Bettina checked the lane to her left, let a truck pass, then sped up and slipped in behind the truck, eliciting a horn blast from the car behind her. "Here we go," she said, making the turn. "Do you see anything along here that looks like a place an SUV loaded with antiques might be heading?"

"Not really." Pamela scanned the buildings that lined the busy thoroughfare: a gym, a restaurant offering fried chicken, a Goodwill store, a hair salon with illustrations of various hairstyles in the window, and a couple of unprepossessing hotels.

The SUV was two cars ahead but easy to keep track of as traffic moved along 14th Street, lurching ahead at green lights, jolting to a stop at red lights, and clogging at corners as drivers made left or right turns. After several blocks of hair salons, gyms, narrow store-front restaurants with neon signs, and clothing shops with impossibly crowded windows, Union Square came into view. The park's greenery was enlivened by food trucks with bright umbrellas, and its broad walkways were lined with huge pots gaudy with flowers. Just past Union Square, the black SUV suddenly peeled off to the left. The light turned red and Bettina stopped, two cars between her and the cross street.

"Oh!" She twisted her lips in disgust. "Don't tell me we're going to lose him right at the end."

"No," Pamela said. "We won't." She jerked the door handle toward her, shoved the door open, jumped into the street, and darted around the front of Bettina's car onto the sidewalk.

Chapter Nineteen

Pamela's feet pounded along the concrete as she turned the same corner the SUV had turned. It was only a block away, cruising slowly northward. She checked the street sign and discovered she was on Irving Place.

The SUV was taking its time, so Pamela slowed to a walk, catching her breath though her heart was throbbing from exertion and excitement. Here, a block off 14th Street, it was like another world—a world of charming brick buildings no more than a few stories high. They were restaurants and shops, with multi-paned windows, signage that featured gilt lettering, and window boxes planted with delicate flowers in tasteful colors.

At the next corner, the SUV turned right. Pamela sped up until she reached that corner and gazed in the direction the SUV had gone. There it was, stopped in midblock—in front of one of those charming brick buildings. She crossed the street but made sure she was hidden from the view of the SUV's occupants by edging close to the brick wall of the shop at the corner.

Then she leaned out far enough that one eye could survey what was happening.

The passenger-side door of the SUV opened and the mysterious man in the possibly seersucker suit got out. The driver's side door opened and the thin, young man got out. He circled to the back of the SUV and opened the tailgate. Content that the SUV had reached its destination, Pamela began to retrace her path along Irving Place.

She had gone a block and was hurrying past a restaurant whose white tablecloths and gleaming table settings were visible through its multipaned windows, when Bettina's car careened around the corner from 14th Street. It slowed, and an anguished voice not like Bettina's at all called, "Pamela!" Framed in the open car window, Bettina's face looked like she'd aged ten years in the last ten minutes.

"I'm okay, I'm fine," Pamela called back, extending her arms as if to show she was indeed all in one piece. She hopped off the curb and approached the open window. "He's around that corner," she said, pointing in the direction she had just come from. "The tailgate is open, and they're probably unloading the stuff right now." She stepped back and scanned the street for parking signs. "I don't think people are supposed to park along here, so stay in the car and cruise around a little bit. I'll walk past the SUV and see what's going on. I'll meet you up there." She nodded toward where Irving Place dead-ended into what looked like another park.

Bettina pulled away and Pamela crossed the street once again. Affecting a careless air, as if she was a most leisurely person out for nothing more than a pleasant stroll through a charming pocket of the city, she made her way up to the corner from which she'd surveyed the SUV. It was still parked in the same place and the tailgate was still open. In fact, one of the huge cardboard boxes remained within, but no one was in sight. She set out down the block, glancing here and there, admiring the window boxes, the row of sidewalk trees with delicate iron fences ringing their bases, and a chandelier visible through a window.

When she was parallel with the car, she glanced in that direction, only to notice the mysterious man standing near the open tailgate. She lifted her eyes to the elegantly lettered sign above the window—now, clearly, a shop window, because the sign read J & J ANTIQUES.

"I've got a plan," Pamela said as she climbed into Bettina's car, which was idling at the curb in front of an impressive stone townhouse. The park at the end of Irving Place was Gramercy Park, a lush block-long rectangle protected by a spiky iron fence and planted with carefully manicured trees and shrubs.

"I hope it's better than jumping out into traffic and running after someone who, for all we know, is a killer," Bettina said, still looking shaken. Even her hair, usually groomed to perfection, had become disarranged.

"It's an antique store," Pamela said. "J & J Antiques. We'll come back tomorrow, dressed in good clothes, and browse in the shop. We'll strike up a conversation with the owner—you're good at that—and see what we can find out."

"Come in and have some lunch," Bettina said as she pulled into her driveway. "Wilfred is still steering clear of the Co-Op, so he went out to the farmers market in Newfield this morning. I'm sure he brought back goodies."

Sure enough, the results of Wilfred's excursion were laid out on the pine table in Bettina's spacious kitchen: a huge cluster of tomatoes—heirloom (to judge by their unusual shapes and colors), avocados, an oval loaf of bread encrusted with seeds, a length of hard sausage that gave off a tantalizing aroma of garlic, and a large round pie. "It's a quiche," Bettina said, leaning over it and studying the surface, baked custard with the rich golden glow of cheese.

He'd left a note nearby. "*Dear Wife—Gone out again. Help yourself.*" It was signed with a heart.

"The mysterious man has to be related to Randall Jefferson," Bettina said, as she set out two of her hand-made plates from the craft shop and arranged portions of quiche on them. "He looks exactly like him."

Pamela meanwhile was slicing the largest tomato onto another handmade plate. "In that photo of the people standing in front of the house, there were two boys," she said. "Brothers, most likely."

"But nobody should be helping themselves to Jefferson's things yet, not even a brother, unless the estate has been settled." Bettina rummaged in her silverware drawer for forks.

"How's he getting into the house?" Pamela said. "If he had a key, that suggests they were on good terms."

"But if they were on good terms, why would he help himself to things? And I didn't notice anybody at the funeral who looked like Randall Jefferson." Bettina handed Pamela a cruet of olive oil. "Of course, we were looking for a woman with wild red hair. There were a lot of well-groomed men there—at least judging by the backs of their heads. Or maybe he has a key from long ago, when they were both growing up in the house. Maybe the locks have never been changed."

Pamela let a few dribbles of olive oil flow over the tomato slices. "So it's sibling rivalry then?" she said. "Randall inherited everything when his father died, and the other brother always resented that. Years went by, then something happened that made the other brother snap."

Bettina cut in. "He killed Randall, and now he's helping himself to all the stuff he thought he should have had in the first place. And he's carting it off to sell it to an antiques dealer."

"We'll know more tomorrow," Pamela said. "You're good at getting people to talk."

"Nine a.m.," Bettina said. "And be sure to dress the part."

At home, Pamela collected her mail and climbed the stairs to her office. Roused from a nap on the windowsill, Catrina seemed normal. Pamela waited as her computer completed the cycle of beeps and whirs that brought it to life, then checked her email and got to work.

"How was your day, Mom?" Penny sat at the kitchen table still dressed in the clothes she'd started out in that morning. She wore a white blouse with a sweet round collar, and a festive skirt that might once have been a square dancer's. "What did you do?" she added.

"Nothing out of the ordinary," Pamela answered before turning from the counter, afraid her face would give away her lie. She wasn't a good liar, but she certainly didn't want Penny to know what she and Bettina had been up to. She had sliced dill pickles onto a plate, and she was forming ground beef into patties for hamburgers. A few buns waited nearby. Catrina had been fed and was pacing back and forth between the kitchen and the entry.

Penny reached down and gave Catrina a pat as she veered near the table. "Did she seem normal today?" she asked.

"Pretty much," Pamela said. "I think it's time to make that appointment with the vet. It's not good to . . . do it . . . while they're actually in heat."

"She's pacing now," Penny said. "Is that normal?"

"She used to do it sometimes."

Penny stood up. "I'll go change," she said and started for the entry. "Hey," she called a minute later. "Somebody's coming up onto the porch." Just then the doorbell rang. "I think it might be Wilfred," Penny added. "It's somebody in overalls."

"Open it, can you?" Pamela said from the kitchen doorway. "My hands are all greasy."

Penny swung the front door open. At that moment, a streak of black darted past Pamela's ankles, zigzagged around Penny's feet, and leapt over the threshold. Wilfred staggered back and uttered the closest to a curse he had in his vocabulary, "Criminently!"

"That was Catrina!" Pamela cried, the last syllable of the cat's name trailing off in a heartbroken moan.

"I'll find her!" Penny squeezed past Wilfred and tore down the steps.

Wilfred remained on the porch, looking crestfallen. "It wasn't your fault," Pamela said, joining him. "She's never tried to run out before, but she's in heat." Pamela felt like she was about to cry.

"Dear, dear." Wilfred patted her shoulder. In his free hand he held a large shopping bag. "Heirloom

tomatoes from the farmers market," he said, holding
it up. "Bettina sent them over." He reached for the
doorknob but pulled his hand back. "No good closing
the barn door after the horse has gone," he said and
shrugged.

They watched as Penny bounced here and there
over the lawn in her festive skirt, peering under shrubs
and searching along the hedges that rimmed both
sides of Pamela's lot. After a few minutes, she headed
down the driveway toward the backyard. Then she was
back, empty-handed.

Pamela and Penny spent a sorrowful evening together.

A surprise awaited Pamela when she opened her
front door the next morning on her way to collect the
newspaper. From under one of the porch chairs came
a hesitant *meow*. Pamela looked down and there was
Catrina staring up at her, the cat's yellow eyes as expressive as if she were a contrite human acknowledging a night of debauchery.

And debauchery it had been, Pamela was almost
certain. And that meant there would very likely be kittens on the horizon. "Are you pleased with yourself?"
she asked with a frown. Catrina dipped her head. "Do
you want to come back home?" Pamela gestured
toward the open door.

Catrina's sleek body seemed to flatten and elongate
until she resembled a jet-black weasel. With a wary
glance upwards, she slunk past Pamela's slippered feet
and over the threshold.

"I suppose you're hungry," Pamela called after her
as she headed down the steps to collect the *Register*.

* * *

Half an hour later, Catrina had been fed and Penny seen off to work. Dressed in the best outfit she could muster—a freshly ironed white shirt and a pair of navy cotton slacks, Pamela was standing in front of Bettina's open closet. Four rejected jackets lay on the bed.

"It's hopeless," Bettina said with an exasperated sigh. "If only we were the same size, I could put together a wonderful ensemble for you. But you're not going to make a good impression in a jacket that barely reaches your waist and with sleeves that are three inches too short." She stepped toward her bureau and opened a drawer. "At least maybe a scarf and some earrings can make you look a little bit more polished."

She held up a luxuriously silky scarf with a pattern of elegant gold chains against a dark blue background, folded it on the diagonal, and arranged it to fill the neckline of Pamela's shirt. Then she opened another drawer and brought out a pair of earrings, simple gold buttons with diamonds in the center. Pamela fastened them to her earlobes and studied herself in the mirror on Bettina's closet door.

"It's better," Bettina said, "and at least you're not wearing your Birkenstocks."

The morning crush at the bridge was nearly over, and twenty minutes after leaving Arborville, Bettina and Pamela were zipping down the West Side Highway toward 14th Street.

"We'll need to put the car in one of those expensive Manhattan lots," Bettina said after they'd made their turn and were nearing Union Square. "I checked online this morning, and there's something just around this corner." She swung to the right and made for the large PARK sign jutting out over the sidewalk. Pausing to let a young couple meander past, she maneuvered her car down the concrete ramp into the shadowy gasoline-smelling depths of the underground garage.

Back up in the fresh air, Pamela and Bettina strolled along Irving Place, past the charming brick buildings housing charming restaurants and shops. A few blocks before the street ended at Gramercy Park, they turned right and soon were standing in front of the shop whose elegantly lettered sign identified it as J & J Antiques. Arranged behind the multipaned window was a display of china so delicate it was translucent—tea cups so very antique they dated from before tea cups had handles, matching saucers, a fat-bellied teapot, and a sugar bowl much larger than a modern one. All were decorated with intricate scenes that evoked their likely country of origin, China.

Pamela twisted the polished brass knob on the shop's door and pushed the door open, Bettina following. The silvery jingle of a bell announced their arrival, and a bear-like man in a well-starched Tattersall shirt emerged from a doorway in the back wall.

"Good day, ladies," he said with a courtly bow. He had a sandy, well-trimmed beard and wore glasses with gold wire frames.

"Beautiful shop," Bettina said. "Have you always been here?" In her black linen skirt suit and pearls, she looked perfectly at home among the lustrous wooden pieces, the gleaming silver, and the museum-quality art.

"Ten years," the bear-like man said. "Before then we were on the Upper East Side."

"We?" Bettina offered a flirtatious smile. "Which 'J' of the 'J and J' are you?"

"Benson Jasper at your service, ma'am." The words were accompanied by another bow.

"Nice to meet you," Bettina said with another smile. "Who's the other 'J'?" Standing to the side, Pamela marveled to herself. What a slick character Bettina could be.

"That would be Reynolds Jefferson. We're partners in life as well as in business."

Bettina's smile vanished. "Oh, my," she said, opening her eyes wide and raising her hand to her cheek in a display that Pamela thought was more theatrical than strictly necessary. But Bettina knew what she was doing. "Jefferson! He couldn't be . . . he isn't . . ." She paused, then went on. "There was that terrible murder in New Jersey a few weeks ago. He's not . . ."

Benson Jasper nodded. "He is."

"Not a *close* relative, I hope," Bettina said, reaching out a flawlessly manicured hand to give the antiques dealer a comforting pat.

"I'm afraid he is," Benson Jasper said. "Randall Jefferson was my partner's brother."

"That must be hard on you both." Bettina offered another pat.

"Randall took it quite well, actually. I was surprised." Benson Jasper's lips parted in a melancholy smile. "They weren't close." The smile widened and he glanced from Bettina to Pamela and back to Bettina. "Are you ladies looking for anything special? Decorating a new condo? Rounding out a collection?"

Pamela suspected that the clientele J & J Antiques served had little interest in deviled eggs, let alone platters to serve them, so she kept her mouth closed about that. But there was more sleuthing to be done, particularly given the excellent start Bettina had made. If Benson Jasper and Reynolds Jefferson were partners in life as well as in business, Benson was certainly in a position to say whether Reynolds was with him the night before Arborfest—or not. In which case Reynolds could have been in Arborville clunking his brother on the head with a rock.

But how to ask? *What* to ask?

Bettina's voice interrupted her ponderings. "Aren't these just too precious!" She was standing in front of a tall cabinet with glass-fronted doors. Through the carefully polished glass could be seen a row of porcelain greyhounds, posing on little mounds of porcelain grass.

"Staffordshire," said Benson Jasper from across the room. "Authentic, you can be sure. Not the repros."

Pamela returned to her musings. Maybe she didn't need to ask about *Saturday night.* If the same person who killed Randall Jefferson Saturday night put the aardvark on his chest the next day (and Pamela didn't think it made sense to believe that two people were involved, despite the lively discussion the knitting club had had on that topic), then what Reynolds was doing Sunday around noon was just as relevant.

Bettina was truly a mind reader. No sooner had this thought occurred to Pamela than Bettina turned from the cabinet and took a few steps toward Benson Jasper. "My sister would absolutely *love* these. Will you be here Sunday?"

Never mind that Bettina didn't have a sister. Benson Jasper didn't know that. "Of course!" The antiques dealer nodded enthusiastically. "Sunday is our busiest day."

"So 'J' *and* 'J' will be minding the store?"

Though to outward appearances Pamela was casually examining a set of sterling silver flatware, she was in fact listening intently, wondering whether she'd soon be crossing Reynolds Jefferson off her list of suspects. If both partners were always in the shop on Sundays, Reynolds couldn't have been at Arborfest.

"Reynolds *will* be here this Sunday," Benson Jasper said. "But some Sundays I have to go it alone. Much of our stock comes from estate sales. High end, of course, but they often happen on Sunday. Reynolds has an unerring eye for treasures."

Bettina gave Pamela a sidelong glance and turned back to the cabinet. "This pair of greyhounds with the little gold collars . . . so adorable." She reached toward the filigree knob on the nearest door. "Do you think I could . . . ?"

"Of course." Benson Jasper was at her side in a minute and after another minute, the greyhounds—whose porcelain bodies were glazed a refined shade of russet that set off their delicate gold collars—were sitting side by side on the well-polished surface of a nearby table.

"I can't wait for my sister to see these," Bettina said, and launched into a tale about her imaginary sister's collecting habits.

If Sunday was a busy day for J & J Antiques, Thursday—or at least Thursday morning—was quite slow. Pamela and Bettina were the only people in the shop, and Benson Jasper seemed happy to chat with Bettina while Pamela browsed among the china, glassware, and silver. She stopped to admire a serving plate rather like a deviled-egg platter but clearly designed for raw oysters, as attested by the meticulously rendered strands of seaweed that meandered along its gilt-edged border. As she pictured the feasts such a platter might grace, the quiet murmurs coming from Bettina and the antiques dealer bubbled up into laughter.

"Me too," Bettina said when the laughter subsided. "Of course I love her now, but when I was growing up with my sister, I'd have given anything to be an only child."

"It's hard when there are two of you," Benson Jasper said. "Both too many and too few. With a larger family, things don't get so intense."

"Did Reynolds have other brothers, or was Randall the only one?" Bettina asked as Pamela moved on from the oyster plate to a pair of gilt and marble candlesticks.

"I believe there was a black sheep, disinherited. Mustn't have been much of a story though, or I'm sure Reynolds would have told me all about it." His voice modulated from chatty friend to businessman. "Shall I set these greyhounds aside for your sister to take a look at Sunday? Or perhaps a gift-giving occasion is coming up, and you'd like to . . ."

"She can be so fussy," Bettina said. "I wouldn't want to take a chance. So I'll see what she's got on her agenda for this weekend, and I hope to see you again Sunday."

Chapter Twenty

"Too early for lunch," Bettina said with a sigh. "And these aren't the kind of places where you can pop in for coffee and a sweet roll." They were strolling back toward Irving Placc and had paused in front of a restaurant called Chez Marguerite. Through the window, complete with a window box artfully planted with ivy and begonias, they could see rows of tables covered with starched white cloths. In a few hours, servers would be scurrying among them bearing menus, wine, and baskets of rolls, but just now the restaurant was dark.

"I'm sure there are places around Union Square where we can find coffee," Pamela said. "Do you want to get something before we head back to Arborville?"

"I do," Bettina said, pulling herself away from the restaurant window. "Shopping for antiques makes me hungry. And these Manhattan parking lots cost the same for three hours as they do for one. We might as well get our money's worth."

So fifteen minutes later, Pamela and Bettina were sitting, not at a table covered with a starched white cloth, but at one whose scarred wooden surface still featured crumbs left behind by previous occupants. Cardboard cups of coffee bearing the Starbucks logo sat before them, along with napkins bearing slices of lemon-poppy seed cake, rich yellow flecked with black dots of poppy seeds. Sharing the table, which spanned nearly the width of the shop, were two twenty-somethings staring raptly at their smartphones and another attached to his by earbuds. A backpack occupied another chair.

"I liked the story about the sister who collects greyhounds," Pamela said.

"They *were* cute," Bettina said. "Probably out of my price range though, and my taste in dogs runs more to homely creatures like Woofus."

"What do we know that we didn't know before?" Pamela asked. Bettina broke off a morsel of lemon-poppy seed cake and conveyed it to her mouth. As she chewed, she wrinkled her forehead in thought. Pamela answered her own question. "We know the person who's been raiding Randall Jefferson's house is definitely his brother."

Bettina swallowed and added, "So . . . motive for murder: like we said before, Randall inherited everything and Reynolds resented that. Something made him snap, and he did away with Randall so he could claim what he thought should have been his."

Pamela nodded. "He obviously has a taste for pretty things, since he ended up in the antiques business. It must have been particularly galling to him that all the family treasures went to his brother." She reached for her cardboard cup of coffee and took a sip.

"But—we don't know what Reynolds was doing on the day of Arborfest." Bettina twisted her lips into a disgusted pout.

"You really tried though," Pamela said. "That was a good angle—Sunday is the busiest day and all."

Bettina broke off another morsel of lemon-poppy seed cake. "Was he out scouting estate sales for antiques? Or was he in Arborville's park waiting until the coast was clear so he could perch an aardvark on the chest of the brother he'd killed the night before?"

Pamela broke off a morsel of her own lemon-poppy seed cake. "That *is* the question," she said. "Of course, the other question is where does the aardvark come into all of this? Why return to do that unless it was fiendishly important for some reason?"

Bettina left off nibbling at her morsel of lemon-poppy seed cake to shrug. "Make Brad Striker seem guilty?" She finished the morsel. "You know what bothers me?" she said. "Benson Jasper was so nice. Could he be in on this?"

"Not necessarily," Pamela said. "Reynolds could have set out Saturday night claiming he was driving up to . . . let's say Connecticut, to be on hand at eight a.m. for a particularly tantalizing estate sale. But really he drives to Arborville and kills his brother. Then he sleeps in the family home—remember, we think he had his own key. Sunday he stops by the park to nab an aardvark and perch it on the corpse's chest. Then he drives back to Manhattan to report to Benson that he scored big at the estate sale, and he'll be picking up things and bringing them to the shop a few boxes at a time."

"Why would he take an extra aardvark?" Bettina said.

Pamela felt a little jolt, as if she'd shifted position in a chair with one short leg. "Because," she said, much louder than she meant to, and Bettina chimed in, "*there was another brother.*" They stared at each other.

Pamela slapped the table with both hands. One of their tablemates looked up from her smartphone in alarm.

"We've got to talk to Reynolds," Pamela said. "Maybe there's a greyhound in your future."

"I'm off again," Bettina said as she pulled into Pamela's driveway and Pamela started to get out of the car. "Someone from the nature center in Timberley is bringing turtles to show the kids in the summer youth program, and I've got to cover it for the *Advocate*."

Pamela had no sooner turned the key in her front door than her phone began to ring. Dropping her purse on the chair in the entry, she hurried to the kitchen to answer it.

"Hi there," said an unfamiliar female voice in response to her "Hello." The voice went on. "Got the note you stuck under my door. Very old school way to communicate. I like that. Nightingale here, in case you hadn't guessed—or do you go around leaving notes all over the place?"

"Oh . . . no. I . . . hardly ever. That is . . ." Pamela struggled to collect herself. Her heart had sped up as soon as she heard the word "Nightingale." She'd hoped for a response to the note, of course, but she hadn't planned what her response to the response would be.

"So . . ." Nightingale had a pleasant voice, rich and deep, like the voice of an actress—or maybe one of those lady DJs on the jazz stations. "You like the hat. I'll give you the pattern, sure. Always glad to commune with a fellow knitter—or do you even still want it? I've been gone awhile. Needed some sea air. There's ions in it, you know. Clears out the brain, like cleansing. When did you leave that note, anyway?"

"Monday, I think," Pamela said. "Shall I pick it up? The pattern?" *Say yes,* she whispered. *I need to talk to you in person.*

"I could photograph it with my phone," Nightingale said, and Pamela held her breath. But then Nightingale added, "Except I don't have one of those fancy things. And you know what? I like it that way. It's restful. Why would I want to be staring at a little screen all the time?"

"I'll be right over," Pamela said. "I'll photograph it with *my* phone." She'd report to Bettina after Bettina got through covering the turtle demonstration. Before she left, Pamela tucked the yarn, hat, and knitting needles from under the pillow into one of her canvas bags. Bettina was so good at getting people to talk, but Pamela didn't want to wait. She'd do the best she could.

Nightingale was attractive, in a flamboyant way. The red hair indeed was wild, curly and uncontrolled, framing a face in early middle age, with large eyes, strong brows, and an expression of amused worldliness. She was wearing a T-shirt with a heart on the front and a gauzy skirt that reached her ankles. Her feet were bare. The apartment, a studio, featured a huge bed covered with an Indian-print bedspread, a beat-up chrome and Formica table, and a pair of purple velvet chairs.

A rumpled page that looked like it had been torn out of a magazine sat on the table. Shown in the black and white illustration that accompanied the directions, the hat was not nearly as eye-catching as Nightingale's garish renditions.

"Have at it," Nightingale said, waving toward the

table as Pamela retrieved her phone from her purse. She watched as Pamela focused on the page, clicked, and turned the page over. "Those things can be useful, I guess."

Pamela finished, made a show of checking that the photos were in focus, and smiled. "Thank you so much. The knitting club will be delighted," she said as she slipped the phone back into her purse. Nightingale smiled back. "Nancy Billings is a lovely person," Pamela added. "Do you have other connections in Arborville?"

"No," Nightingale said dryly. "And I try never to go there. The place might as well be named 'Bourgeoisville.'"

Pamela suppressed a laugh. She actually thought the "Bourgeoisville" quip was rather funny. "But your niece," she said. "You made her the hat."

"Maybe she can still be rescued," Nightingale said. "But I doubt it. I go there for Christmas. That's it."

"Arborville can be a bit dull," Pamela said. "But there was that murder." She watched Nightingale's face carefully and went on. "Randall Jefferson." There was no reaction. "Not many people were close to him though," Pamela said.

"I wouldn't know." Nightingale picked up the knitting pattern and glanced around the room as if trying to recall where it came from.

"That page looks like it's been handled a lot," Pamela said. "Is this pattern a favorite?"

"Who'd make this thing more than once?" Nightingale wrinkled her nose.

"Well . . ." Pamela reached toward where the canvas bag sat on one of the velvet chairs. Trying to ignore the tight feeling in her throat and the tremble in her hands, she slowly drew out the orange and chartreuse hat and the knitting needles with the beginnings of the tail.

Nightingale stared at the spectacle. Then she attempted an unconcerned shrug and said, "So? Somebody else has a copy of the September 1961 issue of *Yarn Fancies*. What of it?" She used her fingers like a comb to push her tangled mass of hair away from her forehead.

"It's exactly the same yarn as in the hat you gave your niece," Pamela said. "That's quite a coincidence." She was feeling calmer now.

Nightingale frowned. "What are you, anyway? An undercover cop?" Pamela didn't answer. She concentrated on looking stern. "Okay," Nightingale said at last. "It's my project. But I don't know how it got to wherever you found it."

"It was under one of the pillows on Randall Jefferson's bed." Pamela locked her gaze onto Nightingale's, recalling the few times she'd had to exert her motherly authority to find out what Penny was up to.

"Can't think how it got there," Nightingale said. She fidgeted with her hair again. Perhaps nerves were making her perspire and her forehead needed air.

"I could return it to where it came from," Pamela said, tucking the project back into the canvas bag and clutching the bag closed with both hands. "Police are bound to find it, and they'll use DNA to trace it right to you. They've released their chief suspect because he turned out to have an alibi. So they're back to square one."

"I thought you were the police," Nightingale said.

"Never mind what I am." Pamela slung the bag over her shoulder and took a few steps toward the door. "The relationship you had with Randall Jefferson seems very suspicious, especially if you're not willing to acknowledge it."

"I knew him." Nightingale grabbed Pamela's arm and steered her toward one of the purple velvet chairs. Pamela lowered herself into it, still holding tight to the canvas bag. Nightingale sat in the other. "We were casual friends," she said. "We got together every once in a while to chat about . . . about . . . *opera*. I'm a huge fan."

"The knitting project was under one of the pillows on his bed," Pamela said.

"That's not his bed," Nightingale said firmly. "It's the guest room bed."

"He kept his clothes and his glasses and his bedtime reading material in the guest room?" Pamela said. "Seems odd."

"Okay. Um, well." Nightingale licked her lips. Her glance flickered around the room as if she was an actress frantically searching for a cue card. "*He* must have taken it up to his bedroom and put it under the pillow. We were chatting in the kitchen. Over coffee. I knew I'd left my knitting somewhere, but I couldn't remember where." She ventured a smile. "You know how it is when you love to knit—you carry it around with you wherever you go." Her eyes begged Pamela to acknowledge their kinship as fellow knitters.

"That's very far-fetched," Pamela said. "And I don't believe it. Neighbors saw you visiting him late at night, and then leaving again." She stood up and started toward the door. "The hat's going back under the pillow."

"Why?"

Pamela turned. Nightingale was still sitting in the purple velvet chair, her face with its strong features looking like a tragic mask, and her tangled hair vibrating as if alive. "You were having a relationship with him," Pamela said. "You're a grownup, he was a grownup, so why lie about it unless there's some reason you don't want anyone to know you knew him? Like the fact that you killed him?"

"I didn't kill him," Nightingale moaned. "I didn't. I really, really didn't."

"So why not admit you were involved with him? You might have information that would help the police find his killer." Pamela retraced her steps and perched on the chair again.

"It wasn't a conventional relationship," Nightingale said, her eyes focused on her hands, which were gripping each other tightly in her lap. She wore several large rings, and Pamela hoped the combination of large rings and intense squeezing wasn't too hard on the fingers involved.

"Lots of relationships aren't conventional," Pamela said encouragingly.

"He paid me." Nightingale sneaked a furtive glance at Pamela, then her gaze returned to her hands.

"Oh?" Pamela tried to make the word sound non-judgmental.

"It wasn't sexual!" Nightingale straightened her shoulders and raised her head. She fixed Pamela with a defiant stare.

"No?" Pamela tightened her lips to suppress any hint of amusement.

"He had insomnia, okay?" Now Nightingale sounded angry. Perhaps she'd had to explain one too many times that accepting money for visiting a man late at night didn't always mean what people thought it meant. "His mother was a knitter. The only thing that helped him get to sleep was hearing the click of knitting needles while a woman's voice told bedtime stories. He especially liked *Snow White and the Seven Dwarves.* He envied Sleepy."

Pamela couldn't contain herself. Laughter bubbled up, driven partly by amusement and partly by relief. She'd begun to like Nightingale and was just as glad to cross her off the list of suspects—especially now that Reynolds Jefferson was looking so guilty.

"I *did* feel bad when I heard he'd been killed. And those local radio stations can be so ghoulish with all the gruesome details."

"So why didn't you come forward and say you knew him? The police were interviewing everybody they could find."

"I went away," Nightingale said. "I didn't want to hear about it anymore." She sniffed vigorously and blinked a few times. Perhaps she was struggling with tears. She leaned toward Pamela. "I liked Randy," she said earnestly. "He could be stuffy, but it wasn't his fault. His dad was stuffy—that's what he said anyway. Determined for his sons to be *gentlemen.* Ivy League schools and all that. I didn't want it to come out that he had to have somebody tell him bedtime stories in order to fall asleep. I didn't want people to laugh at him."

Pamela hated to think of herself as a nosy person, and she'd learned everything she needed to learn. But she couldn't resist asking one more question. Nightingale saved her the trouble.

"You're wondering how I met him, aren't you?" Nightingale asked, looking more cheerful. She nodded in response to Pamela's surprised expression. "I can be kind of psychic. I knew what you were thinking." She tapped her forehead with an index finger.

"How *did* you meet him?" Pamela leaned back in the purple velvet chair. Perhaps an entertaining story was in the offing.

"I do voice-over work," Nightingale said. "Through an agency. He contacted the agency. The knitting came later—the bedtime stories alone just weren't doing the job." She nodded toward the canvas bag on Pamela's lap. "He gave me an old knitting magazine that had been his mom's. At first I didn't have a clue, but I figured it out, more or less. The main thing was for him to hear the needles clicking. The hat was probably a little overambitious, but the first one came out pretty good, so I just kept on with the hats." She shrugged. "They make good gifts. And he paid for the yarn, so what's not to like?"

Chapter Twenty-One

Bettina's car was still gone when Pamela got back home. She had a lot to report, so much, that instead of distracting her friend from the nature center's turtle presentation with a phone call, she'd wait until Bettina returned. Besides, it was nearly two p.m. and the mid-morning lemon-poppy seed cake hadn't been sufficient to serve as an early lunch.

Catrina was dozing on the sofa as Pamela entered and looked up briefly. "How are you?" Pamela said. She stepped into the living room and studied the cat. How soon could you tell if a cat was pregnant, she wondered. Perhaps Nell would know.

In the kitchen, she poured a can of lentil soup into a small saucepan and set it to heat on the stove. She buttered a slice of the bread Penny had brought back from the Co-Op, wondering when the "Killer Aardvark" issue would finally be resolved, so that she herself could shop there again.

After her quick meal, she called Nell. The story of how she'd allowed Catrina to dash through the open door and spend the night outside felt like a confession, but Nell was kind.

"The urge to mate is very powerful," Nell said. "Creatures find a way. When I was in college, I used to sneak out of my dorm's laundry-room window to spend the night with Harold."

"What I need to figure out," Pamela said, "is how can I tell if she's pregnant? Bettina says there's a tomcat in the neighborhood."

"You won't know for a few weeks," Nell said, "but even they can get morning sickness. You'd better hold off on getting her fixed though. Wait till you know what's going on."

Catrina had wandered into the kitchen. She jumped onto a chair, and from there onto the table. Pamela absentmindedly stroked her as Nell described her own recent encounters with the natural world, in the form of her garden.

"Bare spots," Nell said. "The winter was hard on things."

"My daylilies are quite overgrown," Pamela said. "Why don't I dig some tubers and bring them up the hill? I've got to spend the afternoon working on things for the magazine, but I'll deliver the tubers tomorrow morning."

Pamela had no sooner headed up to her office and turned on her computer than the doorbell summoned her back downstairs. Through the lace on the oval window she recognized Bettina, who was tapping on the glass for good measure.

"Did you know female turtles can lay thousands of eggs in their lifetimes, but out of all those eggs only a few turtles survive?" she asked as she stepped into the entry.

"I didn't," Pamela said. "But I've got things to tell you too."

As they headed toward the kitchen, Catrina strolled by. "That reminds me—" Bettina paused and watched the cat make her slow progress toward the sofa. "Does she seem . . . *different* . . . at all?"

"It's too soon to know," Pamela said. "At least according to Nell."

"Wilfred feels terrible. He thinks it was totally his fault that she got out. If there are kittens, we'll take them. I promise. All of them."

"Let's wait and see," Pamela said. She quickly made coffee and they sat at the kitchen table as she described her meeting with Nightingale.

"Sounds nutty," Bettina commented. "But kind of believable. It looks like Reynolds is our guy. Unless Clayborn discovers that there's really a connection between the doll full of pins and the murder. Or decides Marcus Verteel is worth looking into after all."

"Does Detective Clayborn know about Reynolds?" Pamela asked.

"They tracked him down and interviewed him, of course, right after the murder," Bettina said. "But he doesn't know what we know, and I can't tell him what we know because then I'd have to tell him about how we've been snooping in the house and all of that." She added more cream to her coffee. "I'll figure out when we can be sure Reynolds is on duty in the shop, and we'll go back and talk to him. Maybe I can get Wilfred to call and ask when he can confer with the partner who does the buying, to discuss the houseful of furniture he just inherited."

* * *

Pamela finally did get to settle down at her desk, and she worked without stopping until she heard the front door open and then Penny's voice. The words were indistinct, but as soon as she opened her office door and started down the stairs, she realized that she wasn't the one who was being addressed.

"Did you have a nice adventure?" Penny was murmuring. She was crouching on the floor stroking Catrina, who was stretched out on her side in a pose made all the more languorous by her closed eyes and slight smile.

Penny looked up. "How does she seem?" she asked.

"It's too soon to say."

Penny hopped to her feet and Catrina opened her eyes, looking resentful that her rub had been interrupted. "I'll run up and change," Penny said. She'd dressed for work that morning in a pleated navy-blue skirt and a white blouse with red polka dots.

After dinner, Pamela ventured out into the May evening, taking with her a section of the day's newspaper and a canvas bag that had long since been superseded by newer canvas bags. The sky was still bright, with sunset nearly an hour away. In the garage, she exchanged her sandals for an old pair of clogs and retrieved a shovel and her gardening gloves.

A clump of daylilies returned year after year in a sunny spot between the side of Pamela's garage and the hedge that separated her backyard from Richard Larkin's. She stepped gingerly among the long spikes of leaves and the slender stalks bearing cheery blooms shaped like fragile six-armed starfish.

Daylilies were nearly indestructible, she knew. Any

bare spots would fill in quickly as the hardy plants spread. She set the curved edge of the shovel blade against the ground in a spot where one plant seemed to leave off and another begin. She stomped down hard to drive the blade into the soil, twisted the shovel, moved it to the right, and stomped again. A few more stomps and she leaned on the shovel handle to lever out the clump of loosened earth with the fingerlike daylily tubers. She laid the clump on a sheet of newspaper and moved to a spot a few feet away to repeat the process.

Soon she'd accumulated six clumps of tubers, the trailing leaves making them resemble exotic offerings in a market's produce section. She knelt on the grass to roll each in its sheet of newspaper and tuck the rolls into the canvas bag. She'd leave the bag out in the cool night air and deliver it to Nell the next morning.

As she clambered to her feet, a rustling in the hedge caught her attention. She looked toward where a spray of leaves near the ground was vibrating, and as she watched a cat emerged. It was a huge ginger cat, and it stalked past the stand of daylilies with as much self-possession as if it weren't countless generations removed from its wild forebears. Just before it veered off to make its way down the driveway, it turned and gave Pamela a long stare. She could have sworn that it was smiling.

The next morning, Pamela set out after coffee and toast, the canvas bag full of daylily tubers slung over her shoulder. The air was clear, the day was bright, and May was so far advanced that even at ten a.m. it was worth crossing the street if a row of trees offered a respite from the sun. By the time she'd climbed the hill and reached the corner of Nell and Harold's street, she was sweating and panting a bit. If she hadn't stopped right then to wipe her forehead, catch her breath, and shift the daylilies to her other shoulder, she might not have known about the new development in the Randall Jefferson murder case until she heard it reported on the radio.

As it was, she stood on the corner waiting for her breathing to return to normal and enjoying the cooling sight of the lush foliage in the surrounding yards. Randall Jefferson's yard was particularly lush, even overgrown, with him no longer on hand to schedule landscapers' visits. The plantings that bordered the meandering slate steps nearly hid the steps in some spots. When she and Bettina had visited, they had zigzagged their way up, pushing foliage aside, to reach the impressive double doors . . . and—Pamela blinked—one of those doors was ajar right now.

She blinked again. Not so odd though, really. Randall Jefferson had used the door leading to the driveway to carry his boxes of goodies out, but perhaps someone with a legitimate errand was inside now, even a Realtor. Perhaps enough time had passed that the chores involved in settling the estate could begin. Or perhaps the police were scavenging for overlooked clues. Detective Clayborn might step out onto the porch at any moment.

She crossed the street and skirted the edge of Jefferson's sloping yard, heading toward Nell and Harold's house. As she made her way past the forest of azaleas and rhododendrons that took the place of a lawn, she glanced toward the imposing buff-colored structure, wondering who its next occupant would be. But her

eyes paused midway up the rise that gave the house its
imposing air. A glint of silver amid the greens and
blooms seemed out of place. She stopped and stared.
Something else seemed out of place as well. Just visible
beneath the lowest branches of a towering rhododendron was a man's shoe.

She backtracked to view the scene from another
angle. Standing on the lowest step of the slate walkway
that led to the front door, she could no longer see the
silver object. But she could see what the shoe was attached to—a leg. And next to it was another shoe and
another leg. The legs were wearing trousers—cuffed
trousers—made of some light-colored fabric. Between
the trouser cuffs and the shoes, brownish in color,
were ankles sheathed in dark-colored socks.

Curiosity overcame the sudden attack of nerves that
had made Pamela's heart speed up. Ignoring the urgent
thudding in her chest, she set down the canvas bag
containing the tubers and continued climbing the
steps. Halfway up, she stepped off the walkway and
detoured around an azalea that reached nearly to her
shoulders. Pushing the blossom-heavy branches of the
azalea aside, she edged toward the giant rhododendron
and stooped toward where the legs emerged from the
thick, dark green foliage.

The trousers were seersucker, the classic blue and
white stripe. The silver object that had first caught her
attention proved to be a teapot, large and round as a
pumpkin, with a raised design featuring an impressive
dragon, and a spout and handle modeled to resemble
bamboo. She stood and peered around the large
shrub in order to get a better view, and realized that
the teapot lay as if it had just slipped from the grasp of
a hand that was now visible.

Pamela backed away from the rhododendron as her mind raced. Summon the police, obviously, but her habit when walking was to leave her phone at home and let her thoughts wander. She'd hurry on to Nell's—that would be the best plan. Something was nagging at her though. The seersucker pants. Could it be that Reynolds Jefferson was no longer a suspect in the killing of his brother? Because he himself had just become a victim?

She stepped toward the rhododendron and slid a hand past one of its huge wine-colored blossoms. She did the same thing with her other hand. Then she grasped a branch with each hand, pushed the branches aside, and leaned into the leafy interior of the plant, inhaling its earthy, woody smell. Below she could see a torso, also clothed in seersucker, and enough of a face to recognize the man who had been filling his car with boxes of goodies looted from his dead brother's house. But the V-shape between the jacket's lapels, where a shirt and bow tie would have been visible, was hidden from view—not by an intervening branch, but by a splash of unexpected color. Turquoise to be exact.

Whoever was responsible for the fact that Reynolds Jefferson was now dead and reposing under a rhodo-dendron in the front yard of his family home had finished off the job by plopping one of the Arborville knitting club's aardvarks on his chest. Pamela let go of the branches and they snapped back into place, brushing her cheeks with their stiff leaves. She squeezed past the azalea and launched herself down the slate walkway toward the sidewalk. She'd run to Nell's, only a few houses away. But at the bottom of the steps she stopped.

Instead of turning toward Nell's, she hurried toward

the corner and then up the hill toward Randall Jefferson's driveway. At the driveway's end she paused just long enough to observe that a black Mercedes SUV with New York plates was parked near the back door.

An accomplice had pulled up in the SUV the day Bettina and Pamela watched Reynolds Jefferson stage the boxes on the driveway. Loading the boxes in the SUV and transporting them to J & J Antiques had evidently been a two-person job. Had Reynolds come back alone today? Or was the accomplice lurking somewhere, afraid to meet the same fate that had just befallen his boss? Or was he perhaps the killer, observing her from the shrubbery?

That thought set Pamela in motion. She whirled around and sped toward Nell's house, grabbing up the canvas bag with the tubers en route. Her feet struck the sidewalk with bone-jarring thuds and the bag flopped against her back. She arrived on Nell's porch, chest heaving as frantically as if she'd run a mile rather than half a block—though the steps that led up to the front door of Nell and Harold's substantial house *were* challenging—and pressed the doorbell. A faint chime echoed inside and time passed—probably no more than a second, but things were happening in slow motion now, and she found herself pounding on the door, desperate for a response.

The door swung back to reveal Nell. "What is it? What's happened?" Nell asked, hunching forward and peering intently at Pamela.

"There's a body!" Pamela gestured in the direction of Jefferson's house, and her arm began to flail uncontrollably. "And an aardvark! Under a rhododendron!" She felt a catch in her throat.

"Oh, my dear!" Nell reached out and drew Pamela over the threshold.

"Has something happened?" Harold Bascomb stood in the arch that led from the entry to the living room.

Still hugging Pamela, Nell turned her head. "Call the police, Harold," she said, sounding somewhat annoyed. "There's been another one of those aardvark killings."

Nell insisted that Pamela accept a cup of tea. At some point the canvas bag with the daylily tubers slipped off her shoulder and was tossed to the side in the entry, and she found herself seated at Nell's kitchen table. The tea kettle hadn't even begun to whistle when, heading up the hill, came the sound of a siren, like the high-pitched whine of an angry animal—and then another, and another.

The kettle finally whistled and Nell set loose tea steeping in a cheerful pot. In a few minutes she pronounced the brew drinkable and prepared a cup for Pamela, adding a spoonful of sugar and a dollop of milk. "Now you sit here and drink this," she said, slipping the cup in front of Pamela, "while I—" She stepped into the hallway. "Harold?" she called, and when there was no answer, added, "Now where has he gotten to?"

Pamela sipped the tea, feeling as comforted by Nell's solicitude as by the sweet, fragrant liquid. She heard the front door open and Nell call, "Harold! You come back in here right now. They don't need your help."

Harold came panting into the kitchen, followed by Nell. "They found the murder weapon," he announced. "Another rock, just like before. I saw them looking at it, and I heard one of them say it had blood on it, but they didn't pick it up. They have to wait for those guys in the white coveralls, from the sheriff's department. But Clayborn is already out there. I told him you were the one who found the body, and that you were sitting in our kitchen."

Detective Clayborn wanted a private interview, not a cozy chat in Nell's kitchen with Nell and Harold as audience. As he escorted Pamela down the sidewalk toward where his police car was parked, it occurred to her that she was in something of a predicament. It wasn't that she could possibly be a suspect—certainly he'd already realized that this second murder, so similar to the Arborfest murder, was the work of the same killer. And he'd rapidly dismissed her as responsible for Randall Jefferson's death.

No—the problem was that she knew much more about the victim than the police did. A wallet, which perhaps they'd already recovered, would tell them his name and address. And they'd make the connection to J & J Antiques soon enough. (She paused in her ruminations to reflect sadly that the other "J" in "J & J" had just been deprived of his partner—in life and in business, as he had put it.) But she could hasten things along for them, if only there was a way to do so without revealing her own snooping.

Sometimes it was best not to overanalyze.

"He's Randall Jefferson's brother," she blurted out as Detective Clayborn reached to open the passenger-side door of his police car.

He paused, his fingers on the door handle, his eyes on her. His homely face tightened. Then it relaxed, as if he'd thought better of the expression. He smiled slightly. "Let's talk about that," he said, swinging the door open and gesturing for her to get in. He settled in the driver's seat and took out a small notepad and a pen.

"But," he said, turning toward her, "why don't you tell me first how you happened to discover the body?"

"I was walking past Randall Jefferson's house," Pamela said, "on my way to Nell and Harold Bascomb's, to deliver some daylily tubers." Her mind flashed to the tubers, abandoned in their canvas bag in Nell's entry. "I looked up toward the house—it *is* quite impressive. There was something silver in the bushes, shiny. It seemed out of place, so I stopped and looked closer. Then I saw a shoe, sticking out from under a big rhododendron bush. So I walked up the path and waded through the azaleas till I got to the rhododendron, and I pushed some branches aside, and there he was underneath, with the aardvark on his chest."

"And you knew right away he was Randall Jefferson's brother?" His expression was neutral, with a hint of skepticism.

"He looked so much like Randall," Pamela said. "His face. There's a definite resemblance. And the clothes . . . the seersucker suit. Randall always dressed formally too, like somebody who really belonged somewhere else, somewhere fancier than Arborville." The hint of skepticism became more pronounced. "And right here in front of Randall's house, and the front door was open, so it seemed that, yes, he was probably Randall's brother. Someone has it in for the whole family. That's logical, isn't it?" Pamela nodded, set her lips in a firm line, and looked directly into Detective Clayborn's eyes.

"The killer's motive is not something for you to

concern yourself with," Detective Clayborn said with a frown that made him look more like himself.

"There's an SUV with New York plates around the corner in the driveway," Pamela said. "But you probably noticed that already."

"We did," he said, and the frown deepened.

Chapter Twenty-Two

Detective Clayborn wanted to talk to Harold and Nell too, but just as he was twisting his key in the ignition to drive half a block farther down the street, one of the uniformed officers tapped on his window to summon him back to the crime scene.

"I'll ask someone to take you home," he said as Pamela reached for the door handle on her side.

"It's okay," she said, hopping out. "I left something at Nell's, and I don't live that far away."

The canvas bag with the daylily tubers still lay in the corner of Nell's entry. Pamela scooped it up as she followed Nell to the kitchen. Proceeding down the long hallway, she noted the empty hook that had held the key to Jefferson's house, almost hidden among the masks and baskets and puppets. Apparently Nell had never noticed that the key was gone. "Detective Clayborn is coming to talk to you," she said to Nell's back.

"*I* didn't see anything," Nell said without turning around. "But since it was Harold who called the police, I suppose they think he's relevant." She continued on through the kitchen and into the mudroom, where she opened the back door and called, "Harold! The police are coming to talk to you!"

Harold followed her back to the kitchen, trailed by Joe Taylor, whose hands were covered with dirt. "I'm wrapping up for the day," Joe said, "but it sounds like big doings down the street. I suppose the cops will ask me if I saw anything, since I was in your yard all afternoon." He shook his head. "It's a shame—not what you expect in a town like this."

"Where's that bag?" Nell said. Pamela handed it over, and Nell passed it to Joe. "Daylily tubers," Nell said. "Whenever you have a chance to get them in the ground."

"You got it, Mrs. B," Joe said, and headed back the way he'd come.

Pamela convinced Nell that a second cup of tea wasn't necessary. She was anxious to hurry back to Orchard Street and update Bettina on the latest development. But instead of walking past the crime scene, she turned in the other direction and descended the hill by the route that ended up at the edge of Arborville's commercial district. As she made her way along Arborville Avenue, Wilfred's ancient Mercedes pulled over to the opposite curb and he waved at her.

"Heading home?" he called. Pamela nodded and hurried across the street. Wilfred chuckled as she climbed in. "Good news," he said. "I just spent twenty minutes in the Co-Op, and no one said anything to me about the 'Killer Aardvark.' I think the crisis has passed, and I came away with the makings of chili, plus crumb cake and a pound of Bettina's favorite Stilton from the cheese counter."

Pamela sighed. She reached over to touch Wilfred's shoulder. "It's starting again," she said. "Remember how there were two missing aardvarks . . . ?"

* * *

"I guess that means we can cross Reynolds Jefferson off the list of suspects." Bettina spread mayonnaise on whole-grain toast and added slices of avocado. She arranged the result on one of her craft-store plates and slid it in front of Pamela. "You'll feel better if you eat something," she said. "It's almost noon." Wilfred had delivered Pamela not to her own home but to Bettina's welcome ministrations, and the three of them were sitting at the pine table in Bettina's kitchen.

Pamela obediently bit into Bettina's creation, but she scarcely tasted it. The image of Reynolds Jefferson lying dead under the rhododendron was still vivid in her mind. But she was equally troubled by the fact that she and Bettina were no closer to figuring out who had chosen to implicate the knitting club in his (her?) crimes by adding aardvarks to the crime scenes.

"I suppose there's nothing new on Marcus Verteel," Pamela said after she'd eaten half her sandwich.

"Why would he kill Randall Jefferson's brother?" Bettina raised her hands, palms facing upwards. She twisted her lips into a puzzled knot. "The rivalry was between him and Randall."

"True." Pamela nodded sadly. "I suppose this new development also means that Randall wasn't killed by a disgruntled student who made a doll of him and stuck it full of pins."

Wilfred spoke up from his end of the table. "Unless there are two killers with two motives."

"Both using rocks and perching aardvarks on the corpse?" Pamela's voice was mournful.

"Copy-cat killer?" Wilfred said.

"I suppose Clayborn will want you to examine the aardvark and tell him if it's one of ours," Bettina said.

"I suppose so," Pamela said.

Bettina rose and set to work at the counter, creating sandwiches for herself and Wilfred. Pamela lingered at the pine table, finishing her own sandwich and resisting Bettina's encouragement to accept another.

Pamela stepped outside to discover a knot of reporters waiting on her driveway. She took a deep breath and crossed the street, answered their questions as quickly as she could, and gratefully took refuge in the comfort of her own house. Upstairs, she lost herself in editing three articles for *Fiber Craft*, and the afternoon went by with no calls from the police department. It took Catrina's piteous meowing to bring her back to reality and notice it was dinnertime—for both cat and human.

Penny came in as Pamela slouched on the sofa, dozing with a British mystery unfolding on the screen before her and the beginnings of the ruby-red tunic resting on its needles in her lap. Catrina leapt gracefully to the floor and greeted Penny with an ankle-rub as Pamela opened her eyes and offered a groggy, "Hi."

"Everybody's talking about the new murder," Penny said. She'd been to the movies with old friends from Arborville.

"Do they have any brilliant ideas about who did it?" Pamela pulled herself into a sitting position and regarded her daughter, who was dressed in the T-shirt and jeans she still favored when she wasn't heading for work. "Probably not the person who made the Jefferson doll—at least not if the doll was the result of being mad about a bad grade. Reynolds Jefferson was an antiques dealer."

Penny laughed. "Oh, Mom," she said. "I know all about the doll now. The girl who made it *was* mad that Mr. Jefferson gave her an F—but she didn't kill him. Lorie Hopkins's little sister is still at Arborville High. Remember what I said about mean girls? Lorie's sister isn't a mean girl, but she told Lorie all about the doll. A girl named Heather made it, and one of her frenemies thought it would be funny to leave it on our porch."

"I don't think anybody ever really thought the person who made the Jefferson doll was the killer," Pamela said, "but I suppose I should pass that information along to Detective Clayborn."

Chapter Twenty-Three

Focus on the positive and praise it. That had been Pamela's philosophy in raising her daughter, and the result had been a happy and confident young woman. Now Pamela stood at her kitchen window, sipping the last of her morning coffee and watching Richard Larkin. He was wearing the torn and faded jeans that, on a man less fit, would have looked foolish or just plain sad—but which she now realized weren't a fashion statement but a testament to his frugality. He'd finished off the outfit with a T-shirt, equally distressed, but it clung to his torso in a way that revealed exactly how fit he was. And he was pacing along the edge of his perennial border. He bent forward, plunged a hand among the foliage, and came up with a ragged fistful of crabgrass.

This industry deserved praise if Miranda Bonham's perennial border was to be coaxed back to its former glory. Pamela finished her coffee and rinsed the cup. In a few minutes, she was striding past Richard Larkin's recycling bins. She stepped into his backyard just in time to greet Joe Taylor, arriving from the other direction with a wheelbarrow full of plants in plastic nursery pots.

"Foxgloves," Joe said. "Just the thing to fill in those bare spots. Not perennials, strictly speaking, but they provide a great contrast to the lower, bushier areas."

Richard turned around while Joe was speaking, but instead of looking at Joe, he looked at Pamela. The expression on his face was so serious Pamela wondered if she was welcome. "Oh, uh . . . hello," he said, taking a step toward her, reaching out a hand, and then retracting it. "I didn't know you were here. I—" He seemed to think better of his action and retreated, stumbling backwards into the perennial border and catching his balance between a peony and a stand of goldenrod.

Joe hid a smile and busied himself lifting the foxgloves out of the wheelbarrow, placing them at intervals among the other plants that made up the border.

"The garden is looking good," Pamela said. "Very good."

Richard's strong features softened. "You're all right, I hope. After yesterday. It was all in the *Register* this morning."

"I'm fine," Pamela said, "but that peony—"

With one long step, Richard was once more on the grass. "And Nell and Harold? Nell was quoted in the article, so I guess reporters were all over the place up there."

"And I'm sure Detective Clayborn will get interested in the knitting club again." Pamela shrugged. "But I wonder if the police will ever figure things out. They certainly hadn't gotten anywhere with *Randall* Jefferson's murder." Joe knelt on the ground behind Richard and began digging a hole next to a patch of salvia. "Of course," she went on, "this second murder could actually be a clue—take the focus off Randall's role in the community and put it on the Jefferson family."

"Did he actually have a role in the community?" Richard seemed less nervous now that there was a clear topic of conversation. "I got the impression from Wilfred that nobody much liked him."

"People respected him," Pamela said. "But as far as *knowing* him goes, Nell knew him about as well as anybody. She knew his parents too, and her children went to Arborville High with the Jefferson boys. She's lived up in the Palisades forever, and she could probably tell a lot of tales if she wanted to."

Joe dislodged a foxglove from its plastic pot, set it in the hole he'd dug, and patted the loose earth into place around it. He scooted along the ground to where another foxglove waited to be planted and began to dig.

"She seems too sensible to tell tales," Richard said. "I like her—even if she wasn't the one who brought those deviled eggs to the barbecue."

"She's not a gossip by any means—far from it," Pamela said, "but Detective Clayborn can be very persistent—and I think he's embarrassed about arresting Brad Striker and then having to let him go. I'm sure he wants to make progress now, and fast."

"Good point." Richard nodded. "If I was him, I'd sit down with Nell and not get up until she'd told me everything she knows about the Jeffersons. Two brothers killed within two weeks? It's got to have something to do with family secrets."

Pamela had gotten out of bed that morning determined not to think about Randall or Reynolds Jefferson, so she said, "Penny has really loved getting to know Laine and Sybil."

"I'm afraid they won't be in Arborville this weekend."

Richard stepped to the side as Joe changed position to attack his new hole from another angle. "It's Laine's birthday and my parents are in town. We're all going out to dinner."

"The whole family," Pamela said.

Richard nodded. "The whole family."

Back at home, Pamela found Penny, still in her nightgown and with uncombed hair, sitting at the kitchen table poring over the *Register*. She looked up, a worried crease marring her smooth forehead. "Did the police ask you if the aardvark was one of yours yet?"

"Not yet."

"I always thought it was kind of a dumb mascot." Penny frowned in mock seriousness and pounded her fists on the table. "Varks! Varks! Go, Varks, go! Why couldn't we be the Lions or the Bears or something?"

"Laine and Sybil are staying in the city this weekend," Pamela said.

"Dinner with their grandparents." Penny nodded. "The whole family." She jumped up. "Lorie and I are going to the mall," she said, "I've got to get dressed."

"Breakfast?" Pamela called after her.

"We'll eat at the donut place in the food court," Penny answered from halfway up the stairs.

The whole family. That couldn't be the answer, could it? Pamela stood in the middle of the kitchen staring at nothing. But what if it was? Details of the library display drifted back to her. She reached for the phone.

Nell answered right away. Pamela pictured her in her kitchen, still lingering over her morning tea. She asked the question that had popped into her mind as she stared at nothing. Nell started to answer, but then she interrupted herself. "There's someone at the door," she said, "and Harold has gone to the farmers market in Newfield. Just one minute."

Still holding the phone, Pamela ran to the window. Three foxgloves planted and three to go, but no sign of the gardener. "No, Nell!" she squealed, barely recognizing her own voice. "Don't answer the door. Call the police."

Pamela grabbed her keys. She wouldn't walk—there wasn't time. She didn't even stop for the stop sign at the corner of Orchard Street and Arborville Avenue, only dimly aware of an amazed Mr. Gilly pausing behind his lawnmower to stare as she shot into the intersection.

He was there, at the top of the stone steps that led past the viburnums, pounding on Harold and Nell's front door. Pamela jumped out of her car and screamed, "She's not going to let you in, and the police are on the way."

Joe Taylor turned and stared. "Why should the police be on the way?" he asked. "I left my big shovel here, and I need it for Rick's yard."

For a minute Pamela wasn't sure what to do. Maybe he was telling the truth, and the picture that had formed in her mind when the last puzzle piece slipped into place was no more than a work of her imagination. But the look on his face told her that he was worried about more than a missing shovel.

"They were your uncles, weren't they?" she said. "Your father was the third brother and the black sheep of the Jefferson family."

"No!" he said. "You're crazy!"

From down the hill came the sound of a siren, as piercing and insistent as one of Catrina's cries in the grip of her first mating season. It rose and fell, growling, shrieking, growling again. At the top of the steps, Joe froze. He looked frantically toward Pamela, and then he looked in the direction of the siren, his handsome face distorted more by confusion than by fear.

As Joe stared toward the siren, Harold pulled into the driveway from the opposite direction. He got out of his car and opened the trunk.

The siren got closer. Joe swung around and leapt off the porch into the shrubbery. Pushing branches aside, he struggled toward the sidewalk. The bushes rustled and Harold looked up, puzzled.

"Stop him," Pamela cried. "He's the killer!"

Harold stood still for a minute. He stared at Joe, stared at Pamela, stared back at Joe, and gave a resolute nod. He reached into the trunk of his car and came up with a potato, which he threw at Joe. The potato struck Joe's forehead and bounced off. Joe staggered slightly.

"You killed Randall and Reynolds, didn't you?" Pamela said. "I know you did it, and I think I know why. You shouldn't have told me your lottery number."

Harold threw another potato. It hit Joe on the cheek and he slumped back into the shrubbery. "My dad was just a guy," Joe said, his voice breaking. "He liked football and girls and hanging out with his friends drinking beer, and when he graduated from Arborville High, he joined the Navy. He didn't deserve to be disinherited. He never married my mother, but when she took off he raised me. And then when he died—" Joe pulled himself to his feet and lurched ahead, pushing branches out of the way. "All I wanted was a little help . . . to make something of myself. I thought my uncles would be proud that I had ambition, but they treated me like I was nobody." He dodged around an azalea. "I'm getting out of here, and you're not going to stop me."

Harold threw a third potato, and then a fourth. Pamela joined him on the driveway, grabbing potatoes from a canvas bag in the trunk. For a minute or two, all that mattered was the feel of the potatoes in her hand, the tightening of muscle as she slung her arm back, the jerk and the satisfying snap of her elbow as each potato went flying. Meanwhile the siren grew louder and louder.

A police car swung around the corner and pulled up at the curb. The siren's shriek faded to a resentful moan and then silence. Two officers sprang out. Joe Taylor leapt over an azalea and bounded along the driveway toward the sidewalk.

Nell appeared on the porch. "Stop him!" she yelled toward the officers. "He's the killer!"

One of the officers took off after Joe. "What's going on here?" the other asked. It was the pleasant-voiced officer who had shown up at the booth the day Pamela discovered Randall Jefferson's body.

"He killed those two men," Pamela said, "and he came up here to kill Nell because she knows the Jefferson family secrets."

The pleasant-voiced officer took off after his partner, and soon the two of them had wrestled Joe to the ground. They linked his wrists together with handcuffs, led him to the police car, and bundled him inside. The wail of another siren suggested that reinforcements were on the way.

Pamela leaned shakily against Harold's car as Nell started down the steps. The potatoes had still had dirt on them, and Pamela's hands felt gritty. She rubbed them together.

Harold gazed toward the shrubbery. "Nell isn't going to like these potatoes going to waste," he said. "I'd better try to gather them up—but what was that business about the lottery number?"

Chapter Twenty-Four

The blueberry cobbler was cooling on Pamela's kitchen table, which had been spread with a freshly ironed cloth. Bettina was setting out cups and saucers from Pamela's wedding china on a painted wooden tray. Coffee beans had been ground and loose tea spooned into the teapot.

"I'm just sorry the police whisked him off so fast," Bettina said. "All the trouble he caused and we couldn't even get a picture of him in handcuffs for the *Advocate*." She reached for Pamela's cut-glass sugar bowl. "This is getting low. Shall I fill it?"

"Sure. And there's cream in the refrigerator." Pamela held out the matching cut-glass cream pitcher. "The *Register* had a shot of him appearing in court," she said.

"I saw it," Bettina said. "And that quote from Benson Jasper. Poor man. I know how I'd feel if I lost Wilfred."

"It's a sad way to come into a fortune." Pamela counted out six forks and six spoons.

"We certainly jumped to conclusions, didn't we?" Bettina said.

"It all made sense, or seemed to." Pamela's lips formed

a sad smile. "Killing Randall and helping himself to his brother's beautiful things."

"We just didn't know that Randall and Reynolds had jointly inherited the house and everything in it. Then, when Randall was gone, it all belonged to Reynolds, and now it belongs to Benson." Bettina opened the refrigerator and reached for the cream.

Their conversation was interrupted by the doorbell. Pamela hurried to the entry, and in a minute Nell and Roland were stepping over the threshold. Roland had apparently come directly from work and was dressed in one of his flawlessly tailored suits and a shirt whose starchy perfection had outlasted a ten-hour day in a corporate office. Nell wore nondescript pants and a faded blue chambray shirt that matched her eyes.

Roland offered a quick greeting and headed for his usual seat on the sofa, but Nell lingered in the entry. "How is Catrina doing?" she asked. Catrina had been dozing in the chair by the mail table. She looked up sleepily and blinked her yellow eyes.

"She seems the same," Pamela said. "I mean, the same as she used to be, before . . . before she started acting strange."

"I have to warn you"—Nell chuckled—"cats are very efficient breeders. You might end up with a whole family." She started toward the living room but paused. "Richard Larkin certainly is a nice man," she said. "He was getting out of his car as I walked past his house just now. He made a point of asking if I was okay, and he was concerned about you too. He seemed very solicitous."

Bettina chimed in from the kitchen doorway. "He planted the rest of the foxgloves," she said. "I ran into him yesterday. He told me he's determined to keep the perennial border in good shape. He wanted you to know."

"Ummm." Nell studied Pamela with an appraising smile. "He's single, and good looking. Is it possible he's—"

"Is it possible you're both more interested in my business than I am?" Pamela tried to leaven the question with a smile of her own.

"You're not getting any younger," Roland piped up from the sofa.

"For heaven's sake!" Pamela retreated to the kitchen, where she counted out six dessert plates for the cobbler. She knew about the foxgloves. She'd watched from her kitchen window as Richard labored in his yard all Sunday afternoon.

The doorbell rang again and Pamela stood in the kitchen doorway as Bettina welcomed little blond Karen and her gregarious friend, Holly.

"What you did was *amazing*," Holly squealed, catching sight of Pamela and displaying her perfect teeth in a dimply smile. "You're totally a hero. And Nell—" She turned toward where Nell had joined Roland on the sofa. "You were so brave."

"I was inside the house the whole time," Nell said with a shrug. "I hardly knew what was happening until the end."

"And Harold coming to your defense like that—I can't wait to hear the whole story from him." Holly advanced toward the sofa but took a seat on a footstool nearby. Karen perched on the rummage-sale chair with the carved wooden back and needlepoint seat.

"There's room here on the sofa," Nell called to Bettina.

Pamela stepped back into the kitchen to finish preparing for the refreshment break. She reached down her electric mixer and fitted it with its beaters, and she set out the deep bowl she'd whip the cream in for the cobbler. Bits of conversation drifting in from the living room suggested the group had all read the *Register*'s report of Joe Taylor's arrest as thoroughly as if preparing for an exam. They were now happily rehashing the details. She lingered over the table, arranging and rearranging the already-neat stack of napkins.

When she finally joined the group in the living room, they had settled down to work on their projects. Nell was casting on for another scarf—bright blue this time, Holly's giant needles were twisting and looping her giant yarn into another section of her chic jacket, and Karen was shaping another tiny sleeve. Roland was toiling at the pink angora dog sweater, which had barely grown since the previous meeting. "Busy week," he murmured when he noticed Nell observing him, "but I'll get in a solid two hours of knitting tonight."

Pamela offered the comfortable armchair to Karen and then to Holly, but they insisted she take it. She settled against its soft cushions, pulled out the ruby-red yarn and the needles with the beginnings of the tunic's back, and abandoned herself to the rhythmic motions that stitch by stitch, row by row, would create the glamorous garment pictured in the pattern book.

But suddenly Holly spoke. "How *did* you figure it out?" she asked, looking up from her project. "That's one thing the *Register* didn't explain."

"I—what?" Pamela was startled. She sensed that she was frowning and made an effort to smooth her forehead.

"How did you figure out it was Joe Taylor? And just in time to rescue Nell?"

"I was in the house the whole time," Nell protested from the sofa.

"He could have broken a window," Holly said. "He wanted to kill you. He would have found a way, if Pamela hadn't told you not to answer the door and to call the police instead. And then to drive up there, and stop him from escaping—" The look she gave Pamela was so admiring that Pamela felt embarrassed.

"It was Harold who thought of the potatoes," Pamela said.

"Don't get me wrong—" Nell had apparently reconsidered her comment. She leaned forward and caught Pamela's gaze. "It was very brave. And how *did* you figure it out? I want to know too. Harold told me about the lottery number, but there must have been other clues as well."

"The Jeffersons had three sons," Pamela said. "You must have known that, Nell, and when I called you it was to check on what I suspected about number three. There was a photo in Randall's study, obviously taken in front of the Jefferson house long ago—"

"Randall's study?" Nell's voice scaled an octave. "How did you—?"

Pamela grimaced. She hadn't meant to give that part away.

"Did Harold give you that key?" Nell half rose from the sofa and Pamela shrank against the cushions. But Nell laughed and sank back down. "I guess it's water over the bridge, as Wilfred would say. You're okay, and Joe Taylor is in jail."

Roland looked up. "And all those aardvarks we worked so hard on are in a box at the Co-Op. What are we going to do about that?"

"They're not at the Co-Op anymore," Nell said. "They've

been donated to the women's shelter in Haversack, for children staying there with their mothers."

"Nice idea," Bettina murmured, but Holly was squirming impatiently on the footstool.

"The photo, the photo," she said, looking like an excited child with her wide eyes and flushed cheeks. "What about the photo?"

"It showed a man and two little boys," Pamela began. She realized that she was enjoying herself, at least a little bit, like she sometimes felt when she helped a fellow knitter with a pattern she herself understood clearly. She went on, "But the edge had been cut off, as if there was someone else in the photo that the owner of the photo wanted to erase from memory."

"The black sheep!" Bettina spoke up from the sofa.

Pamela nodded. "Bettina and I found out that Randall had a brother, Reynolds, and that Reynolds was an antiques dealer. This was before Reynolds was killed, obviously. We went to his shop in the city and his partner told us that there was a third brother, but that brother had been disinherited."

Nell was frowning and Pamela knew she disapproved of the sleuthing. So she was relieved when Roland, who had been listening closely, cut in. "I don't see any connection at all," he said with a dismissive laugh. "Lots of families have black sheep. Why should a black sheep in the Jefferson family mean Joe Taylor was the killer?"

"Aardvarks," Pamela said. "The team, not the animal. Joe's father was a football star at Arborville High. The library has a display about the high school's athletic program up now, and a yellowed clipping from the *Advocate* shows Joe's father in jersey number 43. The team won the state championship in 1985. Joe let slip one day that when he plays the lottery he always uses the same number, 431985. And when he got a look at the aardvarks out on display at the Knit and Nibble booth he said, 'Nice varks.' Only somebody who'd listened to his father relive his glory days on the football field at Arborville High would call them 'varks.'"

Roland grunted. "Impressive reasoning, I have to admit. And meanwhile, what were the police doing with our tax dollars? Privatizing some aspects of law enforcement might—"

Nell's knitting flew across the room, and she sprang up from the sofa. "That is the silliest thing you have ever said," she exclaimed.

Pamela jumped up too. "There's blueberry cobbler," she said hastily, "with whipped cream, and coffee and tea of course."

Bettina was on her feet. "I'm certainly ready for a break," she said.

"I'll help with serving." Nell retrieved her knitting and gestured at Karen and Holly to stay put.

In the kitchen, Pamela poured cream into the deep bowl and set to work with the electric mixer. Bettina got water for coffee and tea started in the kettle while Nell scooped portions of the cobbler, deep purplish blue with golden-brown crumbles of crust, onto plates. Soon they were all reunited in the living room, plates of cobbler topped with whipped cream in hand and the tray with four coffees, two teas, and the cut-glass sugar bowl and cream pitcher waiting on the coffee table.

"My turn next week," Holly said, showing her dimple. "I can't wait to have you all at my house. This group is so amazing."

"I feel bad about the people who gave their aardvarks away," Karen said. "Maybe they would have wanted them back."

"It was their free choice to part with them," Roland said. "No recourse now."

"The children at the shelter are loving the aardvarks," Nell said.

"I'm sorry I missed out on doing the aardvarks," Holly said. "A group effort like that must feel amazing, and having a booth at a town event is such a great way to show everybody what an awesome hobby knitting is."

"Actually"—Bettina was adding sugar to her coffee but she paused—"there's going to be a craft fair. The craft shop sent a press release to the *Advocate* last week, and they're looking for groups to get involved. It's to be in the parking lot behind the library, and each group will set up a booth, and—"

Roland cleared his throat. Karen's face puckered up as if she was about to cry. Nell closed her eyes. Pamela focused on her plate of cobbler.

Holly looked around nervously. "I didn't mean that soon," she said. "I meant, like maybe—"

"Like maybe never again?" Nell said.

"Like maybe never again," the rest said in unison.

KNIT

Cozy Cat

He's not cool. In fact, he's very square, and if you can knit basic squares and rectangles you can make a knitted stuffed-animal toy.

If you've never knitted anything at all, it's easier to learn the basics by watching than by reading. The Internet abounds with tutorials that show the process clearly, including casting on and off. Just search on "How to knit." You only need to learn the basic knitting stitch. Don't worry about "purl." That's used in alternating rows to create the stockinette stitch, the stitch you see, for example, in a typical sweater. If you use "knit" on every row, you will end up with the stitch called the garter stitch. That's a fine stitch for this cat. A skein of medium-weight acrylic yarn from the hobby store will provide plenty of yarn. Use medium-gauge needles, size 8, 9, or 10. You'll also need acrylic stuffing from the hobby store and two buttons for eyes.

The cat is created from three rectangles and six squares. Start with the body. Cast on 24 stitches, using either the simple "slip-knot cast-on" process or the more complicated "long tail" process. Knit until you have a rectangle 6" by 12". Cast off, leaving a yarn tail of at least two inches when you clip your yarn.

For the head, repeat the process but cast on 16 stitches and knit 8". Cast off. For the legs, make four squares, each 4" by 4", by casting on 16 stitches, knitting 4", and casting off. The ears start out as small squares. Cast on 6 stitches, knit 1½", and cast off. The tail is another rectangle. Cast on 6 stitches, knit 6" to 8", depending how long you want the tail to be, and cast off.

Now you are ready to assemble your cat. For the body, fold the large rectangle so that you have a 6" square. Using a yarn needle (a large needle with a large eye and a blunt end) and matching yarn, sew the sides, leaving the top open. Stuff the square with enough acrylic stuffing to fill out your cat's body nicely. Fold the medium-sized rectangle in half and sew the sides. This will be the head. You will find it easier to sew on the buttons for the eyes if you do it now, using sewing thread if the holes in the buttons are small, or you can embroider a cat face instead. Stuff the head. Hide all the yarn tails by tucking them into the stuffed openings. When you have both squares stuffed and the yarn tails hidden, center the open end of the head over the open end of the body and sew them together, back of head to back of body and front of head to front of body—though, obviously, at this point the front and back of the body are indistinguishable. There will be little openings left on the shoulders because the head is not as wide as the body. Sew them closed.

Make the legs by folding each 4" square in half so that the knitted edge becomes the long side and the edges where you cast on and off are the ends. Sew the long side and one of the ends and stuff each leg. With the open end of each leg facing the body, attach the legs to the cat, two at the bottom of the body and one on each side of the body at the shoulders. Sew all the way around the open end so that each leg stands out nicely from the body instead of flopping.

For the ears, fold the smallest squares to make triangles. Sew the two open sides closed and sew the long sides of the triangles to the top of the head. You want the right-angle points to stick up.

Fold the last rectangle in half to make a long, skinny tail and sew one end and the long side closed. There's no need to stuff it. Attach it to the cat on the back of the body between where the legs are attached.

Now it's time to hide any yarn tails that are still visible. Thread your yarn needle with your first yarn tail and work the needle in and out of the knitted fabric, preferably along a seam, for an inch or so. Pull the yarn through and cut off the shorter yarn tail that's left.

You can add a ribbon bow at the cat's neck, and even a bell. Cozy Cat can also become a bear or a rabbit—just vary the ears and tail.

For a picture of a finished Cozy Cat,
visit PeggyEhrhart.com.

NIBBLE

STRAWBERRY SHORTCAKE

Make this when it's really strawberry season and strawberries are at their peak of natural sweetness. Two pints (32 oz.) of strawberries makes 8 servings, but you can always use more berries if you like. This shortcake recipe makes a classic biscuit-type shortcake, not like the packaged sponge cakes often displayed near strawberries in the produce department. You'll also want to have heavy cream on hand.

Ingredients for the shortcakes:
- 2 cups flour
- 4 tsp. baking powder
- 1 tsp. salt
- 1 to 2 tbs. sugar
- 5 tbs. butter, plus extra for spreading
- Milk to moisten the dough—about ⅔ cup

Preheat oven to 425 degrees. Mix the dry ingredients in a bowl. Slice the butter into thin bits and add it to the bowl. Cut the butter into the dry ingredients with two knives, a pastry blender, or your fingers, until the mixture resembles sand. Sprinkle the milk over the mixture, tossing with a fork until the dough holds together. Flour your hands and a pastry cloth or board and knead the dough briefly until it forms a smooth ball. With a floured rolling pin or your hands, flatten it until it is about ¾" thick. Now, using either a biscuit cutter or an inverted glass, cut out eight 2" rounds. You can use your fingers to shape the scraps into rounds or ovals too. Arrange your biscuits and scraps on a buttered baking sheet and bake at 425 degrees for 10 minutes, or until they are golden.

While the shortcakes are baking, prepare your strawberries. Wash and core them, and, depending on their size, slice them or cut them into halves or quarters. Sprinkle them with a tiny bit of sugar, a few teaspoons or less, to bring out the juice.

For a classic old-fashioned presentation, split the shortcakes while they are still warm and butter the cut surfaces. Put one half of each shortcake (cut side up) on a dessert plate, heap sugared berries onto it, and top with the other half shortcake (cut side down). Pour the heavy cream over the assembled shortcakes. If you prefer whipped cream, whip the heavy cream with a bit of sugar and top the shortcakes with it.

You can eat your baked scraps later with butter and jam.

For a picture of the finished strawberry shortcakes, visit PeggyEhrhart.com.

Please turn the page for an exciting sneak peek of
Peggy Ehrhart's next
Knit and Nibble mystery,

KNIT ONE, DIE TWO,

coming soon
wherever print and eBooks are sold!

Chapter One

Pamela Paterson tried to keep her voice neutral, even pleasant. "Will Caralee be here tonight?" she asked her neighbor and best friend, Bettina Fraser.

Bettina turned from her cupboard and placed two pottery mugs on the pine table that dominated her pleasant kitchen. "I know she didn't make a very good impression last time," she said. "Margo warned me that her niece could be prickly. But Margo is a good friend and it's not like Caralee wants to become a permanent member. She just needs a little help with her knitting project. It's for a good cause, after all. The Arborville Players contribute a lot to the cultural life of our little town."

"That they do," Pamela said. "I'm looking forward to seeing their version of *A Tale of Two Cities*." She reached for the mugs and lined them up next to the others already arranged in a neat row. "One more," she said, "for Caralee."

"Two," Bettina said, reaching into the cupboard again. "Wilfred spent all afternoon working on that pie. I'm sure he'll want a piece."

An apple pie reposed on a colorful mat in the center of the table. Flaky golden-brown pastry formed an intricate lattice top, and syrupy apple slices dusted with cinnamon peeked out between the interlocking strips.

"I didn't really mind Caralee," Pamela said. "I thought she made some good points about small-minded people in small-minded towns. But I wish somebody had tipped her off that Roland is a lawyer before she got started on the legal profession."

"It was touching that Nell defended him," Bettina said. "Considering they almost never see eye to eye about anything."

"Knit and Nibble has been going for a long time now," Pamela said. "We're like a family—and people in families love each other even if they don't always get along." Knit and Nibble was the nickname of the Arborville knitting club, and Pamela was its founder and mainstay. She surveyed the table. "I think we're all set here. Eight mugs for the coffee or tea, eight dessert plates, eight spoons and eight forks, eight napkins."

"I bought some of that new coffee they've been getting at the Co-Op," Bettina said. "From Guatemala. We tried it this morning and it's very good. And I've got tea bags for Nell and Karen—not very elegant but I don't think they'll mind." She added a sugar bowl and a cream pitcher to the arrangement, smooth sage-green pottery like the mugs and plates.

They were interrupted by the cheerful *ding-dong* of Bettina's doorbell. Woofus the shelter dog tore in from the living room and took refuge under the table, nearly knocking Bettina over. She reached the front door with Pamela close behind and pulled it open to reveal Karen Dowling and Holly Perkins standing on the porch.

"Are we early?" Karen said nervously. She was a

slight blonde woman, still in her twenties, and as shy as her friend Holly was outgoing.

"Of course not!" Bettina opened her arms in a welcoming gesture that turned into a hug. "Come in!"

Bettina's living room was as welcoming as Bettina herself. A comfy sofa stretched along the windows that looked out on the street and two equally comfy armchairs faced it across the long coffee table. Cushions covered in bright hand-woven fabrics provided extra seating on the hearth and enlivened the sage-green and tan color scheme.

The door was still open and Karen and Holly barely settled on the sofa when a cheery voice called, "Hello! Shall I come in?" Nell Bascomb entered the living room, her step lively despite her advanced years and the fact that she'd walked half a mile from her house, which was partway up Arborville's steepest hill. "Roland is just parking," she said. "Is Caralee coming?"

"As far as I know," Bettina said. "She told me they're not rehearsing her scenes tonight and she needs to make lots of progress on the knitting in time for the dress rehearsal." Bettina motioned toward one of the comfy armchairs. "Please," she said. "Have a seat. And leave the door open for Roland."

But instead of Roland, the next person to step through the door was a woman. Her height and slenderness would have made her striking enough, without the perfectly straight jet-black hair that skimmed her bony shoulders and bisected her high forehead with precision-cut bangs. She wore an austere long-sleeved black sweater despite the warm mid-September evening.

"Am I late?" she asked, looking around. Her voice was deep and musical.

"Not at all." Bettina was the only person smiling.

Pamela rallied to her friend's side. "Not at all," she

echoed, commanding her lips to form a welcoming smile. Pamela herself was tall. She found looking up to meet another woman's gaze an odd experience, but that was the case now.

Caralee Lorimer stood uncertainly at the edge of the carpet. "Where do you want me to sit?" she asked.

"Anywhere. Of course." Bettina waved a hand toward the unoccupied armchair, then toward the hearth. "Pamela, you sit down too. Please."

"There's room here." Holly spoke up from the sofa. "Room for two more even." She moved closer to Karen, who had already taken yarn and needles from her knitting bag. Thus it was that Pamela found herself sitting next to Caralee Lorimer, who pulled her knitting from her bag and started in without another word.

"And here's Roland!" Bettina clasped her hands and gave a welcoming nod as Roland stepped through the door. He scanned the room, then turned and closed the door carefully behind him.

"I see I'm the last to arrive," he said. Carrying the briefcase that he used instead of a knitting bag, he threaded his way past the coffee table towards the hearth. "No, no," he said, waving off Bettina's attempt to point him to the remaining armchair, "I'll be fine on a cushion. You take the chair."

Pamela reached into her knitting bag and pulled out a partial skein of yarn in a dramatic shade of ruby red and a pair of needles with the beginnings of a sleeve. She'd started the project the previous June, a departure from the conservative designs she'd favored in the past. It was to be a sleek high-necked tunic with cut-outs that revealed bare shoulders. The woman at the yarn store had suggested it would be perfect for après-ski, a fashion need Pamela could not foresee having, but she had allowed herself to be talked into the extravagant project.

Next to her Caralee unfurled her project. The yarn was a nondescript shade of gray, and bulky, befitting the project's destiny. Caralee's role in *A Tale of Two Cities* was that of Madame Defarge, married to one of the revolutionaries—a wine-shop proprietor—and characterized by her constant knitting. The gray rectangle hanging from her needles was to be her prop.

"I like that color," Caralee said with a hesitant smile, nodding toward the skein of ruby-red yarn resting between her and Pamela on the sofa. "I didn't get a chance to say anything last time. You were sitting way across the room."

"Thank you," Pamela said. "It looks like you're making progress." Caralee's project had indeed grown longer since the previous week, but left to her own devices she seemed to have forgotten the principles Pamela and Bettina had tried to impart when she first requested their help in preparing for her role. The swathe of knitting that dangled from her needles was lumpy and puckered, as if stitches had been dropped and not picked up, and knitting and purling had been interchanged at will. But Pamela supposed Caralee didn't really care, since the point was just to create something that looked realistic from a distance and gain enough skill to handle needles and yarn convincingly.

Caralee was silent then, and Pamela focused on her own work, occasionally glancing around the room but soothed by the quiet hum of conversation. Nell's busy hands were shaping the beginnings of a toy elephant. At present it was merely a fuzzy lavender oval, but during the time she'd been a member of Knit and Nibble Nell had turned out whole herds of elephants in a rainbow of colors. The elephants, destined for the children at the woman's shelter in nearby Haversack, were only one of Nell's many do-good projects.

In the armchair flanking Nell's, Bettina was making an elephant of her own, a gift intended for her new granddaughter. As Pamela watched, Bettina leaned toward Nell and pointed to the oval taking form on her needles. Nell studied it for a moment and then nodded, eliciting a smile from Bettina.

"New project, Roland?" Bettina asked, leaning the other direction, toward where Roland was perched on the hearth, casting on from a skein of pink angora yarn. Roland frowned, waved a silencing hand, and began to count out loud, "Twenty-seven, twenty-eight, twenty-nine, thirty—"

"I'm sorry," Bettina whispered. "I didn't mean to throw you off."

Roland nodded and continued counting, more quietly. Watching him, Pamela reflected that it would be hard to conjure up a more incongruous sight. In his well-cut suit, aggressively starched shirt, and expensive but understated tie, Roland DeCamp was every inch the corporate lawyer, his lean face as intent on his knitting as if he was studying a particularly opaque legal brief. "There," he said, looking up. "Now what were you saying?"

"Are you starting a new project?" Bettina repeated.

"Well, *duh*," Holly piped up from her end of the sofa. "He *is* casting on." But she smiled one of her dimply smiles and followed it with a laugh. Bettina was always ready to join in any sort of merriment and she laughed too.

"It's going to be a sweater for Melanie," Roland said. "She liked the one I made for Ramona so much I decided to make her one too. I'm getting a head start so I can give it to her for Christmas." Melanie was Roland's chic wife, and Ramona was the DeCamps' dachshund. Pamela had her doubts about whether Melanie would find a way to integrate a pink angora sweater into her wardrobe, but Roland's doctor had recommended knitting to calm him down and lower his blood pressure, and she knew Melanie had noticed an improvement.

"Christmas will be here before we know it," Nell observed with a sigh. "Time certainly flies."

Next to her on the sofa Caralee twitched. "Original thought," she murmured under her breath.

"Not too soon, I hope," Holly said, addressing Nell. "I love this time of year—the leaves starting to change, and Halloween—"

"And children making a mess all over town with silly string and eggs and toilet paper"—Roland shifted his intense gaze from his knitting to the assembled group— "and whose tax dollars go to pay for the cleanup?"

"I do enjoy the parade," Nell said. "The children have so much fun dressing up."

"Extra police on duty." Roland scowled. "And I forgot to mention pumpkins rotting on people's porches for weeks afterwards."

"It *is* a shame that people insist on carving them," Nell said. "So much nourishment going to waste. Harold and I leave our pumpkin whole and then eat it when Halloween is over."

"You do?" Holly leaned forward. Pamela couldn't see her face, but her voice combined admiration and amazement. "Do you just bake it? Or . . . ?"

"Pies usually," Nell said. "Not too sweet though. A little sugar goes a long way. And I dry the seeds to put out for the birds and squirrels."

"I'd love to learn to make pumpkin pie," Holly

said. "Will you teach me? I'll keep my pumpkin whole this year."

"It's a deal," Nell said. "I usually steam the pumpkin flesh and mash it, and I freeze it till Thanksgiving. Bring yours over and I'll steam it too. Then at Thanksgiving we'll work on pies."

"That would just be wonderful!" Holly wiggled with glee and the sofa trembled. She turned to Karen and said, "You save yours too and we'll all make pies together."

"Okay," Karen said in her small voice. Karen and Holly began to talk about a new home-improvement project Holly and her husband had embarked upon. Like the Dowlings, they were young marrieds engaged in restoring a fixer-upper house.

"Bourgeois topics," Caralee murmured, in a voice so low Pamela suspected she alone had heard the comment.

Holly was scarcely the image of a suburban matron however. She and her husband owned a hair salon and tonight she sported green streaks in her luxuriant dark hair, with matching green nail polish on fingers and toes.

In the armchairs that faced the sofa, Nell and Bettina worked industriously on their elephants, chatting quietly. The occasional word that reached Pamela's ears suggested they were discussing the exhibit of work by local artists that had recently gone up at the town library. Bettina had written an article on it for Arborville's weekly paper, the *Advocate*.

After several minutes passed, Pamela began to smell coffee. No one else seemed to notice it, or if they did they didn't comment, and Bettina continued knitting, occasionally nodding in response to a comment from Nell. But Roland was becoming restless on his hearth cushion. He set his knitting down and pushed back his flawless shirt cuff to expose his elegant watch. Frowning, he studied its face, then he surveyed the group.

"It's eight o'clock," he announced. "Don't we usually take a break at eight o'clock?"

"Oh, my!" Bettina jumped from her chair. "Time certainly does fly"—a strangled groan reached Pamela's ears from the direction of Caralee—"and here Nell and I were just chattering away."

Pamela looked up to see Wilfred Fraser standing in the arch between the dining room and the living room, a genial smile on his ruddy face and an apron tied over the bib overalls he'd adopted as a uniform after he retired. "I took the liberty of making the coffee, dear lady," he said as Bettina joined him. "And water is a-boil for the tea drinkers."

"I'll help," Pamela said, rising from the sofa and hurrying across the room. Her words were echoed by Holly, who hopped to her feet.

"No, no!" Bettina waved her hands at Holly. "Three people is plenty."

"Too many cooks spoil the broth," Wilfred added.

"Wilfred made apple pie," Bettina said, pausing on the edge of the dining room as Pamela and Wilfred proceeded to the kitchen. "And there's ice cream to go on top. Just sit tight."

The kitchen was fragrant with the bitter spiciness of the coffee, which waited in a large carafe on the stove. Wilfred began to cut the pie and ease slices onto Bettina's pottery dessert plates.

"Caralee seems to be on her best behavior tonight," Bettina observed as she stepped into the kitchen.

"She *has* been quieter at least," Pamela said. She

took a carton of cream from the refrigerator and filled the cream pitcher.

"Margo is such a good friend of mine, and an *old* friend," Bettina said. "I'm sure she's got her hands full with Caralee as a permanent house guest now. But family is family." She sighed and handed Pamela a small wooden tray for the cream and sugar. "Too bad about the divorce. I'm sure Caralee felt much more at home in the city."

"How many for ice cream?" Wilfred asked as he laid the knife and server inside the empty pie plate and transferred the pie plate to the counter.

"I'll deliver the cream and sugar," Pamela said, picking up the wooden tray, "and take orders for à la mode."

She was back in a few minutes. Six steaming mugs of coffee were ready to be served and two teas were steeping alongside them. Bettina arranged four mugs on a larger wooden tray, along with forks, spoons, and napkins—the latter a homespun gray and green stripe from the craft shop. As Bettina headed for the living room, Pamela relayed the ice cream orders to Wilfred: "Seven with, but Nell and Roland just want a little bit, and Caralee doesn't want any at all and not a huge piece of pie."

"One pie for eight people," Wilfred said. "None of the pieces are huge."

"They're just right," Pamela assured him as he deposited a glistening scoop of vanilla ice cream on the flaky lattice surface of a pie wedge.

Bettina delivered the remaining mugs and Pamela delivered pie. When Wilfred entered carrying the last two slices, Holly followed his every motion as he handed Bettina her plate and then lowered himself next to Roland on the hearth.

"You are just awesome," she said. "And this pie looks amazing."

"Eat up, eat up!" Wilfred said jovially.

A companionable silence descended on the group, punctuated only by occasional moans of enjoyment. When the plates were nearly empty and people had reached the coffee-sipping stage, Nell spoke up. "How are your rehearsals coming, dear?" she asked, directing her kindly gaze at Caralee.

Caralee twitched on the sofa, as if surprised to be spoken to. "They're good," she said. "They're fine." She reached forward to set her empty plate on the coffee table.

"Such a powerful story," Nell said. "I love the movie, the old one, with Ronald Colman as Sydney Carton. And the actress who played Madame Defarge—such a dramatic role. You'll be perfect." Caralee grunted noncommittally and focused on her coffee.

"Oh, I love that movie too." Bettina's fork, laden with a bite of pie, paused halfway to her mouth. "And I remember reading the novel in English class so long ago."

When all that remained on the plates were pastry flakes and trails of melted ice cream, and all the mugs had been drained, Wilfred began to gather things up. Holly insisted on helping and hopped up to lend a hand. On the hearth, Roland was methodically thrusting needles and looping yarn, oblivious to the cheerful hubbub around him. Karen was blushing as Nell inquired how she was faring in her early stages of pregnancy—in June she'd announced that she and her husband were expecting their first child. Holly was congratulating Wilfred on his pie and interrupting herself to compliment Bettina on the design of her pottery mugs. And Bettina was assuring Nell that a little sugar had never hurt anyone, especially when combined with something as healthful as apples.

Pamela remained on the sofa, not quite ready to pick up her knitting again. Next to her, Caralee squirmed as she murmured, "Quite warm in here," and began to push up the sleeves of her black sweater.

Normally Pamela was not a nosy person, and Caralee certainly wasn't a close friend—hardly really a friend at all, though Pamela felt a certain sympathy for her. Perhaps, like many creative people, Caralee had never been willing to renounce uncompromising honesty in order to win social acceptance, and she seemed shy as well. Pamela herself was shy. When meeting new people, she sometimes had to remind herself that what she called her "social smile" was in order.

So not being a nosy person Pamela wouldn't have made any comment at all as the sleeve on the arm closest to her slid up above Caralee's elbow and she saw what was revealed. But she didn't think fast enough to suppress the horrified gasp she suddenly realized was her own.

Chapter Two

"Yes, it's quite a bruise, isn't it?" Caralee said dryly.

Nearly half of Caralee's forearm was covered by a dark blotch that shaded from blue-gray to olive green. Down the center a scab like the stroke of a pen marked a long scratch.

"What on earth happened?" Pamela found herself whispering, despite the fact that Wilfred, Holly, and Karen had disappeared into the kitchen, Roland was intent on his pink angora, and Bettina and Nell were on the other side of the room and deep in conversation.

"Last week a pile of stuff fell on me in the storage room where the Players keep their scenery. It knocked me down and almost knocked me out. I still have a cut on my head too." She shrugged. "Perils of acting, I guess. I usually get to rehearsal before everybody else, so I was rummaging around for some chairs to set up. Some fool had jammed them in so tight I had to struggle to get them out. Then it all came down."

"Did you see a doctor?" Pamela asked, reaching out to touch Caralee's hand but then pulling back. She studied Caralee's face. It was quite emotionless. Apparently she saved her emotions for the stage.

Caralee shrugged again. "I was basically okay," she said, "and the show must go on, though I didn't realize how bad it was till the next day. The odd thing is, that night I told a couple of the guys what had happened and we rearranged the storage room to make sure nothing else could fall. But the same thing happened again, just last night. Luckily I jumped out of the way in time."

Caralee was silent then and returned to her knitting. Pamela watched for a minute, but the project taking shape on Caralee's needles was almost as disturbing a sight as the bruise on her arm. The yarn was coarse, the shade of gray reminded Pamela of her basement floor, and the stitches were a jumble of knitting and purling with no apparent logic.

At the other end of the sofa, Holly and Karen were back from the kitchen and had returned to the topic of home improvements, conferring about paint colors and wallpaper patterns suitable for a baby's room. Bettina joined the conversation, lamenting that the "Boston children," as she called her Boston-based son and his wife, had forbidden any gender-specific décor, clothing, or toys for their baby daughter.

"I was so looking forward to dolls, and doll clothes," she said. Her other two grandchildren, offspring of the "Arborville children," were boys.

"I wouldn't mind a doll for my little . . . when she comes." Karen's shy voice trailed off.

"I would love to give her a doll," Bettina said. "I just don't see the point in being so . . . *rigid*. Girls will be girls." Bettina tossed her head and her earrings bobbed. They were jade pendants, set off by her bright red hair, and they matched her gauzy jade-colored shirt and wide-legged pants. "Why, look at Roland here, with his pink angora sweater for Melanie, and I'm sure she'll be thrilled."

"Did Ramona like her pink doggy sweater?" Holly leaned past Caralee toward where Roland sat on the hearth.

Roland looked up, as startled as if he'd been asked an unexpected question in a corporate meeting room.

"The pink sweater you made for Ramona," Nell said. "Holly is wondering if Ramona liked it."

"I'm . . . I'm not sure she noticed it was different from her old one." Roland licked his lips. "Dogs . . . I don't think they see colors the way we do." He frowned for a minute and then added, "In fact, I'm quite sure they don't."

"I love those programs on the Nature Channel," Bettina said. "Such things you learn."

"Yes," Nell agreed, and she launched into a description of a recent series on rhinoceros conservation. Pamela felt awkward carrying on conversations that required nearly shouting to be heard across a room, but Caralee hadn't proven to be a very forthcoming conversational partner. Nevertheless Pamela felt awkward too sitting next to a fellow knitter in complete silence. So she was just as happy when Roland once again consulted his impressive watch to announce that it was nine o'clock and time for him to say goodnight.

Caralee reached under the coffee table and pulled out the attractive carry-all she stored her knitting in, and Holly and Karen began to pack up, chatting now about window treatments that could serve as a baby turned into a little girl and then even a teenager.

From across the room, Bettina caught Pamela's eye. "Don't leave yet," she mouthed, as Roland and Nell stood up.

People made their way toward the door, Holly taking

Nell's arm and insisting she accept a ride back up the hill since Holly and Karen were going almost that far anyway. Pamela and Bettina watched as the three of them headed toward the street and Roland followed toward where his Porsche waited at the curb. As Caralee paused under the porch light, from across the street came a male voice. Pamela couldn't make out the words, but Caralee turned and raised an arm. The gesture was either a wave or a motion like one would make to shoo a fly away. Pamela wasn't sure which.

Caralee crossed the street, then Bettina nodded toward the house next to Pamela's. "Well," she said, "he'll be back in a few days."

"Who?" Pamela said.

"Richard Larkin, of course. I know you've been looking after things for him."

A slight line appeared between Pamela's brows and she tightened her lips. "I told him I'd pick up stray mail and make sure newspapers didn't pile up in his driveway. That's all. It's what any neighbor would do."

Richard Larkin was a recently unattached man who had bought the house next to Pamela's the previous year. "You know he's interested in you," Bettina said, controlling a giggle. Sweet-natured as she was, she occasionally enjoyed teasing her more serious friend.

"I don't know that at all." Pamela stepped off the porch onto the path that bisected Bettina's carefully groomed lawn.

"You're barely forty," Bettina added, "and he's an attractive, eligible man."

"Thank you for hosting the group," Pamela said somewhat stiffly, "and thank Wilfred again for the pie."

Bettina reached out and gave her a hug. "See you tomorrow," she said. "I've got to cover a morning event at the senior center but I'll drop by after. I'll bring some Co-Op crumb cake."

"I'm really not interested in him," Pamela said, a little less stiffly. Bettina meant well. "See you tomorrow." She set off down the walk.

A minute later, she was stepping over the curb on her side of the street. She paused to let a few people go by—apparently the Players' rehearsal in the auditorium next door was just breaking up, then paused again on her own front walk. A tall and thick hedge separated her yard from the grounds of the church, but just now she could hear voices as clearly as if the voices' owners were standing on her own lawn.

"This is the last time I'm going to discuss this with you," said an angry woman's voice. It was a familiar voice, and Pamela suddenly realized it was Caralee's. "So don't talk like that again. Just don't. Because it's not doing you any good and I don't want to hear it."

"You don't understand," said a male voice, more sorrowful than angry, but equally loud. "I can't help how I feel—" The voice broke and Pamela heard a gulp. Despite the gulp, the voice went on, gasping for air between words. "Don't be so mean. I'm just asking you to listen."

"I don't want you to mention this ever again," Caralee said. "Goodnight. You're pathetic!"

Pamela was still staring at the hedge when Caralee spoke from the sidewalk. "You heard that?" she said, still sounding irritated. "Sydney Carton, aka my fellow actor Craig Belknap and my colleague at Hyler's Luncheonette. He's the one who goes to the guillotine at the end."

She strode past Pamela and hurried up the street.

Chapter Three

Pamela was not alone in her house, despite the fact that her architect husband had been killed six years earlier in a construction-site accident and her only daughter, Penny, had returned to her college in Massachusetts at the beginning of September. She climbed her front steps, traversed the wide porch that had attracted her and her husband to their hundred-year-old house so long ago, unlocked the heavy oak door with its oval window, and peered cautiously inside. But nothing stirred. The lamp in the corner of the entry illuminated the aged parquet floor, the worn but lovely Persian rug, the small wing chair where she sat to read her mail.

She made her way cautiously to the kitchen and then along the hallway that led to the laundry room, tiptoeing as she got closer to her destination. Trusting the hall light to reveal all she needed to know, she slowly pushed the laundry room door open. From the floor two eyes, glowing amber, met hers. The rest of the cat, a sleek swathe of jet-black fur, blended into the shadows. But a few sleeping kittens—the ginger ones that took after their dashing father—were just visible, clustered around their mother in the comfortable bed Pamela had arranged for their mother's confinement.

"Goodnight," she whispered, backing away and tiptoeing back to the kitchen.

Upstairs, she stopped in her office and brought her computer to life, waiting through the attendant chirps and hums. No new messages had arrived from her boss at *Fiber Craft*, though she was sure there would be a work assignment in the morning—her boss was an early riser. But Penny had sent a note to say she'd gotten an A on the test she'd been so worried about.

Back downstairs, in pajamas and robe, she applied herself once again to the ruby-red yarn and the in-progress sleeve, while a mystery with a plot as genteel as the actors' British accents unfolded on the screen before her.

Pamela stood at her counter grinding coffee beans while Bettina set out portions of crumb cake on dessert plates from Pamela's wedding china. The grinder growled and whirred in spasmodic bursts, making conversation momentarily impossible. On the floor, a black kitten and a ginger one tussled near Bettina's sandaled foot, stopping their play to investigate her toes.

"They already have sharp little claws, and this ginger one is a tough character," Bettina said.

"All the girls are," Pamela said. "They take after their mom." Catrina had been adopted as a stray the previous fall after surviving many frosty November nights outside.

The kettle's whistle summoned Pamela to the stove, and a minute later she was pouring boiling water through the fragrant, fresh-ground coffee she'd spooned into the filter cone. As the coffee dripped into the carafe, she set out two cups and saucers from her wedding china. Pamela saw no point in saving her pretty things for some imagined future time. And anyway, aside from her wedding china, most of her pretty things were tag-sale finds valuable to no one but her, like the cut-glass cream and sugar set that waited on the kitchen table.

"I do know who Craig Belknap is," Bettina said, returning to an earlier topic of conversation after they were settled on either side of the table with their coffee and crumb cake, "but I don't know why she would have been arguing with him. If anything, she owes him a favor."

"The job at Hyler's?" Pamela asked, teasing a forkful from the golden crumble-topped sponge cake in front of her. "He's got an in with the management?"

"He works there," Bettina said, "but you never see him because he's back in the kitchen."

Pamela finished chewing and swallowed. "What was Caralee doing when she lived in Manhattan?" she asked.

"Same thing," Bettina said, "but a grander place than Hyler's Luncheonette, I'm sure—and the tips for a tuna melt with fries probably don't match what a server gets from somebody who's just dined on a dozen raw oysters and a filet."

They sipped their coffee and finished off their crumb cake, chatting about Bettina's grandchildren and Penny's reports from college. When the last crumbs had been forked up from the wedding plates and the last drops of coffee had been drained from the wedding cups, Bettina climbed to her feet, careful not to step on the tussling kittens, whose number had grown to five.

"I'm off to the mall," she said. "Feel like taking a break from work today?"

"Too much to do," Pamela said. "I've got four articles to edit for the next issue, and my boss wants them back today. Besides, you know . . . I'm not really . . ." She looked down, taking in the none-too-new jeans and simple cotton blouse she'd put on earlier that morning.

"You could dress up more," Bettina said. "I certainly would, if I was tall like you and had your figure."

"You *do* dress up," Pamela said, smiling fondly at her friend. Bettina had an extensive wardrobe, and she dressed for her life in Arborville with as much flair as a Manhattan fashionista. For her visit to the town's senior center to cover an event for the *Arborville Advocate*, she'd chosen a silky wrap dress in a swirling print of navy, bright pink, and turquoise. She'd accessorized it with turquoise wedge-heeled sandals, revealing bright pink toenails, and accented her hazel eyes with turquoise shadow.

After Bettina left, Pamela inventoried her cupboards. She certainly wasn't hungry after a mid-morning snack of crumb cake, but the previous night's dinner had consisted of a baked sweet potato, one chicken thigh remaining from a chicken she had roasted on Saturday, and a homegrown tomato. The grocery list fastened to the refrigerator door with a tiny magnetized mitten reminded her that she needed a loaf of the Co-Op's special whole-grain bread, as well as butter and cat and kitten food. Catrina was eating several times a day to keep up with the demands of the five kittens she was nursing, and the kittens themselves were starting to sample solid food. As far as provisioning herself

for the next few days' meals went, she'd wait to see
what looked good at the Co-Op.

After retrieving several canvas bags from the closet
in the entry—her canvas bag supply was an homage to
Nell, who spoke frequently about the virtues of re-
nouncing paper and plastic—she stepped onto the
porch to collect the day's mail. It consisted of a utility
bill, a card offering one month of free lawn service,
and a catalogue featuring just the type of jewelry she
would have worn if she was a jewelry person: stones
that were pretty rather than precious and designs that
evoked exotic lands.

Scanning her own mail reminded her that she'd
promised Richard Larkin to make sure no mail accumulated in his box while he was gone—the mail carrier could be a bit forgetful about whose mail was to be
held and whose delivered. She darted around the
hedge that separated her yard from his and peered
toward the metal box fastened to his house's shingled
facade. Nothing was sticking out, and anyway he'd be
back tomorrow.

She wasn't sure how she felt about that, but she
wished Bettina would stop trying to play matchmaker.
Yes, she'd once let slip that with Penny off to college
and on her way to being independent, she might con-
sider dating. But Richard Larkin, attractive as he was,
might not be the right person. The shaggy hair that
had originally marked him in her eyes as too bohemian
had proven to be the effect of a temporarily demand-
ing work schedule that left no time for a visit to the
barber. But still, she wasn't sure. Or maybe she just
wasn't really ready yet, despite the fact that even Penny
had urged her to remedy her solitary state.

Her own mail deposited on the mail table in her
entry, she was on her way. Arborville's walkability had

attracted Pamela and her husband long ago when they were shopping for a house, and Pamela still did most of her errands on foot. Arborville's tiny commercial district, with the Co-Op Grocery and an unpretentious collection of narrow storefronts, including Hyler's Luncheonette, was only five blocks distant and the route was a pleasant one—up tree-lined Orchard Street and then left at the stately brick apartment building that faced Arborville Avenue. Pamela often detoured through the parking lot behind the apartment building, where a discreet wooden fence hid trash cans and whatever else the building's inhabitants had recently discarded. One person's trash truly was another's treasure, and she had recently rescued an ornate picture frame that exactly suited an antique sampler she had found at a thrift shop.

Today was a perfect mid-September day. Yards were still green, trees were still leafy, but the sun's angle was no longer the direct blaze of midsummer, and the sidewalks were littered with acorns. Pamela took her time, and when she reached the Co-Op she dallied outside for a few more minutes. Besides supplying the inhabitants of Arborville with food, the Co-Op also supplied information. The large bulletin board next to the automatic door had only recently been supplemented by AccessArborville, the town's listserv, and people still consulted the bulletin board for news about town events. Moreover, the bulletin board welcomed postings from anyone with anything to publicize.

Pamela's heart sank to discover that more than one person was offering kittens to good homes. Soon it would be time to find homes for Catrina's lively brood, but how many kittens could a tiny town like Arborville absorb at once?

Inside the market, Pamela selected a cart from the

small collection waiting near the entrance and wheeled
it toward the bakery counter, where a tempting assortment of loaves in various shapes and hues beckoned.
She chose her favorite whole-grain, a gleaming oblong
the color of toasted wheat, waited while it was sliced
and bagged, and moved on to the cheese counter.
There she hesitated between Gouda and cheddar, and
finally came away with half a pound of each.

She maneuvered the cart into the produce section,
where a row of bins piled high with greens of every
sort faced bins of squash and root vegetables across
a narrow wood-floored aisle. She added a head of
romaine to her cart and moved on to collect a bundle
of carrots and a bunch of celery. A special display at
the end of the aisle featured sweet corn, still in its husks,
and billed as "New Jersey's Own." Pamela couldn't
resist, and piled six ears into her cart. A display of local
apples occupied the corresponding spot across the
way. She picked out four, rusty red with golden streaks.

Farther down the fruit aisle, neighboring bins offered peaches, plums, and apricots. September was the
last chance for good peaches, local peaches that tasted
the way peaches were supposed to taste. Pamela pushed
her cart a few yards farther and cupped a peach in her
hand. It was pale gold, velvety, with a rosy blush. It
wasn't soft yet, but she knew peaches were happy to
ripen off the tree. A bowl of peaches on the kitchen
counter could perfume a kitchen for a few days and
then turn into a pie—or a cobbler. In fact peach cobbler
was exactly what she planned to make the following
Tuesday when Knit and Nibble met at her house. She'd
wait a few days to buy the peaches though.

The question of dinner for the next few nights still
needed to be addressed, and she couldn't forget the cat

and kitten food and butter. A quick detour through the canned goods section allowed her to cross the first two items off her list, and she picked up a pound of butter on her way through the dairy aisle. At the meat counter she studied the offerings. The Co-Op had good meat, much of it from local farms, but it was hard to be inspired when cooking for one.

A package of smoked ham hocks caught her eye—not the most exciting perhaps, compared to the marbled steaks, dainty lamb chops, and racks of baby back ribs, but Pamela loved making bean soup. And she liked her meals to reflect the seasons. A salad was the perfect dinner at the end of a long summer day, but by mid-September a steaming bowl of soup ladled from a pot that had simmered on the stove all afternoon would be most welcome. And she could cook today and have a week's worth of meals. She added the ham hocks to her cart.

Pamela was happy to set down the two canvas bags, laden with groceries and heavier than she'd expected them to be, when she stepped up onto her porch. Inside the house, she was greeted by five hungry kittens and their equally hungry mother, and she quickly spooned cat food into a bowl for Catrina and kitten food into the large bowl the kittens shared—though their first ventures with solid food had involved climbing into the bowl.

When the groceries were stowed away, she toasted a slice of the fresh whole-grain bread and ate it with a few slices of Gouda, finishing the meal off with an apple. It was only one p.m. She'd work her way through two of the articles that waited upstairs on her computer, then take a break and get the soup started.

At four p.m. Pamela was back in the kitchen, studying the dried beans in the jars she had lined up on the counter. The beans ranged in color from white to deepest maroon, with a jar of speckled pinto beans at the end. She poured from this jar and that until she'd filled a two-cup measure. In a large heavy pot on the stove, chopped onion, carrots, and celery were already softening in a few tablespoons of olive oil, and sprigs of parsley and thyme from the herb pots on the back porch waited on the counter. When the beans, water, and a ham hock had been added to the pot and all was on its way to a low simmer, she returned to her office and article number three, "Victorian Needlework in the Victoria and Albert Museum."

Pamela worked until six-thirty, when the tempting aroma of bean soup summoned her down to the kitchen. The ham hock had simmered among the beans and other vegetables as she edited her way through the Victorian needlework article and "The Role of Weaving in Modern Mayan Culture." It was time to extract it from the pot and trim off the now-tender bits of ham. She scooped it out onto a cutting board and set to work with her favorite paring knife.

But after a few minutes she paused in her task, letting her knife rest. It was unusual to hear sirens on this block of Orchard Street, or any block of Orchard Street in fact. Emergency vehicles sometimes sped along Arborville's main artery, Arborville Avenue, at the top of the hill, or busy County Road, at the bottom. But this siren was close and drawing closer. She set the knife down and quickly washed her greasy fingers at the sink.

Outside it was still daylight, but the sky behind the

church steeple was reddening. A man and a woman
were standing on the sidewalk in front of the church.
They were looking eagerly up the street, but the
expressions on their faces suggested that whatever
they were waiting for wasn't connected with a happy
event. The siren had become so loud now that when
Pamela turned to look in the direction they were looking she wasn't surprised to see a police car only a few
houses away and bearing down on them. Pamela blinked
as the lights on its roof flashed in sequence, left to right
and back again, like so many flashbulbs.

The police car swerved toward the curb as it neared
Pamela's house and then coasted to a stop in front of
the church. The doors swung open and two officers
leapt out as if jointly responding to an internal com-
mand of "Ready, set, go!"

"This way," the woman called from the sidewalk.
She motioned the officers to follow and she headed
toward the driveway that led to the church parking lot.
The man who had been waiting with her joined the
procession, and the four—the officers in their dark-
blue uniforms with the heavy leather gun belts and
stiff visored caps, and the man and woman in jeans
and T-shirts—disappeared around the side of the
church.

Pamela stood uncertainly in her yard. She was
tempted to follow the procession toward the parking
lot and whatever it was that had seemed serious enough
to summon the police. But she knew that the sensible
choice would be to go back inside, finish cutting off
the ham bits, and add them to the nearly-ready bean
soup. Then a third alternative presented itself.

She was just turning toward her house where the
sensible choice in the form of the ham hock and the
bean soup awaited, when from across the street came

Bettina's voice. She turned back to see Bettina scurrying toward her, with Wilfred several paces behind. Bettina was still wearing the chic wrap dress she had started the day in. Wilfred, judging from his apron, was evidently in charge of the evening meal.

"What could be happening?" Bettina panted. "We heard the siren but we couldn't imagine it was on its way to Orchard Street."

Wilfred joined them. "Most unusual," he said. "The church, of all places."

"Rehearsal," Bettina observed. "The Players are here tonight. I saw Caralee arriving when I opened the door for a UPS delivery a little while ago."

"Uh-oh!" Wilfred held up a finger and closed his eyes. He frowned as if straining to make out a sound. "More sirens." He opened his eyes. Pamela heard them too. This time they were coming from both directions.

At nearly the same moment, another police car appeared at the top of the hill, and an ambulance swung around the corner from County Road. The competing sirens intertwined in a discordant competition of wails and howls, growing so loud that the sound was almost a physical presence. With a few last resentful growls, both vehicles nudged into spots at the curb and were silent.

EMTs in dark pants and white shirts hurried from the ambulance toward the church parking lot, followed by another police officer and a man in a sports jacket and slacks.

"It's Detective Clayborn," Bettina said. "I talk to him sometimes for the *Advocate*."

"This doesn't look good," Wilfred said. Concern had banished the genial expression he usually wore and he seemed almost a stranger. Bettina reached for his arm and he tugged her to his side.